PLASTIC

HEARTS

LISA DE JONG

Printed in the United States of America

Plastic Hearts

Copyright © 2013 by Lisa De Jong
Jennifer Roberts-Hall, Editor
Michelle Preast, Cover Designer
JT Formatting, Formatter
www.facebook.com/JTFormatting

ISBN-13: 978-1482333138
ISBN-10: 1482333139

Dedication

To all those who've ever had a dream and
reached for it...

Prologue

"Another mimosa, miss?" the waiter asked, distracting me from the piece of art in the corner of the dining room.

"No, I'm fine. Thank you," I replied, shifting my attention back to the modern abstract painting. I hated the country club, but I had to admit that the decorator had great taste.

"Are you having a good time?"

I turned to face Ryan, my boyfriend of eight months. I smiled weakly at him. I wasn't having a good time, but I would never admit it. This was my part. To play the happy, successful, put-together daughter who doted on her parents. Being here with our families made me miss the peace of my college dorm. Only four more hours before we had to leave and head back to NYU. Still, it seemed four hours too long.

"Yes, the food is delicious," I said, pulling my muffin apart and popping a piece in my mouth. Honestly, I had barely touched anything. My mother always watched what I put in my mouth and I would rather go hungry than listen to her rattle off how many calories I ate. Though she wouldn't say anything here, of course.

"So, Alexandra, have you decided which field you're going to practice medicine in?" Thomas, Ryan's father, asked.

I cleared my throat and glanced around the table, realizing all eyes were on me. "I'm thinking about pediatrics, but I'm still undecided," I finally replied. The truth was that I hadn't been thinking about it at all. I noticed my father's eyes were locked on me. This was a rare occurrence, but also one that terrified me. His attention rarely came with good intentions.

"As in surgery?" my father asked, his eyes still glued on mine.

I looked down to calm my racing nerves. "No, just general pediatrics. I don't think surgery is for me." Medicine in general wasn't for me.

My eyes met his again and I said a silent prayer, thankful that we were in the club and that the conversation wouldn't continue. He gave me a look that said it wasn't over, but returned his attention to his prime rib. I took a deep breath as I began to move the fruit around on my plate.

Ryan placed his hand on my thigh. "Are you all right? You seem tense."

"I'm fine," I said, leaning in to kiss his cheek.

"Aren't they adorable, Catherine?" Jillian, Ryan's mom, beamed from across the table, leaning in on her elbows.

I glanced over at my mother who sat with her signature fake smile. She looked happy and had a polite demeanor; she always did when we were around her friends. "Yes, they are. How can they not be though? Look at us," my mother said, bringing her third glass of wine to her perfect red lips.

"I see some planning in our future," Jillian smiled. I almost choked on a piece of pineapple. I could just imagine all the time the two of them had spent together, discussing our future. They would like nothing more than for the two of us to make little country club babies.

"Gwen, how are the wedding plans coming along?" I

asked to try and move the attention away from myself.

"Great! We have the menu all worked out and the tuxes have been ordered. Just a few little things left and then we are all set," my sister said, smiling up at her fiancé. They looked perfect together, but that was where the connection seemed to end. So many times I'd wanted to ask her if this was what she truly wanted because I thought the line between her wants and my parent's wants had been blurred.

"When will the bridesmaid dresses be in?" I asked.

"Next week. I'll give you a call when it comes in and you can pick it up at Kleinfeld."

"I hope it still fits with all the bread you've been eating over break," my mother sneered from across the table. I waited for someone at the table to correct her, to tell her she was being ridiculous, but no one said a word.

I needed fresh air. I needed to get out of here for a few minutes to regain my equilibrium. "Ryan, do you want to go take a walk outside for a few minutes?"

"Sure, let me go grab our coats," he said, walking away from the table. Gwen grabbed my hand. "Alex, don't worry. You'll look gorgeous in your dress." She smiled and I squeezed her hand, then turned toward the lobby to meet Ryan.

Ryan helped me with my coat and we stepped outside to take in the cool January air. It was unbearably cold this time of year, but I would rather be anywhere but at that table. Our families had come to the Hamptons for winter break and it had been the longest three weeks of my life. Okay, maybe not the longest, but now that I knew what it was like to be on my own after finishing one semester of college, this was torture. I was constantly trapped under a microscope and couldn't get out from under it, though it wasn't like I ever really tried. This was my life; I was used to it and up until recently, I thought I was happy with it.

"Do you want to go sit in the car? I'm freezing," Ryan asked, entwining his fingers with mine.

I nodded as we walked toward his shiny black BMW. Being alone with him has been awkward during these last few weeks. Things would be so much easier if we had just remained friends. He opened the door for me before moving to the driver's side. As soon as he climbed in, he cranked up the heat, rubbing his hands together as we sat in silence.

"I can't believe classes start again in two days," he said, breaking the silence.

"I know. I'm ready to get back in a routine though. You?"

He shrugged. "I don't know. I won't get to see you again until Gwen's wedding." He grabbed my hand and rubbed his lips over my knuckles. He was a sweet guy, but maybe not the one for me. I had gone back and forth, trying to decide what I should do. I needed to make a decision soon.

"I can't believe she is getting married in two months. It seems like just yesterday we were riding our bikes through the neighborhood." I smiled at the memory. Things were simple then.

"Yeah. Do you remember when we were racing and you fell and tore your new tights?"

I laughed. "Yeah, we buried them in your sand box and tried to convince my mother that I hadn't worn any that day."

"That didn't work though, did it?" he asked. I stopped laughing as I remembered how my mother cornered me until I told her the truth. She always picked up on my lies. Always.

I didn't get to ride my bike the rest of that summer as a punishment.

"No, it didn't," I whispered. Ryan and I created an album of memories between us. Some were good and some were bad, but we experienced it all together. He knew the parts of me that I let him see well. He just didn't hold the key to everything.

He cupped my face in his hands, bringing my eyes to his. I didn't see electric sparks. I didn't see rainbows. I saw my best friend. As he leaned in to kiss me, I closed my eyes and tried to pretend that this was where I wanted to be. That this was what I wanted to be doing, but still no electricity. He pulled away. "I love you, Alexandra."

"I love you, too," I whispered. And I did. I loved him, but I needed to consider what that meant to me. Was he my forever?

"We should probably get back inside before someone comes looking for us," Ryan said, turning the car off.

I followed him inside, reassuring myself that there was only three hours and six minutes before I could leave again. Before I could return to my new normal.

CHAPTER ONE

LATER THAT NIGHT

Dancing for me was a form of expression, a way to release pent up stress and energy. I could go to a club where I knew no one and just let go. It felt good to let the music take my body where it wanted to go. I could forget about all my thoughts and worries and just be myself.

My roommate Jade and I had been dancing for over an hour when my favorite Nelly Furtado song started pumping through the club. It instantly renewed my energy as Jade turned her back to mine and we started to move together. We're very different, but when we went dancing it was like we were one in the same.

I met Jade last semester at the start of our freshman year at New York University. Our first few weeks as roommates were difficult to say the least. She came to college to party and meet guys and I came to study and escape the chaos that was my family. Jade and I both grew up in upper class homes, but Jade's parents were famous photographers who had showered her with love, convincing her that she could be whatever she wanted to be and she really wanted to be a photographer.

My parents, on the other hand, applied pressure on me throughout my life and wouldn't settle for anything less than me becoming Dr. Alexandra Mirabelle Riley. My father was a doctor and my older sister Gwen had just finished her medical residency, landing a position as a pediatric surgeon at one of the most prestigious hospitals on the East Coast. Thankfully, I had three and a half years before I needed to address my post college life and, at least for tonight, I wasn't going to think about anything but letting loose in the middle of the packed club.

Jade took my hand and pulled me off the dance floor. "Let's get something to drink. It's getting really warm in here."

"Yeah, that sounds good. I should probably check on Ryan anyway," I said, following her toward the bar area.

New York City had no shortage of clubs, but Club Max was one of the more popular haunts for NYU students. The cover charge was affordable and you didn't have to be a celebrity to get in. The club was decked out in black décor; floors, tables and ceiling, but the glowing purple lights and chrome accents pulled it all together, giving it a hip, modern look. The bar itself was completely illuminated in purple lighting with a stainless steel top. The whole club was lined with small, high top tables and white leather furniture accented the VIP area. The place was loud and packed with people, but it maintained a certain sense of comfort and relaxation.

We found Ryan standing next to one of the small high top tables. He had one hand shoved in the front pocket of his designer blue jeans and the other wrapped around the beer he had been nursing for the last hour. His expression was blank, but when he saw us approaching the corners of his lips turned up. He was boyishly handsome with blonde curly hair, dark blue eyes and perfect white teeth; most girls would be happy to call him their boyfriend.

"Are you having a good time?" he asked before kissing my cheek. He refused to dance, saying he had to save his moves for the lacrosse field, but he didn't hesitate for a second when I asked him to come here tonight. Ryan was always more concerned that those around him were happy than he was about his own happiness. I used to think it was a good quality, but lately I wondered if he was sacrificing too much of himself. We both lived our lives worrying about others feelings more than our own and I knew I wasn't happy.

"Yes, the DJ's great tonight!" Jade yelled, leaning in so he could hear her over the music. "You should join us." He shook his head as he took a small sip of his beer. She lifted an eyebrow before focusing her attention back on me. "Alex, I'm going to grab a drink, do you want something?"

"Water, please."

"I'll be right back," she said, turning toward the bar.

I focused my attention back on Ryan who was staring at me intently. His eyelids looked heavy as I reached up to run my thumb over his forehead. "Are you getting tired? We can leave if you want."

"No, we can stay." He started to work on the edges of the label on his beer bottle, slowly peeling the corners away. Things had been awkward between us for months, but it was magnified over winter break because we were actually able to spend time together. It had become apparent that just because two people got along really well didn't mean they should date. Ryan and I were an example of this, but ending things would cause so much chaos between our families. I couldn't decide if it was worse to stay with someone who had a piece of my heart, but didn't have it completely, or disappoint my parents. Parental disappointment may be a normal part of any teenager's life, but my parents weren't normal.

Last May, shortly after graduation, Ryan asked me out. We were all at his parent's beachfront property in the Hamptons celebrating graduation when Ryan asked if I would go for a walk with him. I didn't think much of it, but as we started to walk toward the ocean, I felt the nervousness rolling off him. When we reached the water's edge, he grabbed my hand, took a long deep breath and started to tell me how much he liked me; that he thought we fit and how happy we would be together.

"I guess what I'm trying to ask you is if you will go out with me? I should have asked you a long time ago and I know we're both leaving for school soon, but I would really like to give us a chance," he said, dragging his feet through the sand. I cared about Ryan, loved him even, and it was hard to deny him when he looked at me with those eyes.

"Yes," I said, standing on my tiptoes to kiss his cheek. When I pulled back to look at him he had the world's biggest smile plastered on his face. Making him happy made me happy. I sort of lived my life that way.

He was comfortable and always there. At first, our relationship worked well, but there was something essential missing. Maybe I knew too much about him; he was one of my best friends and there was little mystery left to explore. I knew what he liked and what he didn't like and there wasn't much left to figure out once we had begun dating. He was like a present I had already unwrapped.

I had family and friends, but no one really saw me; no

4

one paid attention long enough. I thought Ryan could fill that void, but I was wrong. He was sweet and attentive, but he didn't see the real me. He didn't see the artistic, lonely Alex; he only saw the popular, smart Alexandra.

Our relationship had been anything but perfect the last few months; I went off to college at NYU while he attended Stanford in California. Winter break was the first time I'd seen him since Thanksgiving break and before that it had been Labor Day weekend when he left for school. Even when we were together he didn't make my toes curl or my heart race. He was my comfort and stability. I thought I was happy with that, but I wasn't. Not by a long shot.

Jade set our drinks on the table, ending my thoughts. I was ready to get back on the dance floor and forget again. Ryan was still working at the label on his bottle, looking bored out of his mind. I felt bad leaving him alone so I decided to try to lure him out onto the dance floor one more time. "Why don't you come with us?"

"No, I'll just wait right here." He winked at me as Jade and I stood up to move toward the dance floor. As soon as we found a spot in the middle of the crowd, I stepped behind Jade, closed my eyes, and lost myself in the sound of Beyoncé's voice. It was amazing how easily I could lose myself in the lyrics. They played in my head, leaving no room for worries and stress. I wished there was a way to have them on constant replay all day, every day.

Suddenly, hands gripped my hips and I felt a large hard body pressed up against mine. Ryan hated to dance so I was surprised he decided to join us, but glad he did. I pushed my back into him and covered his hand with mine. Jade was so distracted by the guy standing in front of her that she didn't pay any attention to what we were doing. I felt good tonight. I had worn my favorite blue skinny jeans with a red camisole and black stilettos. Not quite winter wear, but it was standard for the club scene. My long wavy blonde hair was down and my blue eyes had a smoky look thanks to Jade's magic hands.

We continued to dance as Beyoncé's voice was replaced with Ellie Goulding's. The slower song made me want to move closer so I lifted my hand and wrapped it around his neck, keeping my back pressed against him. That was the moment when I realized something wasn't right. Ryan's slightly too long hair was nowhere to be found; instead, my fingers met short-cropped hair. I slowly lowered my arm and turned around to face him. The man standing before me was not Ryan, not even close. He was slightly taller, maybe six two with short brown hair. Our faces were only inches apart and even though the club was dark, I could tell he was easy on the eyes. I opened my mouth and tried to speak, but nothing came out.

His hands rested on my hips and he looked down at me with a cocky smile. I was staring at the face of the most beautiful man I'd ever touched. I felt my face flush from embarrassment. I hoped he didn't get the wrong impression from the way I was dancing with him. Then I remembered that Ryan was here somewhere and my eyes did surveillance to see if he was watching. I wasn't sure how he would react to this kind of thing and I certainly wasn't in the habit of dancing with guys while my boyfriend was in the same club. I didn't see him anywhere so I returned my attention to the stranger in front of me. Looking down to avoid further eye contact, I noticed he was wearing a tight grey t-shirt, highlighting a great set of arms and a defined chest. I couldn't help but notice the tattoos covering every inch of his forearms; he was definitely not someone you could ever bring home to Mommy and Daddy.

I felt a finger under my chin, lifting my gaze back up to his eyes. "Hi," he said. I couldn't quite hear his voice, but I could read his amazing lips under the strobe lights. God, he was beautiful; the type of beautiful that rendered me temporarily speechless. I wasn't sure how long I stood there searching for something to say, but it was long enough for me to completely forget my own name.

"I'm here with my boyfriend," I finally blurted. It came out so quickly I wasn't even sure he understood a word I said. Why did I always turn into a blabbering mess when I was nervous? Did I mention that when he smiled two magnificent dimples appeared? Dammit.

I watched him look around and then he smiled. "I don't see a boyfriend. Sorry, you're going to have to come up with something a little better than that. Try again." Who did this guy think he was?

I pressed my lips into a tight line. "No, I'm really here with my boyfriend. Right, Jade?" I turned around to pull her into the conversation, but she was gone. This was not going well. This mystery man had unnerved me by putting his hands on my body and flashing those incredible dimples and there was no one around to save me. Ryan was probably sitting at the bar, slowly nursing his first beer, while Jade was doing God knows what with a guy whose name she would never know.

I hesitantly turned back toward him until our eyes met again. He seemed amused as he continued to smile down at me. "So do you want to keep dancing? Or can I buy you a drink?" he shouted over the music. I was used to guys hitting on me, but usually when I said I had a boyfriend they got the hint.

"I..."

Before I could finish I felt a hand on my back and turned to see Ryan, who wore the same blank face as before. "Are you ready to go? Jade said to go ahead, she's catching a ride home with Dan," he said, looking down at me. At least she got his name before she left with him, I thought.

I realized that Sexy Stranger's hands were still on my hips and my heart rate picked up. I was in the middle of the dance floor talking to my boyfriend while another guy had his hands on me. I felt like I could faint at any moment. I wasn't the type of girl who usually got herself into these situations. Warm breath hit my ear, sending shivers down my body. "If I were your boyfriend, I would be asking what my hands are doing on your body. Are you sure this is your boyfriend?"

Ryan must have then noticed what was going on behind me because his eyes started dancing back and forth between the two of us and a scowl lined his boyish face. He looked as mad as I'd ever seen him; the look was foreign on him. "Why does this guy have his hands on you?" he asked, rubbing his hands over his eyes and through his slightly too long hair. He looked incredibly tired and I couldn't blame him. We drove four hours from his parent's home in the Hamptons to come back here for the night and he had to catch a plane back to Stanford in the morning.

I shook my head, placing a finger over his lips. "Not here. Let's go back to my room and talk. We're both tired and it's loud in here." He nodded slightly before he looked back over my shoulder. I followed his gaze to find that Sexy Stranger was no longer standing behind me. I was so wrapped up in what was happening between Ryan and I that I hadn't felt his hands leave my body. I grabbed Ryan's hand and lead him outside without saying another word.

Sometimes I wished Ryan would just yell at me, show me some emotion and passion, but this was classic Ryan. He would never argue and he would never yell; he lived his life in a sea of calm. I knew Ryan was passionate about becoming a doctor and helping people, but I wished he showed that type of passion toward me.

I liked Ryan, but lately I realized we weren't going to have the fairytale I'd always dreamed of. I wanted the type of love I could feel from head to toe, the type where I felt every kiss deep down in the pit of my stomach, the type where the mere mention of his name made me smile from ear to ear and ignited a passion within me so strong that even on our worst days our love was better than any other love around us. I couldn't string him along any longer. It wasn't fair to him or me. I planned on discussing it with him in the morning, before he left, but now seemed like as good a time as any. He was comfortable for me, but I couldn't use Ryan like a security blanket anymore. We both deserved something better. I took a deep breath before addressing him. "Ryan, I think we should talk," I said, my voice cracking with every word.

Ryan joined me on the edge of my bed, rubbing his hands together, which I knew was a telltale sign he was nervous. "What's going on between you and that guy from the club? I saw his hands on you, Alex. I'm not a jealous person, but I don't like to see another guy touching you like that." I shook my head in an attempt to reassure him that there was no one else. I hated that he thought there was, but maybe it was a sign of what we'd become.

"I don't even know his name." I started to pick the nail polish off of my fingernails. I couldn't will myself to look into his eyes. I'd known Ryan long enough to know what his eyes looked like when he was sad.

"What? You let some guy, whose name you don't even know, touch you like that? God, Alex, I was right there," he said, raising his voice slightly as he raked his hand through his hair. This was going to be so much harder than I had even imagined.

"I thought it was you. I was dancing with Jade and felt hands on me and thought it was you," I replied, not even trying to mask the frustration in my voice. I briefly looked up at him before returning to my nails.

"I guess I'm just upset that I have to say goodbye to you tomorrow. The last few months have been harder than I thought they would be," he said as I turned back toward him. He ran his fingers along the line of my jaw, adding to the weight of my already heavy heart. "I miss you," he whispered. I could see the ache in his eyes as he looked into mine. I hated that I had to do this. Every single part of me hurt because I was getting ready to let go of one of my best friends.

I was a people pleaser by nature. I did everything I could to not hurt others, even if the result of that was hurting myself. It was time to talk to him, no matter how much it was going to hurt both of us. This was me taking control of a little bit of my life.

My lip quivered as I tried to gain enough composure to speak. "I think we should take a break. We're thousands of miles apart and never get to see each other. I need to concentrate on school and you should be doing the same." I wasn't sure if I saw sadness or contemplation in his eyes, but I decided to grab his hand with mine to comfort him. He didn't pull away, but he didn't do anything to tighten our grip either.

He sat quietly, looking across the room. "I don't think we need a break. God, Alex, where is this coming from?" he whispered. I knew this wouldn't be easy.

"Are you happy?" I asked.

"What?" His eyes jumped up to meet mine.

"Are you happy?"

"Why would you even ask that?" he asked, raising his voice slightly. His eyes were searching my face like it would give him all the answers.

"Ryan, don't you think we both deserve the full college experience without worrying what the other is doing? I'm not saying I don't like you or that I want to be with someone else, but this long distance thing just isn't working for me right now and it doesn't seem to be working for you either."

He sighed. "It is harder than I thought it would be, but I don't want to lose you forever and it feels like I am." His admission tore at my heartstrings, but I knew deep down inside that I was not the one for him; he could find someone better. We were meant to be friends and anything more was forced.

"I would say everything will be fine again this summer, but after that we have another eight months apart. I can't promise you anything." This was not my heart speaking, but my head. I couldn't deal with all the potential pain right now. Not to mention that once my mother found out that I dumped Ryan Hill, I would never hear the end of it. It would be much easier to tell her I needed a break than it would be to tell her we were done. The truth could be addressed later. Maybe he would find someone who would fill the void I never really could; I wanted him to be happy.

His eyes pleaded with me. "Please, don't do this. We can make this work. I'll come visit more often and-"

I cut him off as tears started to roll down my face. "I'm sorry. I just can't do this right now. Please understand."

I watched as his face twisted in pain, causing my tears to fall even faster. I was not enjoying any part of this. "Do you want me to leave?" he asked, staring down at his hands. My heart dropped at the thought of him wandering the city, looking for an open hotel room. Or even worse, spending it in the airport.

"Of course not. You can stay here tonight. I'll just put my sleeping bag on the floor and you can have my bed."

His head snapped up to look at me. "I'm not sleeping on your bed while you sleep on the floor."

"Yes, you are." I threw my sleeping bag on the floor and grabbed a pillow. "I'm going to go get ready for bed." I glanced at him and my chest squeezed when I noticed the sadness in his eyes. I felt guilty for not mirroring that same level of sadness in my own. I cared for him. Scratch that. I loved him, but it wasn't the type of love that made butterflies appear in my stomach or made my heart beat faster when I saw or thought of him. I felt kind of stupid saying that since it had never happened with any of my relationships, but it had to exist somewhere.

The day would probably come where I would have to accept what was expected of me and marry an Ivy League educated man who my parents approved of. Would I find one that makes my heart flutter? Most of me thought it would never happen; I had only seen those types of relationships on TV or read about them in books. I learned a long time ago that most of my family and friends had plastic hearts. Plastic hearts are made so they cannot be broken. Cracked maybe, but never broken. They made decisions based on outward appearances and ignored all emotion. That was applied to all aspects of life, even relationships.

When I returned to my room, Ryan laid on my bed with his back to me. I couldn't tell if he was sleeping or not and I didn't move to find out. Tomorrow was going to be awkward and the sooner I got to sleep, the sooner I could face it.

But there was no such thing as peaceful sleep when you'd just broken someone's heart.

CHAPTER TWO

The next morning was as awkward as I imagined it would be. In all honesty, I was sure he wanted to leave just as much as I wanted him to. I didn't want to lose him forever, but I recognized the need for space and time. We both needed time to digest what had happened last night so we could decide what we wanted the future to look like.

I heard him walking across the floor and quickly rubbed my eyes as I watched him grab his bag and head toward the door. My heart dropped. "Are you leaving?" I asked, lifting my head off the pillow.

"No, I was just going to go shower quick. I'll be back in a few minutes." He didn't look at me as he walked out of the room, slamming the door behind him.

Today was going to be difficult, but once it was over I would feel like I could breathe again. It was hard to make this decision, but there was so much peace in doing it. I would drop him off at the airport and get everything ready for class tomorrow. Hopefully Jade would be home soon so we could watch some sappy romantic movie on Lifetime and share some chocolate chip cookies from the bakery down the street. I needed some girl time, something to make me forget the pain I saw in Ryan's eyes last night. Jade may be the oil to my water, but I really missed her while I was home for winter break. I realized how much oxygen she breathed into me when everyone else seemed to suck it out.

The door opened, taking me away from my thoughts. Ryan met my eyes just for a second before he walked over and sat on the end of my bed. He rested his chin on his chest and kept his gaze locked on the floor.

"I'm going to go jump in the shower. When I'm done, do you want to go grab some coffee? I mean, I know we have to leave soon for the airport, but I thought you might like something to eat before you leave," I said, trying to break the silence.

He sat with his elbows on his knees, never looking in my direction. "Actually, I think I'm just going to call a cab and grab something at the airport," he mumbled. My chest tightened as I listened to the sadness that tinged his voice. It was hard to break anyone's heart, but when that person was Ryan it was magnified times ten. I wished there was a way to do this without hurting him.

"Ryan, please don't leave like this. I can drive you to the airport." I wanted to do the right thing. I knew he wasn't going to leave happy, but I didn't want him to be upset either.

"No, Alex, I think it's better if I just go. Let's not drag this out longer than we have to," he said, his voice strained. He was looking at me again and the awkwardness hung in the room like a thick storm cloud.

"If that's what you want. I just don't feel right making you grab a cab when I can take you," I whispered.

"It really isn't a big deal. I think it's better if I just go," he said, sounding frustrated. Maybe it was best if I let him have this victory.

"Alright. I'll call you a cab." I got up from my bed to grab my cell phone.

He continued to look at the floor. "Thanks."

"I don't want things to be awkward between us. I feel really bad about this, but I think we both know it's for the better." I felt like I was trying to convince myself just as much as I was trying to comfort him.

He stood up to retrieve his bags and walked towards the door, stopping when his hand reached the knob. "I just need some time. Give me some time." As soon as the door closed, I settled into my bed and breathed in the smell of Ryan before I let myself fall apart. Ryan and I had attended our first day of school together; we learned to swim and ride our bikes together. He was my friend before I even knew what a friend was and I never imagined I would have to let that go. I hoped that time would heal us and our friendship would be restored. Eventually I settled into a deep sleep as exhaustion took over my body, leaving the sorrow I felt behind.

The door slammed and startled me awake. Jade. That girl couldn't do anything without making noise and drawing attention to herself. Her eyes danced around the room before they finally stopped on me. "I thought you had to take Ryan to the airport. Where is he?" she asked. Even in the morning, after she completed her walk of shame, she looked good. Her long dark hair was pulled into a knot at the top of her head and her large green eyes didn't have a touch of mascara smeared around them. She was absolutely gorgeous and knew how to use it to her advantage.

"Remember how I said I thought it was time to make a change? Well, I broke up with Ryan last night and he decided to catch a cab to the airport alone this morning," I muttered as I rolled the corner of my comforter between my fingers.

She stared at me, mouth wide open. "Are you kidding me? You dumped Ryan? Wait, did he spend the night here last night after you dumped him?" She was talking so fast that I was having trouble keeping up with all of her questions.

"No, I'm not kidding. Yes, I broke up with him and yes, he spent the night here."

"Wow. How did he take it?" Her interest in Ryan's feelings caught me a little off guard. This was coming from the girl who went through boys at lightning pace and never stuck around long enough to develop any real feelings. She said she was too young to be tied down and just hadn't met her Mr. Right yet. Something told me she was afraid of commitment, but I had my own issues so I just left it alone.

"He took it hard, I guess." I relayed the events of last night and this morning while she sat there, looking at me with a stunned look on her face.

"I didn't think you had it in you."

"There's something missing. I know eventually I'll have to marry someone like Ryan to make everyone happy, but I'm not about to string him along when he's across the country."

She shook her head at me. "I'm so sick of hearing you talk about making everyone happy. That is a bunch of bullshit! The only one who needs to love the person you are with is you." I saw her point, I really did, but she didn't have my pressures. Her parents were totally cool, hence why Jade was the way she was.

When she left the room to shower, I relaxed back into my bed, trying to fall back to sleep, when there was a knock at the door. At first I ignored it, thinking it was one of the

17

girls from down the hall wanting to borrow something; I wasn't in the mood to be social today. The knocking continued a few more times before I heard the person on the other end. "Alexandra Riley, open this door right now. I know you're in there." My heart started to race out of my chest at the thought of having to face her. I knew who that voice belonged to and why she was here. This weekend could not go any further downhill.

The woman behind that door was a constant source of stress and sadness for me. There was rarely a minute that went by when her voice didn't play in my head. You need to be better, Alexandra. Why can't you be more like your sister? Why are you wearing that? You shouldn't be eating that, Alexandra. It played over and over like a bad pop song and no matter what I did, I couldn't turn it off.

I rubbed my forehead with sweaty palms as I climbed out of bed, pacing for a moment before opening the door with a forced smile. "Hi, Mom! What are you doing here?"

She lifted her nose at my frumpy appearance before pushing past me. "Cut the crap, Alexandra, you know exactly why I'm here. Where's that roommate of yours?" My mother was short and thin with a perfect blond bob, brown eyes and perfectly manicured nails. She spent hours every week going through various treatments to maintain her youthful appearance.

I gritted my teeth. "Why does it matter?" She narrowed her eyes at me, causing me to focus elsewhere.

I stood silent, my arms crossed over my chest, as my mother eyed our dorm room with disgust. It was simple, but it served our needs. The white walls were covered with our photos and a few random art pieces Jade and I had picked up around the city. My bed was covered in white while Jade opted for red and black; neither bed was made. Clothes hid the desk chair and hung from the closet door.

"Clean yourself up and meet me downstairs. I'll be waiting in the car; I can't stand to look at this place," she said as she waved her hand in the air. I was still frozen in place when she exited the room, slamming the door shut behind her. I guess my sweats weren't appropriate in my mom's eyes.

My hands shook as I went to my closet to pull out a white turtleneck sweater and a pair of light grey skinny jeans. I dressed quickly, throwing on a pair of black flats and a black pea coat before pulling my unruly hair into a tight bun.

I grabbed my purse and was just about to exit when Jade entered the room, wearing only her robe. She eyed me suspiciously. "Where are you off to?"

"My mom is waiting for me downstairs," I replied, fidgeting with my purse strap.

"Does she know about Ryan? She can't know about that already, can she?"

"I think she does. I have no clue how she found out, but she's not happy," I sighed. This day was really going to suck.

Her eyes grew large. "Oh, fuck. Do you need me to go with you?" She started toward her closet, grabbing some clothes before turning back to me.

I took a deep breath. "No, I'll be fine. Besides, I don't think it was an open invite."

"You'll call me if you need anything, right?" she asked, falling into her bed.

"I'll be fine. Movie and junk food tonight? I need it before we start classes again tomorrow."

She smiled and nodded. "You got it."

I said goodbye and walked out the door. I knew exactly why my mother was here. She had come to patronize me. She did this all the time; if I even took one step away from the life she had planned for me she went crazy and tried to manipulate me back into place. It had always been this way and I'd accepted it. As I opened the front door to walk onto the sidewalk, my heart pounded in my chest and my lips felt numb. I told myself that maybe this wouldn't be so bad and that there was no need to panic, but I couldn't make myself believe it. I'd been down this road too many times before.

My mother's long time driver, Thomas, stepped out of the black Lincoln to open the door for me. I hesitated for a second before sliding onto the black leather seat. Clasping my hands on my lap, I closed my eyes and silently counted to ten.

As soon as the door closed, she started in on me again. "Is that what you call cleaned up, Alexandra? God, have you even showered today?" I shook my head at her; if I lied, she would know. It wasn't worth it. "Look, let's talk about why I'm here. This mess you've made with Ryan, it needs to be cleaned up immediately. It's already causing issues between Jillian and I." She shouldn't be more concerned about her friend than her daughter, but she was. I wondered how Jillian found out, but I wouldn't ask.

"There isn't anything to clean up. Ryan and I need a break so we are taking one. We're separated by a whole continent and we both have classes to focus on." Her eyes narrowed at me as I continued, "It's just a break. It doesn't mean we're over forever." Her lack of concern for me made my skin crawl. I would rather be anywhere but here.

She seemed to consider this for a minute. "You better fix this soon. From what I hear, Ryan's heart is broken. If you ruin this-"

I stopped her, my voice shaking with both anger and sadness; I hated that she viewed my personal relationship and breakup like it was a game. I hated her games. "Ryan and I have been friends for a long time. I won't ruin it."

"Good, that's what I like to hear. Now since you made me drive all the way into the city for this nonsense, let's have lunch." Of course I didn't make her come into the city, but there was no point in arguing with her. She wouldn't listen to me anyway.

We ate lunch at an organic restaurant my mother chose while I listened to her go on and on about a charity event she was putting together. I picked at my salad and nodded every now and then, but didn't speak. I wanted to go back to my dorm room and hang out with Jade. I wanted to go somewhere to cry because it wasn't enough that I broke my best friend's heart; my mother had to tear me down more until there was nothing left. She always did that; she pushed and pushed until I broke. For once I wanted to matter to someone.

As she dropped me back off at the dorm, she reminded me how important my relationship with Ryan was to her. I hated every minute I spent in that black car, listening to her talk about how she felt and what the end of my relationship was doing to her. This wasn't normal, that much I knew, but there wasn't anything I could do to stop it. My mother and logic didn't go well together.

As soon as she dismissed me, I ran into the dorm and stripped off my clothes, throwing my sweats back on. That was my silent way of defying my mother. Maybe one day those little steps toward rebellion would lead me to something bigger, but that was unlikely to happen anytime soon.

I filled Jade in on my visit as we walked to the bakery to pick up some carbs for movie night. She hated that I let my mother walk all over me, but I didn't feel like I had any other option. Besides, it had been a part of my day-to-day life for so long that I didn't know any better.

We spent the rest of the day watching DVD's, eating excessive amounts of junk food, and giggling at anything and everything. The weight on my chest seemed to lift with every moment spent with Jade. She told me about the guy from last night. I had no clue why she felt the need to talk to me about her crazy sex life. I was saving myself for marriage; that was what I told every guy I dated, but I just hadn't felt enough desire to take that next step with anyone. Once I gave that part of me away I could never get it back and I needed it to mean something. I wanted to feel so deeply for someone that I wanted nothing more than to be with him. No regrets and no second thoughts, just pure want. I might never find it, but that didn't mean I couldn't crave it.

Chapter Three

I woke up the next morning feeling marginally better than I had when I went to bed the night before. I had no regrets, but my heart still hurt for the loss of my friend. Many times last night I thought about calling him to make sure he made it back to school okay, but I settled for a quick text. He replied with 'yes'. My heart dropped when I saw the impersonal text; I was used to more from Ryan. I guess we both needed space before we could move forward with what I hoped would be friendship. There was too much history between us to become strangers.

Today was the first day of the second semester. I was more nervous than usual because I had signed up for an Art class. I slipped it past my parents by telling them it was an optional elective for my Pre-Med degree. That much was true. It would fulfill my requirements, but more than that it would give me an opportunity to do something I wanted to do for once.

Art was my passion, the one thing that allowed me to escape all the stresses in my life. I could take all my feelings, thoughts, and concerns and stick them on canvas. I'd never been able to find my voice where my parents were concerned, but my hand found a paintbrush when I was five. I guess you could blame my elementary art teacher, Mrs. Rome, but the first time I held a paintbrush, I knew I was onto something. That day my mom had taken away my favorite doll; she said I was too old to play with toys and it was time to take piano lessons and work with a math tutor. I didn't want to play the piano and I was already way ahead of my classmates in math. I didn't say anything, though. I never did. However, that day I took a brush and stroked it over a large white piece of paper until the bell rang and I realized how much better I felt when class was over. It soon became my form of expression and an outlet for all the things I wanted to say, but couldn't. Art meant everything to me.

I looked at the clock on the wall; I only had ten minutes before I had to start my walk across campus. I glanced over at Jade who was still sleeping and remembered she had a class the same time I did. She could care less if she went to class or not, but for some reason it mattered to me. She was always there for me when I had boy or parental difficulties and this was the one thing I could offer her. I was good at doing what I was supposed to do.

"Jade, you need to get up. I have strict instructions not to let you miss the first day of class!" I yelled as I threw my textbooks into my backpack. Jade missed so many classes last semester that she almost got kicked out of school. She had vowed to do better this term and I had promised to help her. I couldn't guarantee she would make it to all her classes, but the first day was pretty important.

"Who gave you those instructions?" she mumbled, rolling over and folding her pillow over her head.

"You did," I said, grabbing a notebook and pen off my desk.

"Okay, just give me five more minutes." She moved so that her head rested back on her pillow, using her arm to cover her eyes.

"That leaves you with five minutes to get yourself ready," I said, dangling her need to always look good. She rolled out of bed and grabbed her robe so fast you would have thought the fire alarm sounded. She was a little on the side of ridiculous, but I loved her anyway.

"Is that what you're wearing?" Jade asked as she crinkled her nose. I had chosen a pair of old jeans that were worn in the knees and frayed at the bottom and paired it with a fitted royal blue turtleneck sweater. Not my best outfit, but it was appropriate for where I was going. I attended class to learn, not to pick up guys. Her face seemed to lighten as she looked up and saw that I had let my long blond hair fall into soft waves instead of doing my usual ponytail or loose knot at the top of my head. I threw on my puffy black coat and turned back to look at her.

"I start my Art class today and I don't need paint stains on my good jeans," I said, giving myself a once over. By this time she was dressed in black leggings and a long grey tunic and had started to pull on her knee high boots. Why anyone would go through all that trouble to sit through a lecture or two was beyond me. I pulled my backpack on and headed toward the door.

"I'm taking off. Don't forget your textbooks." I began the ten-minute walk to the NYU Art Center and instantly regretted that I hadn't grabbed my hat and gloves; the weather in New York was anything but tropic in the middle of January. Personally, I didn't mind winter. There was nothing better than jeans and sweater weather. A storm a few days before had left a light dusting of snow on the ground and my feet made a crunching sound with every step I took. It was a melodic, relaxing sound that cleared my mind as I inched closer to class.

My pulse picked up as I entered the art studio that would hold my class for the next four months. It wasn't the class itself that scared me; I was walking into a room full of strangers whom I would join three times a week for two hours as we shared our intimate thoughts through art. The people in this class would probably end up knowing more about my inner thoughts than any friend or family member. Art was a way to express everything that I was feeling during a given day; some days it all came out rainbows and sunshine, but on others it was clouded by darkness. While most of my friends had journals or laid out their inner feelings through multiple Facebook posts, I had chosen to draw and paint in my family's pool house. My parents weren't particularly fond of my love for art, but had agreed that the 'little hobby that I would simply have to grow out of' could be done out of sight.

When I walked past a circle of easels in the center of the room, I noticed art desks in sets of two; there was only one set open and it just happened to be in the front row. If I wouldn't have had to deal with Jade this morning I would have made it to class in time to get a better seat, but of course things didn't work out that way. That girl really needed to invest in an alarm clock and a decent amount of self-discipline.

I put my bag down and grabbed a new notebook and pencil as the professor cleared his throat, signaling the start of class. "Good Morning, ladies and gentlemen. My name is Greg Thomas and I'll be your instructor for the next 16 weeks."

Greg Thomas couldn't have been more than five foot

seven and wore a ridiculous pair of dark jeans pulled up a little too high on the waist and a patterned button down western shirt. His glasses looked like they hadn't been updated in years and he had longer hair in the back, some of which was combed forward to his forehead in order to hide an obvious bald spot. I couldn't help but ponder the idea of submitting him to the TV show, What Not to Wear, or the movie Clueless. I needed to find his Miss Geist and set him up.

"This semester we will be going over many different art types, from Abstract to Portrait to Still Life. I know some of you may already have a niche you would like to concentrate on, but this is Art 101 and it's required for all Art majors. Consider it a stepping stone to your future." He began to write week one goals on the board when the door directly to his right opened, causing everyone to focus their attention in that direction.

At first I thought my eyes were playing tricks on me because it was Sexy Stranger from the club. He was dressed the same as the other night, wearing faded blue jeans that sat low on his waist and a brown leather jacket over a fitted white t-shirt. One thing I hadn't noticed before was the amazing color of his eyes. They were the shade of green sea glass and, with the reflection of the light, they showed a vibrancy I didn't know eyes could possess. He looked around for a second, realizing the seat next to me was the only one open. I realized I was staring and quickly looked down at my notebook, hoping he wouldn't recognize me. I talked to him for all of five minutes the other night, but something about him unnerved me. I couldn't place it, but I was definitely feeling a level of uncomfortable that I wasn't used to. As he took the seat next to me my eyes betrayed me, trying to get another glimpse of the new guy. When our eyes met, I felt extremely uneasy, wishing there was a hole to climb into. Eye contact had always been an issue for me; I was afraid someone would see through me and would realize that I wasn't who I pretended to be.

"Excuse me. What's your name?" the instructor asked, bringing my focus back to the front of the room. He was staring directly at my new neighbor with a look of annoyance that I usually only saw from my father.

"Dane Wright," he said, drawing my attention back to him. The hot guy from the club had a name…and a deep masculine voice that had me silently begging to hear more. He looked in my direction and winked before turning back around to face the instructor. My heart rate picked up again; I'd be lucky if I got through this day without having a freaking heart attack. I didn't know a thing about this guy - besides that he went to dance clubs and attended an Art class - but my body couldn't stop reacting to him. I never had this type of reaction to guys, ever.

"Okay, Dane Wright, why don't you tell me what time this class starts?" Mr. Thomas asked, crossing his arms over his chest. Even in his awkward state of fashion, he looked intimidating.

Dane took a piece of paper out of his pocket and unfolded it. "It begins at 9am according to my schedule. If you would like to look at it, I can make you a copy." Dane smiled and looked back at our classmates to see how many were getting a good laugh from the scene he was causing. For whatever reason, this lit his fire. I felt like someone had put me in a time machine and sent me back to high school.

Mr. Thomas placed his hands on his hips. "Okay, Dane Wright. Look at the clock and tell me what time it is now."

"Well, Mr. Thomas, it's 9:11am, but I've been in this chair for at least three minutes, maybe four," he replied. This guy was arrogant and immature; I expected guys to be a little more mature by the time we hit college. I guess not everyone could live up to my expectations.

"Okay class, in honor of Dane Wright, the seat you're in now is your assigned seat for the whole semester. I want our shining star right in the front row where I can see him. He will be in charge of fetching my paints when I need them during lessons and cleaning up any messes." There was another roll of laughter from the back of the classroom as Mr. Thomas returned to the board. I didn't find it funny and I was ready to get class started. The sooner we got through this first day nonsense, the sooner I could put a paintbrush in my hand again.

Dane ran both hands over his short brown hair as he sighed and leaned over to grab something out of his bag. His arm lightly brushed mine as he sat back up in his chair, causing a shiver to run through my body.

"Your first assignment involves getting to know the person sitting next to you. The remainder of class today will be spent interviewing each other. You will have the opportunity to create a piece of art that represents your partner during class on Wednesday and we will present on Friday. You can use any method of art you would like. This will give us the opportunity to get to know each other and for me to see where you are with your art. Go ahead and get started."

And that was the cherry on top of my day; I had to

actually talk to him. I slouched in my chair before sitting up straight again. No matter what I did, I couldn't get comfortable.

He turned in my direction and I caught him looking me up and down like some sort of display in a museum. I didn't think he remembered me. and decided that might be for the best. His eyes stopped on my chest and I was pretty sure I saw his eyebrows rise slightly. Typical male, I thought. I quickly crossed my arms and cleared my throat, causing his eyes to shift back up. "We should probably get started on this project. I want as much information as possible to start my painting on Wednesday."

"Well, why don't you start by telling me your name? The whole class already knows mine." He started to tap the eraser of his pencil on his nose while looking right at me with those eyes. It would be so easy to get lost in them. Those eyes could get me into a lot of trouble.

"My name is Alexandra Riley, but my friends call me Alex. I grew up in Greenwich, Connecticut and right now I'm majoring in Pre-Med, but my dream is to become a Graphic Artist which is why I slipped this class into my schedule. Anything else?" I removed my arms from my chest and reached for my pencil, writing Dane Wright at the top of my page. I couldn't believe I just told him all that. That wasn't something I usually admitted out loud, but for some reason I couldn't stop myself. No going back now.

"Why are you Pre-Med if what you really want to be a Graphic Artist? Lots of people end up changing their major, but that's quite a stretch." I didn't look up at him, but I could see out of the corner of my eye that he was taking notes. I tried to discreetly peek over his arm to see what he was writing, but couldn't read his handwriting. I would love to know what he thought of me after all of this.

"I have no desire to be a doctor. My father is a doctor and my sister just completed her residency. In my family, if you have a brain that's what you're expected to do. My parents are paying for my college tuition so If I switched I would have to take care of everything myself. Plus, they don't really leave much room for negotiation." His brows drew together as he shook his head at me. I turned away, deciding a subject change was in order. "Tell me about you."

"I grew up right here in the city. I'm 22 years old and decided I was going to return to school and make something of myself. I really don't want to work in a bar my whole life. Art is something that I know and something that I'm good at, so here I am." He sat up straight and removed his jacket, revealing his tattoo-covered arms. I couldn't make out all of them without an obvious stare, but it was a collage of various images. It was almost like he started with one and just kept going until he couldn't fit anymore on his arm. Usually, I was turned off by them, but something about the coloring and pattern made me want to explore every inch of his arms with my eyes.

"Did you design your tattoos?" I asked. I wanted to reach out and touch his marked skin. But I didn't.

"Yeah, I drew them out and a friend of mine did them in his shop. I have a dragon tattoo on my left arm and a guardian angel with my sister's name on the other. The other stuff just kind of happened out of boredom." I wanted to ask him why he had a guardian angel tattoo with his sister's name on it, but I felt it wasn't any of my business. He must have noticed my hesitancy because he continued. "Jenna died

31

when I was nine; she was five. Mom had picked her up from dance class and a truck ran a red light, hitting the rear passenger side directly where my sister sat." His eyes looked away from mine and he began to twirl his pencil on top of his notebook again. His face showed vulnerability and under his hard exterior, I saw something honest and sincere when he talked about his sister. I could only imagine the amount of pain losing a sibling would cause.

I placed my hand on his forearm. "I'm sorry," I whispered. I meant it. My sister and I were very different, but I would be torn to shreds if I lost her.

"Enough about me, tell me a little more about yourself. How old are you?" There was a deep sadness in his voice, but it was obvious he was trying to push it down and hide it. All of a sudden having my hand on him felt really awkward so I quickly removed it.

"I turned 19 over winter break," I said as I picked up my pen and started doodling on my notebook. "What kind of art do you do, Dane?"

"I sculpt with metal. Sometimes I weld, sometimes I use fire to heat the metal and then hit it with a hammer to shape it. I can draw, but sculpting is the manly form of art because I get to use power tools," he said, wiggling his eyebrows at me. His rationale made me smile. Most guys I knew never got their manicured hands dirty and here was one who defined his manliness through his art by using power tools.

I glanced up from my paper. "I've never seen anyone do a metal sculpture before. I'd like to watch that sometime."

"You can come to my place anytime," he said, as he ran his tongue over his upper lip. I should be appalled by the underlying meaning of his words, but I couldn't take my eyes off his lips long enough to let them bother me. The grin that formed on his face told me that he knew exactly what he was doing.

"Do you like something you see?" he finally asked.

My mouth went dry. I wasn't used to being around someone so forward. When I looked back down at my notebook, it was covered in little hearts. I blushed as I quickly turned it over before Dane could see my newest work of art. Out of the corner of my eye, I could see his grin widen and I wondered if I was already too late.

"Class, I hope you have everything you need to start the second phase of your project. Please take the last few minutes to start thinking about what you would like to do on Wednesday," Mr. Thomas said, interrupting our exchange. Relief washed over me; I couldn't stand to look at those green eyes much longer. I could, but I didn't want to. I needed some fresh air. I grabbed my things and placed them into my bag before getting up from my chair. As I turned to leave, I heard his voice behind me.

"You looked beautiful the other night. Hope I didn't cause too much trouble with your boyfriend." I didn't turn around to acknowledge his comment, but I felt my face turning red for the hundredth time in the last couple hours. As much as I didn't want to admit it, I was happy that he remembered me.

I went to the student center to grab some lunch before heading to Anatomy. As always, Jade was sitting at a table in the corner of the room that was otherwise filled with boys. During the first week of school last semester, a group of freshman guys came over to flirt with us. I had a boyfriend and Jade didn't date freshman. After we turned down their advances they never really went away and we've eaten with them every day since.

I spotted Jade as she waved me over to the table. "How was class?" she asked as soon as I sat down.

I sighed and gave her the short version of my morning class, including my run in with the Sexy Stranger from the club and our first project.

"Is he cute? I never really got to meet him because I was busy," Jade said, looking at me with her big green eyes as if I was about to give her some big celebrity gossip scoop. She was a gossip addict; I could see her working for People or Us Magazine, taking pictures of famous celebrities. It would merge her two true loves.

"I guess he isn't bad. He has the most intense green colored eyes I've ever seen, but he really isn't the type of guy I find attractive. He has tattoos on his arms and wears a leather jacket. You would eat him up." He really was her type and I doubted that he wanted anything serious so I could see them working.

"You know, you should go after him. He might loosen you up some." She let out a laugh before continuing, "but if you really aren't into him, maybe you could get me his phone number?" She winked at me before getting up from the table. The thought of giving Jade his phone number didn't make me happy. It was one thing to say it, but it was another to picture myself doing it.

I didn't need a man to loosen me up. My focus was on the future and I would have lots of time after my career was established to worry about finding Mr. Perfect. If the right one fell into my lap before then I wouldn't shy away from it, but I didn't see that happening anytime soon.

Chapter Four

Wednesday morning came quickly. I pulled on a pair of old blue jeans and a long sleeved NYU t-shirt before tying my hair up in a loose knot at the top of my head. The project I was going to work on today could get messy and I wasn't going to take any chances.

I remembered to grab my hat and mittens before I walked to the Art Center. Temperatures were only in the teens, but the cold air felt cleansing as it hit my face. Dane flashed through my mind on the way to class. He intrigued me because he came off as a typical cocky college guy, but I saw something more in him. He was different from other guys I knew and I was still trying to decide if that was a good thing or a bad thing. I took a deep breath before I entered the Art Center in an attempt to get my nerves under control.

When I walked into the classroom I noticed that Dane was already there and my heart sped up like it did every time I was in his presence. He glanced up at me, smiling briefly before returning his attention back to his notebook. I had to take a deep breath to settle myself down before class began. Having to prepare a piece of art that I would share with everyone had me unhinged and having Dane as my inspiration just compounded my discomfort.

I spent the entire class painting what I learned about Dane Wright onto canvas using one of the easels at the center of the room. At least I wouldn't have to spend my time sitting next to Mr. Green Eyes.

Stealing a few glances at Dane while painting, I noticed that he hadn't done anything during class other than doodle in his notebook. At one point, I saw Mr. Thomas walk over and say something to him. Dane said something in response and Mr. Thomas nodded and walked away. I was starting to feel anxious that his part of the presentation was going to include a bunch of scribbles on notebook paper. Hopefully, I was more inspiring than that.

When I was satisfied with the work I'd done, I returned to my desk with a few minutes to spare before class was over. I wanted to look over my Anatomy notes because I heard that Dr. Draper had a habit of giving pop quizzes. My notebook hadn't been open for more than two minutes when my stomach growled, reminding me that I'd skipped breakfast in order to get to class on time.

"That sounds like an invitation to ask if you would like to join me for lunch. Nothing fancy, just the cafeteria, but I'll pay," Dane said, eyeing me with such confidence that I was sure that he rarely heard the word no when he asked a girl out.

"Actually, I can't. I have to head over to the Med Center for Anatomy, which I'll have to do every Monday, Wednesday and Friday immediately following this class. Just thought I should let you know so you don't waste your breath asking me again," I said curtly, crossing my arms over my chest. He stared at me for a minute, letting my words sink in before the sides of his lips turned up.

"Okay, have it your way today, but eventually you'll cave," he said, the cocky grin still on his face. Like an answer to a prayer, class ended and we were dismissed. A leggy blond from the back of the room came up and grabbed Dane's arm as he walked out. She whispered in his ear as he placed his hand on the small of her back. I would never admit it out loud, but I felt a little pang of something in my chest. Was I jealous? I didn't know him very well, but I had the distinct feeling he went through women like I went through chocolate. Just another reason to stay far away from Dane Wright.

I did need to eat so I headed toward the cafeteria to quiet the monster that was growing in my stomach. There was no way I was going to make it without eating something and after what I had just witnessed in the art room, Dane probably wouldn't be in the cafeteria. I didn't want to think about what he was doing right now.

Jade was sitting with the usual crowd when I joined her. She eyed me suspiciously, "Are you feeling okay?"

"Why wouldn't I feel okay?" I asked, raising an eyebrow.

"Look at your tray," Jade said, pointing to my tray. Instead of my normal healthy salad or soup, I had chosen a cheeseburger and french fries. It was something I only did every six months or so and today was a special occasion. My mother never allowed me to eat this stuff at home; it was strictly forbidden. It was just another one of the little ways I could show some resistance without rocking the boat.

"The snooze button got me this morning so I didn't eat breakfast," I said, as I picked up a french fry and popped it into my mouth. Missing the alarm had been a very rare occurrence for me. My friends always joked that I was a walking watch and usually I lived up to that statement.

I inhaled my sandwich as I listened to Kevin rave about a new bar downtown called Loft 10. "They have a dance floor and the place is always packed," he said.

"Kevin, we aren't old enough to get served in a bar. Isn't there a campus party with a keg that we can go to instead?" Jade tilted her head to the left and crossed her arms over her chest. Kevin was attractive if you liked the big bulky jock type. He had short brown hair with golden flecks, blue eyes and huge arms; bigger than my thigh, huge.

"I'll take care of it. Bring me a current photo of each of you tomorrow," Kevin smiled, elbowing Chris.

I opened my mouth to speak, but was interrupted by a hand on my right shoulder. I dropped my french fry as Jade and I both turned in unison. "Oh no," I whispered under my breath as I felt a sinking feeling in my stomach. Dane was standing so close that I could feel him against my back.

He knelt down; his mouth was so close to my ear that I could feel his warm breath on my cheek. "Skipping Anatomy to have a cheeseburger, are you? You know, you could have had a free one." I swear all the blood in my body migrated to my face.

"She doesn't have Anatomy until one. Alex would never skip class for a cheeseburger," Jade said. *Thank you, Jade.*

"That makes you free for lunch after Art class. Next time I won't take no for an answer." I tried to look down to avoid eye contact only to realize that my head was level with areas of him that I really shouldn't be staring at. If there were any way to get up from this table without bumping into him, I probably would have run for the nearest exit. He raised an eyebrow when I looked back up. "I'll see you Friday." And just as fast as he appeared he was gone, leaving me speechless and flustered.

Jade didn't turn back around as quickly as I did. "Holy

gorgeous. Please tell me that you're not complaining about that fine piece of ass being your art partner?" she said, grabbing my arm.

Kevin interrupted before I could answer her. "That's Dane Wright. I went to high school with him. He can be a real prick. You don't want to get on his bad side. I think he worked his way through half the girls in our school and I have never seen him with the same chick more than once."

Jade closed her eyes and took a deep breath. "Just once would be fine with me." I was not one for violence, but a big part of me wanted to smack her. Why did I feel so jealous and possessive over this guy who I didn't even like? Not like that, anyway.

"Well guys, I would love to stay and chat, but I have to get to Anatomy," I stood up; I didn't need to hear anymore. I dumped my tray and exited the student center as fast as I could. Dane might have thought he had the upper hand and Jade might have thought he was cute, but this was ridiculous. What gave him the right to bully me into a lunch date? If even half of what Kevin said was true, I wanted nothing to do with him.

It was abnormally cold and windy when I stepped outside. I pulled my hat and gloves on as I started the fifteen minute trek across campus. With all the walking I'd been doing the last several months, I hadn't worried about hitting the gym on a regular basis. This time was also good for centering myself, relieving my stress as I walked from one place to another. My med classes were draining and most of the time I didn't want to be there, but I pushed through just like I always did.

"Do you want some company?" My skin tingled when I

heard his voice. He had to be stalking me; there was no other explanation for this much coincidence.

I pinched my eyebrows together as I looked back at him. "I doubt you have any reason to walk to the Med Center."

"I do if that's where you are heading to," he shrugged with his hands in his pockets. He was looking at me with those eyes again and I felt myself melting under them.

"Don't you have anyone else to stalk?" I asked, letting out an exasperated sigh. I was beginning to think I would never get away from Dane. He was popping up everywhere in my life and it was wearing on me. He was disrupting my quiet existence and I was fighting between annoyance and excitement.

"You're the only one I want to stalk," he said, grinning from ear to ear and leaving me lightheaded. Okay, so maybe a small part of me enjoyed the attention he was giving me.

"So, I'm your victim of the month?" I asked.

"No, you're actually my first victim. I usually don't have to try so hard," he said, shrugging his shoulders.

"Yeah? Well you can try all you want because this is all you're getting," I said, picking up the pace. A part of me wanted him to try harder and another part was telling me to run. Right now the latter was winning, but if he kept this up it might not stay that way.

"Hey, Alex?"

"Yeah?"

"I won't have to try for long. I guarantee it." He looked at me with fire in his eyes and emphasized the last three words by letting them roll off his tongue slowly. I felt warmth spread through my entire body. This guy was really something else.

As we walked we made small talk about the weather and the layout of the campus; I couldn't tell you half the things that were said because I was so distracted by his proximity to my body. I felt his arm brushing against mine from time to time and his cologne tickled my nose. We made it across campus in record time, due to the brisk pace I used to try and make our time together as short as possible.

"See you Friday," he said, moving one step closer to me. I noticed his eyes were fixated on my lips. I moved toward the door before he could get any closer. I wasn't going to let Dane kiss me today - or ever for that matter.

He waved as I opened the door to the main building. "Bye," I mouthed as I disappeared into the Med Center. I rubbed my thumb the over my lips, thinking about what could have been. I was in trouble. Dane was the most exciting and scariest thing to ever enter my plastic world.

Friday arrived faster than I would have liked. I could feel the butterflies in my stomach at the thought of sharing my art with the rest of the class.

Dane arrived before me again and I couldn't help how my lips turned up when I saw him sitting there in his jeans and tight navy t-shirt. I'd never been one to ogle a man's body, but my eyes flew to his with magnetic force every time we were in the same room.

"Wow, you look great," he said as I took my seat. He hadn't taken his eyes off me since I walked in the door.

I felt my face growing warm under his stare. "Thanks, I guess. I figured my old jeans wouldn't make the best impression in front of the class." I had carefully chosen a fitted black turtleneck dress with black knee-high boots. My hair was down, allowing it to flow to the middle of my back.

The presentations started and I was impressed by everyone's artwork. We had several painters in the class and a few were very talented. I wasn't sure if mine would measure up, but there was no going back now.

Dane and I were the last pair to go. My chest tightened as I stood up to present. I was nervous because I had to stand up in front of the class. And nervous because Dane Wright was less than two feet from me and I had to talk about him. Walking over to gather my painting from the easel, I regretted my choice in shoes. I had a serious case of Jell-O legs thanks to my growing nerves.

I placed my canvas on the easel that faced the class. My eyes were focused on Dane, waiting to see his reaction. When he finally looked up his eyes widened and I watched him take a deep breath through his nose then let it out of his mouth. Our eyes met briefly and I quickly glanced away as I tried to speak.

I stood there for a moment, looking at the giant red heart that was centered on the canvas. Within the heart was an angel. I filled the rest of the space on the canvas with a colorful abstract art piece, repeating the word INSPIRE to spell out Jenna at the bottom of the canvas in black paint.

"This is Dane Wright. He grew up in the city and, after taking time off after high school, decided to study art at NYU." I cleared my throat before continuing. "Beneath the leather jacket, he has a tattoo of a guardian angel with the word Jenna underneath. Jenna was Dane's sister who passed away when she was just five. She's the inspiration for most of his art." I took a deep breath as the class started to applaud. I was still nervous about Dane's reaction, but happy that I had my first art project under my belt.

"Thank you, Alex. Dane, you're up," Mr. Thomas said, nodding toward Dane. I glanced at Dane who was frozen in place, eyes still locked on the painting I created. When his eyes finally met mine, I noticed they were glistening with unshed tears. Something passed between us. I was not sure if it was understanding or gratefulness, but having that effect on someone warmed my heart.

Dane started to move and I fully expected him to grab a piece of paper from his bag. My eyes grew as I watched him pick up an object wrapped in white cloth from the table at the side of the classroom. He revealed a metal sculpture that consisted of two objects. On the left was what looked like a brain with a scalpel and a stethoscope etched into it and on the right was a heart with a paintbrush and an easel. It was much more than I'd expected. I couldn't believe he had taken the time to create a metal sculpture based on me. No one ever spent that much time on me. I also realized I had told him some things that I didn't necessarily want the whole class to know; things depicted in this piece of art he was about to show everyone. Panic ran through me. Maybe we both got a little too personal on this project.

"This is Alex Riley. She grew up in Connecticut and her family wants her to become a doctor. She is a Pre Med student, but her real passion is art; that's where her heart is. Her dream is to become a graphic artist."

I felt completely naked when the bell rang. I gave him that information, but I didn't think about the repercussions before doing it. It was something I had never told anyone, with the exception of Jade and Gwen, and now a room full of strangers knew everything because of my moment of vulnerability. I quickly grabbed my bag and began to exit the classroom without giving him another glance. I didn't want him to see the tears forming in my eyes. "Alex, wait!" I kept walking until I felt a warm hand grip my arm, turning me around.

"You aren't mad are you?" His serious eyes held my gaze as my own filled with tears. I wasn't mad at him, but I was furious with myself. I might have been overreacting, but I wasn't used to others seeing inside my shell. I had spent years building and beautifying that shell.

"Just forget about it. I have to go." I turned and walked away as quickly as I could before the tears began to slide down my cheeks. I heard him say my name, but I kept walking. The whole class knew I was a coward now. I couldn't be angry at the truth, but that didn't make it hurt any less.

I immediately dialed Gwen's number when I was safely back in my dorm room. Gwen and I were different in so many ways, but we came from the same place. I constantly struggled to do what I was supposed to do while Gwen simply accepted it. She was engaged to a man she had been dating for three years. He was also a medical resident and came form one of the most prominent families in Greenwich. She seemed happy to be marrying the guy of my parent's dreams, but I always wondered if she truly was.

"Hey, long time no talk," Gwen said as soon as she picked up the phone.

"We spoke yesterday," I replied. Gwen had always been

a bit on the dramatic side.

"Someone sounds a little jumpy today. How did your presentation on Mr. Green Eyes go?" she asked. I called her the other day to fill her in on my first day of classes. She was always a good listener and the most understanding person in my family.

"Mine went fine. He, on the other hand, told the whole class that my real aspiration was art and now they all know I'm a coward. I'm not looking forward to returning on Monday." My eyes started to sting again, just thinking about what happened in class today. I didn't want to cry. I was generally not a crier, but the last week had taken a lot out of me. I broke up with my friend, had a surprise visit from my mother, and had been called out in front of the whole class. I would say it ranked right up there with 'worst week ever' status.

"You told him?" she asked, sighing into the phone.

"Well yeah, it just kind of came out. I wasn't thinking about the presentation when I said it." I rubbed my forehead in an effort to ease the pain that had been building since I left class. I wished there was a way to go back in time and tell him how amazing my life was. I should have told him about my amazing parents, my beautiful home and how I was accepted into the National Honor Society, but there was something about him that brought the truth out of me.

"You like him don't you?" she asked. I could tell she was smiling through the phone. I needed her sympathy, but it seemed I was amusing her instead.

"Why does everyone keep saying that? No, absolutely not!"

"Whatever you say, Alex."

Just then Jade walked through the door with a huge smile on her face, holding what looked like two New York drivers licenses. "I'm going to have to call you back later," I said, never taking my eyes off my roommate.

"Okay, later."

"Bye"

I set down my cell phone. "What are those?"

"These are our tickets to drink in a real bar. You and I are going to Loft 10 tonight. You look like you could use a drink." She handed me my card and sat on the edge of my bed. I recognized my picture; it was the head off one of my many senior portraits. There was no way anyone was going to believe this was real. Adding an arrest or ticket to my week was just what I didn't need.

"I should really study." Or stay in the dorm all night crying my eyes out into a tub of Ben & Jerry's. Ben & Jerry were fabulous dates; they never let me down.

"Come on, I'm not going to let anything happen to you. Besides, you are already dressed to go out, just touch up your makeup a little," she said, circling her finger around my face.

After this morning's events, I really wanted to be alone. However, I had only been out one or two nights my whole freshman year of college and maybe I needed this. "Okay, what time?" I asked.

She threw her arms around me, practically screaming in my ear, "Be ready at 9!" Anger and alcohol aren't the best combination, but if it made me feel better and helped me forget I could hang my reservations for one night. For once I just wanted to forget that I was living by someone else's rules.

CHAPTER FIVE

Loft 10 was not my usual scene. The inside was very dark with green and blue lights illuminating the bar. They same lighting continued around the room, shining through a half wall that divided the dance floor from the bar seating area. Seating consisted mostly of tables and chairs, but there were also a few black leather couches in the VIP lounge area. Even in my knee length sweater dress and knee-high boots, I looked like a nun in comparison to most of the other girls in the place. The club was packed, but luckily Kevin and his friends had arrived early and scored a table a few feet away from the bar.

"Well, look who's here. Can I get you girls something to drink?" Kevin asked, his eyes traveling the length of both our bodies before returning to our faces.

Kevin's stare was making me uncomfortable so I tugged my skirt down as far as it would allow. "No, I'll go get myself something. Jade, what are you drinking tonight?" I asked, in an effort to break the spell.

"Vodka and grapefruit juice, please. Make sure they don't burn it!" she shouted over the noise. I weaved my way through the crowd gathered around the bar and waited for one of the two bartenders to serve me. As I studied the ID that Kevin had made for me, I began to feel the nerves build in my stomach again. There was no way anyone was going to look at this thing and serve me. Then again, I was sure half the bar had to have used fake plastic in order to be drinking this evening.

"Alex." My back went stiff when I saw who said my name. Dane was standing right in front of me on the other side of the bar with a huge grin on his face.

"Uh, what are you doing here?" I asked, trying to mask the annoyance in my voice. It was obvious he was working, but I didn't know what else to say. Could I not get away from him? New York City was not that small of a town.

"What does it look like I'm doing here?" he asked as he threw a towel over his shoulder. My eyes locked on the towel but then journeyed downward, taking in the strong, bulky chest highlighted under his black Loft 10 t-shirt. There were a few times these last few days when I wondered what it would be like to touch that chest; it would never happen, but it didn't mean I couldn't dream. He cleared his throat, startling me from the staring contest I was having with his chest. When I looked back up, Dane was biting on his lower lip, trying to hold back a laugh.

"I need a vodka and grapefruit juice, a shot of whiskey, and a Bud Light, please," I blurted. I was rambling again and I hadn't intended to order a whiskey and a beer, but I was going to need both to get through the night. When I walked out of class today, I took comfort in the fact that I wouldn't see Dane for a couple days and now here he was. Any thought of the consequences of underage drinking in a packed New York City bar left me. I really needed those drinks now.

"You have to be 21 to drink in this bar," he said, looking serious. I handed him my ID and he studied it for several seconds before smiling, "Maybe if you take this down to Jay

48

at the end of the bar, he can help you. I can't do it." I sighed as Dane walked down to the end of the bar to help someone else.

As soon as Jay looked my way, I waved him over and placed my order. He hadn't even blinked when I showed him my ID. Relief washed over me as he handed me my drinks and accepted the cash I handed him. I immediately threw back my whiskey and carried the other drinks back to my table, weaving my way through the crowded club.

"Thanks," Jade said, grabbing her drink out of my hand. I noticed we had a new guest at our table who I had not met before. He had longer dark brown hair that was partially tucked behind his ears and his big brown eyes highlighted by thick dark lashes. He was ruggedly handsome with stubble along his strong jaw; not my type, but cute. "This is Tyler. Tyler, this is Alex. Tyler graduated from NYU last year with a degree in Architecture; he and Kevin went to the same high school," Jade said, as her eyes remained locked on Tyler.

"Tyler was a hell raiser. Can't believe he graduated before I did," Kevin said. Tyler narrowed his eyes at him, causing Kevin to clasp his mouth shut.

"Hey now, I wasn't that bad. I couldn't help it if the ladies loved me and the school had too many rules." I could see why the ladies might love him. He was confident with an aura of danger, much like Dane.

"Whatever. You and Dane were quite the pair," Kevin piped in, placing one arm around the back of my chair as he fingered my sleeved arm. I was loosening up a bit from the alcohol so allowed his harmless advances.

"Dane Wright?" I didn't realize that I had opened my mouth until the words had already spoken. Dane was everywhere I was and it seemed that everyone knew him. Someone had effectively removed me from Earth and planted me in Dane's world. The jury was still out on whether or not they would be getting a thank you card.

"Yeah, you know him? Dude has been my best friend since second grade."

I let out a loud belly laugh that earned me some looks from neighboring tables. "I just have a class with him. He's interesting, that's for sure." I took a swig of my beer as everyone at the table eyed me suspiciously. I needed another shot...or five!

"For a second there I thought you were one of the girls from his love'em and leave'em days. He used to go through girls pretty quickly and now I don't know if he's dated at all since he started to pull his shit together." Tyler motioned the waitress for another round.

"No, Dane and I have never been anything more than classmates and will never be more than classmates." I heard Jade snicker beside me and turned to give her a warning look. "What?" I asked, narrowing my eyes at her.

"Now that may be a first. A girl who has no interest whatsoever in the handsome, emotionally unavailable, Dane Wright," Tyler stated as he eyed me intently. I stood, not paying any attention to the disappointed look on Kevin's face and moved back toward the bar. It was time for another shot. I bypassed Dane and went straight to Jay who gave me another shot and beer. I quickly downed my shot as I glanced at Dane. I had never seen the beauty in watching a man work, but Dane was different. His arms flexed as he lifted cases of beer up to fill the cooler; maybe he knew I was watching because he was putting on quite the show. It was time to head back over to the table before he caught me looking again.

As soon as I sat back down, Dane came over to stand by our table, gave Tyler some weird manly handshake, eyed Kevin, and exchanged hellos with the rest of the table. Suddenly he knelt down so his mouth was right by my ear.

"Can you come outside with me for a minute?"

"No, I'm kind of busy right now," I replied, rolling my eyes. Tyler and Jade decided that now was a good time to get up to dance. Why did she have to leave me alone now?

"Please, I didn't mean to upset you earlier," he said with sympathy in his voice. I still wasn't leaving the table.

"I'm fine, really!" I was still a little upset, but only at myself. He had simply done his assignment.

Kevin turned and asked me to dance. Any other time I probably would have said no, but right now it was a welcome invitation. "Yes, please!" I stood up and took one more look in Dane's direction. "I'll talk to you on Monday." Dane backed away and glared at Kevin, his jaw clenched.

A slow song played when Kevin and I joined the others on the dance floor. I wrapped my arms around his neck, being careful that my body didn't rub too closely against his as he loosely laid his hands on my waist. Dancing always felt so intimate to me when my body was pressed against someone, but this I could handle.

I felt a tap on my shoulder. "Alex, I'm leaving," Jade said, leaning in next to my ear. She nodded toward Tyler with a big smile on her face. "Are you okay to get home?"

"It's only a couple of blocks; I'll be fine. Have fun!"

She winked. "You too." Before she walked away, she looked at me with a sly grin and a naughty glimmer in her eye. My plans for the rest of the night involved some more dancing and a few more drinks. This week had worn me out and I needed to let loose and have fun for once.

The music began to pick up as Kevin moved behind me with his arm wrapped tightly around my waist. Through my buzz, I couldn't really see the any reason to stop him. I started to move again and felt his other hand at the hem of my skirt as it slowly moved up my leg. His hand moved up my waist, stopping just below my breast. "Kevin, stop!" I turned around, narrowing my eyes at him.

"Relax, sorry!" He took my hand, using his eyes to plead to me for one more chance before we slowly started to move again. I don't know if I gave him another chance or if it was the whiskey; it didn't matter at that point. A few more minutes went by before he had secured both hands on my ass, and began pressing me against him so I could feel how turned on he was through his jeans.

I pushed as hard as I could on his chest, "I. Said. Stop!"

Kevin just stood there, looking at me with his head tilted to the side. "I thought you came to let loose a little, Alex? What's the problem?"

The way people were dancing around us, it seemed like everything he was doing was completely normal. I just didn't want to partake in normal. "The problem is that I don't want you fondling me in the middle of the club."

I turned to walk away from him, but his firm hand grabbed my arm. "Will you let me do it in private?" he whispered, pulling me close to his body.

"Absolutely not," I yanked my arm out of his hold. Suddenly I wasn't so happy that Jade had left me at the bar. Why did guys have to act like such assholes? Actually, I knew the answer to that; they thought with their lower anatomy rather than their brains. That is exactly why I chose to focus on my classes instead of wasting my time with men.

I found a seat at the bar. One more whiskey and then I was going to head home.

💔 💔 💔

As I rolled over in bed the next morning, my head was pounding and my mouth felt like it was stuffed with cotton balls. Whiskey always seemed like a good idea until the next morning when the hangover induced regret took over. A mix of coffee and men's aftershave hit my senses as I worked to open my eyes. Panic instantly set in. The dorm usually smelled like a Bath and Body Works store and this was not the smell of Cucumber Melon and Sweet Pea.

The first thing I noticed was the bed; definitely not my bed. The sheets were grey and the comforter was black and gray striped, a far cry from the white down comforter that covered my bed. As I continued to survey the room, I noted that the walls were grey and the floors were covered in hardwoods. The window overlooked the downtown sky scrape instead of my usual campus view. Oh my God! What the heck did I do? I looked down and realized I was still in my dress, but my boots were missing. So maybe I hadn't passed out and done something I'd regret with a complete stranger. That was reassuring.

The hammer in my head was pounding something fierce as I sat up. I needed a bathroom badly. I rolled out of bed and noticed three doors. The first one I attempted to open was a closet which, as I predicted, was full of male clothing. I had a little more luck with the second door. After relieving my full bladder, I rinsed my face with some cold water in an attempt to regain some composure. I desperately needed a shower and a toothbrush, but that would have to wait.

The third door led to a quaint loft space with a small living area and a small kitchen space in the corner. I could hear movement in that direction, causing my heart to race as I walked closer. Who the hell had I gone home with?

"Good morning, sleepy head. Why don't you sit down and I'll bring you something to drink?"

No, no, no! Standing in front of me, in black athletic shorts - and nothing else! - was Dane. Out of all people at the bar last night, why him? Did he kiss me? This was not good. I couldn't remember anything. Did I kiss him back? What if he had the wrong idea? Oh crap, I'd never in my life seen abs like that this close. Ryan had nice abs, but Dane's were incredible. And the tattoos spread from his arms to his chest and back; the sight of him made me blush.

He must have sensed my brain was working overtime. "Don't worry, nothing happened. I think Jay gave you a few too many shots of whiskey and you were pretty much asleep at the bar when we closed. I brought you up here to sleep it off," he added, rubbing the back of his neck with his hand.

I could feel my cheeks turn a deeper shade of red as I stepped toward the window, noting he lived right above the bar. "Oh my God, did I really fall asleep at the bar? I'm so sorry. God, I feel like such an idiot."

Jade. Did she realize I was here? If she went home, she must be worried sick. "Why didn't you bring me home? Did you call Jade?" I rubbed my temples with the tips of my fingers in an attempt to stop the pounding hammer. I couldn't believe I let myself drink so much that I fell asleep in a bar.

"Well, Sunshine, for one I don't have a clue where you

live. You haven't invited me over yet." There was extra emphasis on the word 'yet'. He had this cocky smile on his face that showed a dimple on his right cheek. I wondered how much trouble that dimple had gotten him out of in the past? And where did he get off calling me sunshine? I felt anything but bright and cheery this morning. "Two, I didn't see Jade anywhere and I have no way of getting ahold of her. And, last, I saved your ass from Kevin. I saw the way he was dancing with you earlier in the night and figured you wouldn't like to wake up next to him in the morning." Okay, he was right about that, but it didn't mean that I wanted to wake up in his apartment...in his bed.

"So you thought I would feel better waking up in your apartment? I've known you for what, a week?" Raising my voice was not helping my head any and I moved onto the couch as I rubbed my temples. "Um, can I get that drink and some aspirin if you have it? I'm not feeling too well."

"Of course," he whispered before disappearing into the kitchen. God, why did he have to sound so chipper in the morning when my head felt like it had been slammed against a cement wall? He came back out with a glass of water and two white pills. "Do you want toast or something?"

"Actually, that might help soak up some of this alcohol. Make it plain, though. I don't think I can handle anything else right now." He headed back toward the kitchen as I downed the pills with slow sips of water. I took in the rest of the apartment; it was masculine with black and grey décor. There was a guitar in the corner, a couple of art pieces on the wall and several metal sculptures on top of a sofa table. The place was surprisingly clean for a college guy.

"Here you go. Hope I made it right."

"It's pretty hard to screw up toast." I would have rolled my eyes if my head didn't hurt so much. This wasn't the first time someone talked to me as if I was some sort of spoiled brat. I hated it and the banging in my head made my appreciate it even less.

"Well, it's just white. Not wheat. Not rye. Not whole grain or whatever you chicks eat."

He was looking down at me with his arms crossed and a stupid grin plastered on his face. Part of me wanted to look at that grin forever and the other part of me wanted to slap it off his face.

"I'm good, really. Do you always take girls home from the bar and into your bed? Wait, don't answer that. I probably already know the answer."

"Relax. I helped you up here, took your boots off, and tucked you into bed. Trust me, I could have easily taken advantage of the situation, but I was a good boy and slept on the couch." I looked at that couch. It had a blanket on one end with a pillow in the same grey as the sheets on the bed. "You really shouldn't drink yourself into a stupor when you are in a bar alone. Lots of things can happen to a girl like you." His eyes looked at me with something other than anger. Concern, maybe?

"Well, thank you. I'll keep that in mind next time," I mumbled, trying not to anger my pounding head anymore than it already was. I was embarrassed that I drank so much last night and that I ended up in his apartment; annoyed that he was so happy in the morning and flustered by his early morning lecture. Looking at the clock on the wall, I noticed it was almost noon. "I should probably go home. I have lots of studying to do."

"It's Saturday," he said, lifting a brow in my direction. I couldn't expect him to understand how much study time my degree required. I picked up my purse and coat and started toward the door, muttering a quick thank you.

"Alex, wait." I glanced back at him, but did not move. "I just wanted to say again how sorry I am about yesterday."

I turned so that every part of my body faced him. "Don't worry about it. I kind of created this mess on my own," I said, giving him a slight smile. I turned to head back toward the door, stopping to put my coat on. My issues had nothing to do with Dane and my anger yesterday had been a knee jerk reaction.

I tried to tell him thank you again, but the look on his face stopped me. He looked like he wanted to say something, but instead remained silent. After a few seconds of silence, I left his building and made the trek back to my dorm.

I cursed Jade for leaving me at the bar alone as soon as I walked into the room. Of course she reminded me that she had asked and that I had given her the okay. She had the biggest grin on her face when I told her how I found myself waking up in Dane's bed. From the look on her face, she thought something happened between Dane and I, which was far from the truth. I quickly corrected her, but the sly look never left her face. I loved Jade, but I didn't think she realized how different we were.

CHAPTER SIX

I wasn't looking forward to seeing Dane when Monday rolled around. Okay, maybe there was a small part of me that was looking forward to seeing him. He was the only person I had ever met that could excite me and frustrate me at the same time. I arrived before he did and waited for him to make his grand entrance. With Dane, everything was a grand entrance.

When he walked in wearing faded jeans that sat low on his hips and a charcoal grey Henley, my mouth may have dropped open just a bit. His eyes met mine and he smiled, showing me his signature dimple. "Good morning. I thought you should know that it kind of sucked not waking up with you in my bed this morning." I looked around to make sure no one else had heard him. I didn't need the rumor mill kicked into high gear.

"Well, you are going to have many sucky mornings then," I said, smirking as I pulled a notebook out of my bag.

"No, Gorgeous, I think you're wrong. I think my luck is about to change." He winked. He seriously just winked at me and I felt the elusive butterflies fluttering in my stomach. The thought of spending more time with him excited me, but it couldn't happen. I wasn't a fan of trying something when I knew it was destined to fail.

"Do you ever leave your arrogance at home or does it follow you wherever you go?" He laughed before leaning in so we were only inches apart.

"This isn't arrogance, I'm just honest and soon enough you'll be honest with yourself and admit that you want me as much as I want you."

"You're not my type," I muttered, looking up into his eyes. He ran his hand through his short hair as he studied me with so much intensity I feared he could see right through me.

"Okay, why don't you give me a chance before you draw any conclusions? Go out with me on Thursday night. There's a DJ playing at the club that I've heard is really good. And we already know that we move pretty well together." He sat back in his chair, studying me intently. If he looked at me like that for too long, I was going to lose my resolve.

"Not going to happen." I moved my eyes to my desk, tracing the faux wood marks with my finger before looking back up.

"Just one date and if you don't have a good time, we don't have to go out again. But give me one night." I made the mistake of looking into his eyes then; they were pleading with me to say yes and I couldn't look away this time.

What did I have to lose by going out with him for one night? It might turn into a complete mess, but after that he would leave me alone, or so I hoped. "Fine, I'll go with you on Thursday, but if you try anything, it's over. I mean it, Dane."

"Whatever you say, Gorgeous, whatever you say."

The lecture finally began. Every time I glanced at Dane, he had one side of his mouth turned up. I had to admit I felt a bit of excitement at the prospect of going out with Dane. At the very least, I would have a great dance partner for one night.

I decided not to avoid the student center at lunchtime and joined Jade at our usual table. I had been trying to stay away to avoid another run in with Dane, but that didn't seem necessary anymore. Jade looked up at me with her signature, teeth bearing smile as I took the seat beside her. "Decided to face the music today, did you? I guess since you spent the night at his apartment on Friday, you have nothing more to hide?"

"Actually, speaking of Dane, I agreed to go to the club with him on Thursday. There's a guest DJ playing in town." Her eyes were huge as she processed what I just told her.

"Are you kidding?"

"No. I figured if I said yes, he would leave me alone." I didn't add the part where I was actually a little excited about hanging out with him.

"Oh honey, after you go out with that boy once, you will be eating out of his palm. Trust me." There was some wickedness in her eyes, but I knew she was wrong. I couldn't have him even if I wanted him.

My world was so confusing.

My parents were proud of me when I was dating some rich, educated boy whom I usually had a hard time connecting with, but Jade was proud of me for taking a risk and going for the boy that I knew my parents would never accept. All Jade had talked about since yesterday was my impending date with Dane while I dodged phone calls from my mother. Talking to her and knowing I was breaking her rules made me feel guilty because I wasn't used to deceiving her. How did I get to the point where doing something that made me genuinely happy also made me feel like a bad person? I knew it wasn't right to feel this way, but I couldn't stop it. My parents were constantly in my head, telling me what I should and shouldn't do. The longer I listened to them, the more resentment I felt.

My mother called again on Tuesday night. I couldn't avoid it much longer - she would have her driver come looking for me again - so I picked it up on the fifth ring.

"Hello," I grimaced.

"Alexandra, we need to talk." This woman didn't mince her words and I could only imagine what I had coming. She always called with a purpose and not one had ever pleased me.

"Um, yes?" I said, biting my lip so hard that I could taste blood. I would like to say that my mother didn't scare me, but that would be a lie. She scared the hell out of me.

"Have you talked to Ryan? I saw his mother at the gym today and she was giving me the cold shoulder. I can't have this, Alexandra. We're on the planning board for the Children's Hospital Gala together and I don't need you ruining this for me. This is quite possibly the biggest event of the year and everyone who is anyone will be in attendance." My lip trembled as I wrapped my arms around my stomach, taking in every word. Her words cut me. There was no concern for my feelings, but she was very concerned about her precious gala. Was I used to this? Yes. Did it hurt any less when it happened? No.

"Mother, Ryan and I are a country apart and things just aren't working right now. It's hard to carry on a relationship when we only see each other on break and I think it's important that we both focus on school." I tried to speak in a normal voice, but it was shaky as I choked back the tears.

"All the men in his family attend Stanford. You know that." I wanted to hang up the phone so badly. She didn't get it and never would.

"I know he had to go to Stanford, but it doesn't change the fact that we are hours and miles apart."

"Is this still just a break, Alexandra?" There was so much vile in her voice. This was more of an order than a question. We both knew that.

"Yes," I lied, sucking in a deep breath.

"Good, make it a short one." She hung up, allowing me to let out the air I had been holding in my lungs.

I settled into my pillow, letting the tears fall from my eyes as I tried to let go of the guilt. The guilt that I couldn't be what everyone wanted me to be all the time. The guilt that I couldn't stop the side of me that wanted more than what my parents had given me. Every now and then, someone would tell me they wished they had my life. I may have a nice house, expensive clothes and a generous monthly allowance, but my life was nothing to envy. I would trade it all in a heartbeat for a bit of positive attention from my parents.

Ever since I was younger, I had been obsessed with romantic movies and novels. The couples I envied never seemed to force their feelings; they weren't plastic. I, on the other hand, grew up in the plastic heart society. In the plastic heart society, love and respect are secondary to money and power. If I told my mother about a boy, she would have asked "What do his parents do?" or "Where does he live?" and even "What kind of car does he drive?". I would never hear "What is he like?". No, because where I come from, that doesn't really matter.

As soon as Jade came home she could tell I had talked to my mom. I was curled in the fetal position on the bed, my body shaking with sobs. I didn't even bother to say hi as she made her way across the room, wrapping her body around mine. Sometimes, after a particularly bad conversation, I closed off for days. Jade helped me through it, comforting me, purchasing insane amounts of chocolate chip cookies, and renting comedies until she finally got a laugh out of me. I loved her for that. When there was so much negative in your life, it helped to have someone who could coat it with happiness. I knew she would be there for me this time too.

Chapter Seven

Sexy Stranger had become the guy who made my heart skip a beat every time I saw him. Deep down I knew these feelings had to remain unexplored, but it didn't mean I couldn't enjoy his company. For some reason, I was more relaxed with him than I was with most people. Why was that? I think he could end up being a great friend or at the very least someone who understood 'the artsy side of Alex' and that meant everything to me.

I arrived in class before he did and had already settled into my desk when he walked in wearing a pair of dark jeans, a fitted long sleeve white t-shirt and a pair of worn brown boots. He didn't fuss too much over his appearance, but he always managed to look breathtakingly handsome. The boy had swagger and he wore it well, from head to toe. He always smelled like a mix of citrus and cedar and - I wouldn't admit this out loud - I wanted to find out what he used to make himself smell that way and coat everything I owned in it.

"Hey, Gorgeous, are you getting excited for tomorrow night?" he asked, startling me from my rather delicious thoughts. One side of his mouth was turned up as he looked right into my eyes. I bet he knew exactly what I was thinking.

I was really excited for tomorrow night. I loved music and, even more so, I loved to dance. "I guess. Am I meeting you there?" I asked, downplaying the obvious.

"It's only a few blocks from the dorm. I'll come pick

you up and we can walk there together so neither of us has to worry about driving. Can I see your phone?" he asked, holding out his hand.

"Uh, why?" I replied, lifting my brow at him.

He had a huge grin on his face. "In case you need to call me or you decide you can't wait until tomorrow night to see me again."

"Cocky much?" I asked. I couldn't help the smile that pulled at my mouth.

"I think we already established that." He winked as I handed him my phone.

We didn't talk for the rest of class because there was an abstract painting that was due on Monday. The six hours a week spent in Art class were becoming a welcome retreat from my stressful planned life. I didn't outline what I would put on canvas this time; I just let my mind and heart guide the brush and was amazed by what they created.

Dane was a fantastic artist. I mean, off the charts good. I would never tell him this because his head was already so big I was surprised he could get it in his t-shirt in the morning, but he had talent. I knew so little about him, but I did know he'd been through some very painful events; it showed in his paintings with angry red and black color combinations. I could tell he had pain locked inside of him and wondered if he kept it all hidden, like I did.

When class ended, it didn't seem possible that two hours had passed. If I could spend all day, every day doing what I was doing now, I would be the happiest girl in the world. I grabbed my things as a large strong hand wrapped around my arm. "I'll pick you up at 9. Text me your dorm and room number."

Then he was gone. As I stood there, I could feel my head and heart racing. My head was scared to death because Dane was unchartered water for me and my heart was skipping around like a little girl on the playground. What was he doing to me?

That night I was sitting in my dorm working on a paper for my English Literature class when my phone started to vibrate.

Dane: Miss me yet?

I swear my stomach did a little flip flop when I saw it was from Dane. How the hell did he get my cell number?

Alex: How did you get my number?

Dane: Texted myself when I programmed yours :)

Okay, that was clever.

Alex: Stalker much?

I was flattered, but there was no way I was going to tell him that!

Dane: Only U

Alex: Night!

Dane: Goodnight, Gorgeous!

Even the whole Gorgeous thing was starting to grow on me.

When I woke up the next morning, I was full of nerves. Maybe this was a mistake? Did I really want to go out with Dane? It was only one date, but I didn't want him to get the wrong idea and think this was more than it was. Did I think he was attractive? Yes, but this couldn't go anywhere. I promised him one night and I fully intended to give that to him. After that, we would have to go back to being art partners and friends. I thought about calling Gwen, but I already knew what she would tell me; this couldn't end well and I should stop it before it even starts. Jade didn't have class until noon on Thursday so she was still wrapped in her comforter across the room.

I took a quick shower and headed toward the coffee shop to study before I had to go to my English Literature class. I ordered my favorite skinny mocha and found an empty seat near the window. There was something so relaxing about sitting in a coffee shop. The smell of coffee and chocolate are like lavender for my senses. Maybe it was being outside my normal environment or the noises of chatter, blenders and movement that relaxed me, but it was my thinking place. The walls were a deep espresso brown with red, yellow and green accents. The shop was full of tables and chairs as well as a few comfy couches. The lighting was dim, but accented with the natural light from the window. The whole setup washed me in a sea of calm.

Today I'd had a hard time staying focused because of a certain boy who remained under my skin. I couldn't stop thinking about the reasons I should, and should not, go out with Dane tonight.

There were many reasons I should go out with Dane Wright. First, if I gave him this one date he would leave me alone. I had promised him one date and nothing more. Second, it would get Jade off my back; the girl thought I needed to get out more and have some fun and that was exactly what I was going to do tonight. Third, I wanted to go. Dane and I were so different, but we shared a love for art and he could be really fun to talk to, even if he was a pain in my ass. Last, there was going to be live music and dancing. How could you go wrong with that?

When I thought about the reasons I should not go out with Dane, I realized that list was a lot shorter. First, he could get the wrong idea and think this was more than it ever could be. I got the impression that he didn't do relationships, but that didn't mean he didn't have other expectations. Second, I was afraid of what others would think if they saw us together. I didn't go out too often and hadn't met too many people outside of Jade's friends. I didn't want anyone to get the wrong impression about me. I'd always been far too concerned about impressions; it was driven in to me that it mattered what other people thought about me above anything else.

As I thought through all of this, I decided the reasons I should go far outweighed the reasons I shouldn't. It was just one night. I could go out, have fun, and hopefully come out unharmed. I headed to class, happy with my decision and ready to see what the night would bring.

I was relieved that Jade was in our room when I got back from class. I was hoping to pick her brain over dinner. I had been on dates before, but I had never been on a date with a non-parent approved boy with tattoos and a leather jacket. My legs were already trembling and my hands were sweaty just thinking about it. I needed a distraction to kill the couple hours I had between now and when Dane would arrive.

"Hey, what are you doing for dinner tonight?" I asked. She didn't look up as she continued to paint her nails. She should have been studying, but she was painting her nails instead.

"I'm meeting Tyler for a drink later," she replied, briefly looking up at me with a sheepish grin. I was surprised she was meeting with Tyler, but I liked him and I thought he would be good for her.

"Let's grab something to eat. I have to be back early anyway because Dane is picking me up at 9. Actually, no, we should be back by 7 because you need to help me get ready." I knew I was rambling as I paced back and forth across the room.

She looked up at me, her eyes huge. "Oh, I almost forgot about the big date tonight. We need to make you look hot!"

"This is not a date. I'm just going out with him to get him off my back." At this point, I didn't know who I was trying to convince; her or me.

"Would it be so bad if it was a date?" Jade asked.

"It can't happen, Jade. Just leave it alone."

Jade laughed. "Whatever, Alex. If you get one taste of that man, you will never go back to polos and khakis. That boy is going to rock your world."

I rolled my eyes at her. She thought she knew everything, but she really had no idea what she was talking about here. She hadn't lived with my parents and she had no idea how bad things could get. "You know that will never happen. It can't happen."

"Well, let's go to dinner and then we'll get you spruced up for your big non-date." The way she emphasized "big" led me to believe I still hadn't convinced her this was not a real date. I wasn't going to waste any more of my time trying to convince her when I'd spent so much time trying to convince myself.

We grabbed our coats and headed out the door. One of the only things I missed about home was being able to grab something to eat and drink from the fridge without stepping outside. Really, who wanted to walk a half-mile outside in twenty-degree weather to grab dinner? The food wasn't even that good.

Jade started toward our regular table after we grabbed our food, but I quickly stopped her. I needed some advice without the guys around. There were only two sitting there tonight, but two was too many. "Can we sit alone tonight? I need some help and I don't want testosterone getting in the way."

She stopped, glancing back at me. "This isn't your first date, Alex. Didn't you just get out of an eight month relationship?" She sat at a small table in the corner with only two seats. I hoped it was enough of a hint to deter any visitors.

"We both know Ryan was more of a friend than a boyfriend. I've known him forever," I said, moving my salad around on my plate, but not really eating it. I didn't know why I even bothered to grab any dinner; my stomach was wound in so many knots.

"So, what do you want to know?" Tonight she was

eating chili cheese fries. How she maintained her size four figure and perfect skin was beyond me. Genetics could be so unfair.

I thought about it for a minute. "Well for starters, what do I do if he expects more than I'm willing to give him? I'm not used to dating guys I barely know."

"I can see why you've never been in love." She stopped to blot her mouth with a napkin before throwing it on the table. "Do you know how pathetic you sound? Have you ever followed your heart to see where it takes you?"

"My heart told me it was time to let Ryan go and I did. Seriously though, how do I let him know that we're in friend territory without sounding like a total bitch?" I decided to try a few bites of my salad. I needed something in my stomach if I was going to drink tonight. I would need the alcohol to combat my nerves.

"Look, you don't have to say anything. Just go out, have a great time, and cross that bridge if you have to. Honestly, he seems like a nice guy." I snorted at this. He could be a really nice guy; he proved that the night he took me to his apartment, but he was also walking sex. Everything about him screamed sex.

"Seems nice, yes."

We headed back to the dorm. Jade had just started going through my clothes to find me something to wear when my phone buzzed.

Dane: One more hour. Can't wait.

I couldn't help the butterflies in my stomach as I read it over and over. No one had ever been this forward with me and I found it exciting. I curled my hair into soft spirals and applied my usual amount of makeup before Jade intervened, giving my eyes the same smoky look they had that night at the club. I'd never been a fan of being overly made up or one of those girls who thought the way to a guy's heart was to completely paint on a face that wasn't real.

Jade picked out a pair of dark blue skinny jeans, a fitted teal camisole, and my black healed ankle boots before she left for her own date. I expected a tight little black dress, but this was a welcome surprise. The boots were questionable since we had to walk but I should be able to handle two blocks without much trouble.

Right at 9pm, there was a soft knock at the door. I took one more look at myself in the mirror and grabbed my black pea coat and gloves before heading to the door. If there was one thing I wanted to avoid, it was Dane Wright stepping foot into my dorm room while we were alone.

I opened the door and got an eye full of his gorgeous dimpled smile. "You look beautiful," he said as his eyes traveled the length of my body. I felt myself blush under his stare. What was happening to me?

He didn't look bad himself. He wore faded blue jeans, which were a little worn in the knees, a white button up and the infamous leather jacket. That leather jacket was really starting to grow on me. I wondered if it would smell like him if I buried my nose in the jacket. "You don't look half bad yourself," I said, as I tried to shake myself from my thoughts.

He held out his hand. "Ready to go?" I didn't offer my hand and instead stepped out closing the door behind me.

"Ready," I replied. He walked with his hands in his pockets while I fidgeted with the buttons on the front of my coat. We enjoyed some small talk about our latest art project on the way to the club which relaxed me a bit. Before I knew it, we were there. I handed the bouncer my fake ID before we found an empty table.

"I'm glad you decided to come out with me tonight. I don't get out too often because I work every Friday and Saturday night at the bar and sometimes pick up a weeknight when they need me." If I didn't know better, I would say that Dane was a little nervous as he rolled the corners of a napkin between his fingers.

"How did a college student get stuck working every Friday and Saturday night?" I was genuinely curious. Dane didn't seem like the type of guy that would skip the opportunities that weekends brought.

He shrugged his shoulders. "I need the money and those are the money nights."

Fortunately, I didn't have to worry about that as long as I kept my parents happy. I couldn't imagine what it would be like to have to support myself through school. Finding the time to study was hard enough.

"Your parents don't help you out?" I regretted the question as soon as it left my lips. He looked down at the table. I saw sadness in his eyes; not the usually happy and confident look that I was accustomed to.

"No. Dad left when I was really young and I've only seen him twice since. Mom barely makes enough to support herself and my little brother." This was the first time he had mentioned a little brother. I had assumed he was an only child after his sister's death.

"How old is your brother?" I asked.

"Eighteen. Come on, let's dance." He offered me his

hand for the second time tonight and this time I accepted. Turn on the Lights, by Future, was playing and I loved this song. There was a brief moment of awkwardness because I wasn't quite sure where to place my hands. He lightly ran his hands down my arms before settling them on my hips, never taking his eyes off mine. I placed my left hand on his shoulder and lifted the other one in the air as I started to move to the music. My eyes closed as I began to relax; this didn't have to be any different from any other time I'd danced. I was in the middle of the dance floor with a sexy man wrapped around me, beats flowing through my body. When I opened my eyes again Dane had a serious look on his face as he watched me move, but it turned into a smile as soon as he noticed me staring at him. Something silently passed between us. He wasn't Dane Wright, the annoying jerk from Art class anymore. He was Dane Wright, the guy I sort of liked and understood.

I wasn't sure how long we stayed like that, but once Dirty Dancer by Usher came on I turned so that my back was pressed against his chest, just like the first night we met. His strong arm wrapped around my stomach, pulling me as close as I could get to him. I could feel every part of him as our bodies moved together with the rhythm of the music. I'd never danced with someone who could move like Dane and my whole body was alert in a way I didn't even know was possible.

The DJ announced he was going to slow it up for a couple of songs. I decided this would be a good time to go back to our table and have a drink, but before I could say anything Dane turned me to face him. I could read the question in his eyes. My heart and mind battled before I answered him by wrapping my arms around his neck. He wrapped his arms around my waist, pulling me close. I couldn't stop myself from smelling the leather jacket when I pressed my face to his chest. The scent was better than I imagined; a combination of cedar, citrus, and leather with a hint of mint. It was so intoxicating that I completely lost myself in it. "You smell good," he said, burying his head in the crook of my neck. After a few minutes I felt his lips brushing my delicate skin. That was my wake up call; it was getting too comfortable. We were too close and I needed to end it before it went any further. The whole gesture felt too intimate and the warning signals were going off throughout my body.

I stepped back out of his grasp, "Let's go have a drink."

His brows pulled together as he rubbed the back of his neck, but he didn't say anything as he followed me back to our table. I ordered a beer and whiskey before Dane told the waiter to bring the beer and forget the whiskey. I lifted an eyebrow in his direction. "Don't you have class tomorrow?" he asked. Point taken. He ordered himself a beer before turning his attention back to me.

We sat in awkward silence for a few minutes before he started to speak again. "Are you having fun?" I was actually having more fun than I'd had in a long time, but I didn't want to tell him that. I wished I could do this every night....with him, but I couldn't.

"Yeah, I love this place." I gave him a small smile before taking a long drink from my beer.

He looked at me like he really wanted to say something before finally opening his mouth. "Do you have plans for Sunday night? There's an urban art exhibit at the gallery near campus and I thought you might like to go."

"Look Dane, I said I would go out with you one time and I did. You're a really nice guy and I'm sure you can find someone else to go with you, but you and I can't do this again."

I watched as his jaw tensed and I wasn't sure if it was sadness or anger I saw in his eyes, but I knew I'd disappointed him. I felt awful and wished I could just tell him everything about my controlling and judgmental parents, but that would almost be like admitting he wasn't worth the risk. "I'm only asking you go to an art gallery with me, nothing else. We both like art and I thought it would be fun. I didn't think you were too good to go with me." He stood up, glaring right into my eyes. "Let's go. I should probably get you back before I start cramping your style."

His words stung. I picked up my coat and immediately started toward the door as anger ran through my veins. If he wanted to be an ass, he could be an ass, but I wasn't going to put up with it for another minute.

"Alex!" I heard him call after me, but I continued to walk. He quickly caught up to me, but didn't say anything as we continued to walk.

"You don't have to walk me home. I'm a big girl and I don't need a chaperone!" I yelled.

"I'm not letting you walk home alone. Just keep walking and you can continue to pretend that I'm not here. If you prefer, I can walk a few feet behind you so no one suspects that we're together." He used finger quotes to emphasize "together", pissing me off even more.

"Quit being an ass," I said through my teeth. I couldn't remember the last time I was this mad and had let someone else see it. Dane had a way of bringing emotions out of me, good and bad.

"I'm not the one who started it," he said, picking up his pace to walk next to me. Neither of us said another word as we made our way to my dorm building. I wanted to get inside my room and forget this night ever happened.

"Looks like you're off the hook now," I said, grabbing my key from my purse. I wanted to get away from him as quick as possible.

"So this is it?" he asked, as I placed my key into the lock.

I opened the door and quickly stepped into my room, shutting it in his face before he could follow me in. As I threw my purse onto my bed, I heard him yell, "Shit!" I stood still in the middle of the room until I heard him stomp down the hall. I let out the breath I had been holding in.

I was a mixture of confused, relieved and sad. I was confused, because my heart was telling me one thing when my head was telling me another. I was relieved, because the date was over and I wouldn't have to fight whatever this feeling was any longer. I was sad, because all those wants and feelings would have to be left unexplored. I could imagine him, but I couldn't have him. It was more obvious than ever that given the opportunity, Dane Wright could break me.

CHAPTER EIGHT

Friday and Saturday were a complete blur. Jade asked me about my "date" on Friday morning and I left out some of the more colorful details, telling her we had a good time dancing, he walked me home, and that was it. She stared at me, waiting for mention of a kiss or more, but was disappointed.

To be honest, I was a little disappointed in myself. I should've told him that he was good enough when he thought he wasn't. I shouldn't have let him leave thinking he was the problem, but I didn't know how to tell him I was the problem.

Dane arrived in Art Class before me on Friday. He didn't greet me with the smile that he normally would, causing my stomach to drop. I didn't know what I expected, but I hoped everything would just be normal when I walked into class. I sat in my seat and whispered "hi", but he still didn't look up at me. I had always been the girl everyone liked, the one who was always nice and never hurt anyone's feelings, so I wasn't sure what to do with this.

On Saturday, my guilt reached an all time high so I decided to send him a text.

Alex: I'm Sorry. Friends?

I spent the next two hours checking my phone every five

minutes, waiting for the text that never came. Jade asked if I wanted to go out with her and I turned her down, telling her I had yet another date with Ben and Jerry.

When Sunday morning arrived I still hadn't heard anything from him. I hated it when someone completely ignored me; it felt worse than being yelled at. Jade hadn't come home last night which gave me extra time to think... and drive myself crazy. I paced the room before doing some angry cleaning. I decided to try another text.

Alex: What gallery is the exhibit at?

Again I waited with no reply. I guess I could add stubborn to the list of words to describe Dane.

It was times like this that I thanked my lucky stars for Google. I googled Urban Art Show, New York, NY, January 29, 2012 and Expressions Gallery popped up. I wrote down the address and started getting ready. I had no idea if this was a dress up kind of art show or a more casual one so I decided on something in between. I settled on a knee-length black shirtdress that flowed slightly at the bottom with a thick red belt around my waist and my black boots. I topped it off with a black and white checkered scarf and a black beanie. I slipped on my jacket, grabbed my car keys, and headed out the door.

There was no guarantee that he was going to show up, but I was hopeful that he would. A man took my coat as I entered the packed gallery. I took a quick look around and when I didn't see him I started looking at various sculptures, large paintings in vibrant colors, and collages of items that would be junk to some people, but put together in the gallery were absolutely beautiful.

I turned a corner and standing right in front of me, talking to an older couple, was Dane. He wore black dress pants with a grey sweater that fits snug around his arms and chest. I liked this Dane, but had to admit I missed the leather jacket. I imagined the way it smelled and how it felt to hold him with it on. The other night I was stupid to think I could just walk away from this. He saw me and stopped talking for a second before he returned his attention back to the couple. I felt rejected, but not enough to give up so easily. I looked at the metal sculptures that were arranged behind him and discovered that the artist was Dane Wright.

They were of couples; one was dancing, one was hugging, one appeared to be sitting on a bench and one was holding hands. They were so simple, yet beautiful. I knew he was talented, but I had no idea he could do this.

"Does my work live up to your expectations?" he asked, startling me. He stood so close to me that I could feel his breath on the back of my neck.

I turned around, leaving us separated by only inches. "They're beautiful," I whispered.

"Really?" His voice was controlled, but there was a hint of sarcasm. I didn't say anything; I deserved his tone.

"Really." I took a deep breath and said what I had come to say. "Look, Dane, I'm really sorry for what happened the other night. I had a great time with you and I let my head get in the way."

He moved his head a little closer to mine. The way he looked at me, I was sure he was going to tell me to go away, but before I could process what happened, his lips were on mine. At first, I didn't react, but then my body took over as I wrapped one hand behind his neck, tasting the mint on his lips and savoring the soft feel of his mouth. The connection made me pull him closer until there was absolutely no space between us. As his tongue begged for entrance, I granted it. We stood there for what seemed like forever, like there was no one else in the room. His kiss was soft, yet passionate, and at that very moment I knew it was the first meaningful kiss I had ever experienced. I needed him and I was his if he'd have me.

He broke away, putting his forehead to mine. His eyes were hooded and I wanted nothing more than to have those lips back on mine. I felt naked and vulnerable as I waited for him to say something. "We can't be friends," he finally said as he closed his eyes. I nodded my head and began to turn around, feeling defeated and rejected, before he caught my arm. "Where are you going?" His eyebrows were drawn as he searched my face.

"I came to apologize, but obviously it wasn't enough, Dane," I said, my voice shaking.

"We can't be friends, I meant that," he stepped closer to me, never breaking eye contact. "I want you to be my girl," he whispered. For a second I didn't think I heard him correctly, but then my heart went aflutter.

"What?" I had heard him, but I wanted to hear him say it again.

"I want you to be my girl," he said, a little louder this time. I started that internal battle between my head and my heart, but this time my heart won. This man standing in front of me right now could break me into a million pieces, but if I didn't let him in I'd never feel that deep down in my stomach kind of love; I'd forever be unbreakable. I wasn't sure how to respond so I did what I'd wanted to do since his lips left mine and kissed him again. He wrapped his arms around me until I couldn't get enough air in my lungs to breathe.

He backed away just enough to speak. "Wait for me. I have to stay here until 7 and then I want to take you out to dinner." I nodded before reaching up to give him one more kiss. It was hard to leave him as I toured the rest of the gallery. I wondered what my parents would think if they knew what I was up to right now, but I quickly buried it away. I made the decision to stay in the moment and not worry about anything else. I stole a few glances in Dane's direction and whenever our eyes met he threw a sexy smile my way. It melted my heart every time. I was happy.

After the show was over, he took me to a little Italian place around the corner from the gallery. It was quaint with soft yellow walls, black and white photos of old Italy, and white table clothes. It was a quiet Sunday night and I felt relaxed just being here and talking with him.

There were some things I needed to say before we could move forward and there was no time like the present. I grasped the end of the table with both hands. "Dane, I'm really sorry about the other night. I just freaked out, I guess. I've never felt this type of connection with anyone and it scares me."

He reached across the table, grabbing one of my hands in his. "Alex, I've never tried this with anyone. I run from things like this; I don't like getting close to people, but I can't avoid what's already there. For the first time in my life, it's easier to just feel."

Heat radiated through my chest. He felt the exact same way I did. We were two people running from ourselves who found each other. "I know," I finally replied. "I guess we're going to do this together in more ways than one." He squeezed my hand before turning his attention to the waiter who had arrived at our table at some point during our exchange.

After the waiter took our order, he told me about his father who left them after his sister died. Things had turned really bad between his parents and his father began drinking heavily. His mother had never worked when his parents were married and had to take on a couple of minimum wage jobs to support him and his brother, Nolan. She wasn't around much, so Dane took care of his brother. He began having problems at school, getting into fights and barely passing classes before he found art and music as a release for some of his anger.

"How did you do it? You were a kid yourself," I asked, staring at him intently. His life was like a sad storybook that would give you nightmares if you read it. I admired him more and more. How he could go through all of this and still be the kind of person he was today was beyond me.

"Sometimes, when your back's against the wall, you can do things that you didn't know were possible. We were in survival mode, you know?" He shrugged like it was nothing, but the sadness in his eyes told me otherwise. He looked so vulnerable and young. I wanted to wipe his pain away.

"I'm sorry," I whispered, reaching up to rub the lines that formed on his forehead. He grabbed my hand and kissed my palm before clasping our hands on the table.

"Don't be sorry. I used to wonder what my life would be like if that day never happened, if my sister was still here, but I learned to let go of the things I can't change. Mistakes make us who we are." Tears welled in my eyes as I listened to him. He was so honest with himself; I wished I could grab onto some of his strength and use it as my own.

"For what it's worth, I think you're doing a great job. You're in school, you're working and you're creating some of the most beautiful sculptures I've ever seen." His expression relaxed.

"Thank you."

I couldn't help but smile at the beautiful person in front of me and my heart warmed when he smiled back.

"Tell me a little more about you," he said, leaning in toward me.

I told him about Jade and how we hated each other for a couple weeks before deciding we actually really liked one another. I told him about Gwen and he asked me some questions about Ryan. I avoided talking about my parents; going there would only remind me why I shouldn't be here and right now this was the only place I wanted to be.

When we left, he walked me to my car. "Where's your car?" I asked, remembering that I had never seen it.

"I sold my truck before school started to pay tuition. Now I just have my motorcycle and it's a little cold out here for that puppy. I'm just going to grab a cab."

"Get in the car." He smiled, but didn't argue.

We took the short drive in silence. I was content to steal occasional glances at him and breathe in his familiar scent. Every time I stole a peek at him, he had an incredibly sexy smirk on his face. I wasn't sure if I was the cause of that smirk, but I sure hoped so.

I pulled up in front of his building and put my car in park, leaving the engine running. "Do you want to come upstairs?" He had a hopeful look on his face and I hated to wipe it off, but I had homework to do and I wasn't quite ready to be back in his apartment alone.

"I should really get back. I have a paper to finish and it's getting kind of late." I gave him a soft smile, which he returned. I had never felt so much emotion from one smile. There was something so genuine and warm and I tried to capture it in my mind to hold for later.

"I understand." He reached over and cupped my cheeks in his hands, planting a light kiss on my lips. "See you in class tomorrow, Baby".

"I thought I was Gorgeous."

"You are gorgeous, Baby."

He rubbed his thumb over my lower lip and I couldn't help but kiss it. "I kind of like the sound of that," I whispered, leaning into his hand.

"Goodnight, Baby."

"Goodnight." He kissed me one more time before getting out of the car and disappearing into his building.

At that moment, I felt like everything was right in the world. It was something I had never felt before and if this was what following my heart felt like, I might never get back up again.

CHAPTER NINE

When I woke up Monday morning, Jade was moving around the room making way too much noise. I'd lived with her for over four months and I'd never seen her up this early. "What are you looking for?" I said, pulling the blanket over my head.

She plopped herself down on my bed, clapping her hands together. "Nothing, I wanted you to wake up and tell me all about last night. Don't leave anything out."

Really? It only takes a little bit of girly gossip to get her out of bed?

I sighed, pulling the covers down off my face. I texted her yesterday and told her my plans to make things right with Dane in case she happened to come home last night. Since she was out when I arrived home, I didn't get a chance to tell her how it went. "Well, I went to the gallery, which was really nice by the way. Dane was an exhibitor. Jade, you should see his work; it's unbelievably good. I didn't know what was going to happen when I saw him, but it didn't go exactly as I had expected." I paused while I debated whether to tell her the rest. I liked that Dane was mine, and part of me wanted to keep him as my little secret, but it would have been for completely selfish reasons. Plus, I couldn't stop the huge smile that touched my lips whenever I thought of him. The moment he kissed me and asked me to be his girl was one of the best moments of my life. I could still see the look in his light green eyes and taste the mint on his lips.

She studied me like my expression would tell her everything. "Keep talking. I can tell there's more, and you better spill it." She looked right into my eyes; I couldn't lie to her. When I was a kid, I tried to tell little lies about where I was or whether I had stolen a cookie from the cookie jar, but I always failed. I couldn't look someone in the eyes and lie. Honesty is a positive personality trait, but sometimes I wished I could twist the truth a little without feeling guilty.

"Well, he planted the best kiss of my life on me. Said that we couldn't be friends and then told me I was his." I bit my lip, watching Jade's eyes double in size. Before I knew what was happening she had me wrapped in a hug, swaying us back and forth.

When she finally pulled back, her smile hadn't diminished at all. "So, are you guys together? By the sound of your voice, I would say you are." My mother may not like my current boyfriend if she ever met him, but Jade was over the moon. Having one person who supported me made me feel more at ease. Dane made me happy and for whatever reason, I felt like I could be myself around him. What happened yesterday made me forget everything I was supposed to be for one day. I was exactly who I wanted to be and no one could ever take that away from me.

"I think so," I said with a sheepish smile.

She hugged me again before jumping off the bed. "Well then, I'm going back to bed." She walked back over to her side of the room and wrapped herself back up in blankets. "Alex, love can change your life. Don't run away from it," she said before she drifting off to sleep. It took a minute for her words to sink in, but when they did it all made sense. The way this felt right now, I would never want to run from it, but it may not be up to me. Life can be unfair and unkind, but sometimes we just have to let go and let fate take over. I believed there was a reason Dane came into my life and I was done fighting my attraction to him.

My phone buzzed.

Dane: Good Morning, Baby

This one simple text put a huge smile on my face.

Alex: Good Morning

I got up and started to pick out my clothes for the day when it buzzed again.

Dane: What kind of coffee do you drink?

Alex: Skinny mocha, why?

Dane: I'm going to bring one to class.

Alex: Really? Thx!

Dane: See You Soon.

I could get used to this if he was going to bring me a coffee to class every morning. Guys had done nice things for me in the past, but it meant something coming from Dane. He was slowly tearing down all my second thoughts and reservations. Maybe he couldn't be my forever, but while he was my now I was going to enjoy every minute of it.

I returned from the shower wearing my robe with my hair wrapped up in a towel and was about to apply lotion when I heard a knock at the door. I wasn't expecting anyone and Jade would never invite anyone over this early. She mumbled something that sounded like "get the damn door", but it was hard to tell with her head wrapped under the comforter. I opened the door just enough to see Dane standing there with two coffees.

I stood there for a moment just staring at him. His green eyes sparkled and he looked edible in his long sleeve black t-shirt and jeans. I'd never seen a guy pull off simple like Dane could. I finally found my voice as I moved my focus back to his face. "What are you doing here?"

His smile fell slightly. "I'm bringing you coffee. I was going to bring it to class, but I couldn't wait to see you."

"Oh," I said as I fidgeted with the belt of my robe. I was at a complete loss for words as I stood there staring at him.

He looked behind me. "Can I come in?" I glanced down at my robe and contemplated whether or not this was a good idea. I was wearing next to nothing and my super sexy boyfriend wanted to come in my dorm room. I decided it was relatively safe since Jade was here and we had to leave for class soon.

I opened the door all the way and motioned for him to come in. He handed me my coffee before placing a kiss on my cheek. "I'm sorry it took so long to let you in. I'm not used to having guys in my room, much less with me in my robe. Thank you for the coffee by the way," I said, trying to hide my blush.

I noticed his eyes scanning my robe-covered body as the corner of his mouth turned up. "I'm glad I stopped by. I may make this a daily habit," he said as he winked at me. I felt my heart rate pick up. Dane was a total flirt and it was starting to grow on me.

"If you want to bring me a coffee every day, go right ahead. I won't tell you no."

He sat next to me and it dawned on me that Dane Wright was on my bed while I was one cotton garment away from naked. "I just might," he said, wiggling his eyebrows.

Something about the way he looked at me paired with his proximity to my body sent heat through me. For the first time ever, I felt desire to be close to a man, desire to fall and let him catch me. It was a dangerous game I was playing and one I wasn't sure I could win.

Dane and I talked while I got ready for class. I still needed to put my clothes on, but that wasn't going to happen while he was still in my room. "I need to get dressed," I said, as I pulled clothes out of my closet and placed them on the bed.

"I'll turn around, no peeking I swear." His mouth turned up at one side as he looked at me with mischief in his eyes. While I trusted him, he was still a guy and they couldn't be trusted under these circumstances. I stared at him for a moment, silently pleading before he spoke again. "I'll step out in the hall if you do one thing for me first."

I eyed him suspiciously, "And what's that?"

His eyes lowered, "Kiss me."

My stomach fluttered as I stood on my tippy toes to kiss his cheek, but before I could react he cupped my face in his hands and locked his lips on mine. His mouth was warm and soft as he massaged my lips with passion and desire. He worshipped my tongue with his own as his fingers coiled in my hair, sending a tingle through my body. I'd never done anything crazy like bungee jumping or skydiving, but I imagined this was what falling must feel like; the euphoria and bliss mixed with a little bit of danger. Just as I reached behind his back to bring his body closer to mine he pulled away, looking at me through dark, hooded eyes. I could feel his warm breath on my face, but my body felt cold and my knees were weak. I needed the connection back.

I wanted to kiss him again, but he stopped me by placing his finger on my lips. "You better get dressed," he whispered, rubbing his thumb over my lips. He kissed me softly one more time before he left my room without saying another word.

I stood there motionless for several minutes, rubbing my fingers over my lips. Every time he kissed me it was better than the last. Was it possible for every kiss to be the best kiss? It was when your boyfriend was Dane Wright. I turned to grab my clothes from the bed and dressed quickly. I was going to walk to class as Dane Wright's girlfriend; someone may need to pinch me.

Dane carried my bag as we walked to class. At one point, he reached for my hand, entwining our fingers. No one would've guessed a couple weeks ago that Dane would be holding my hand as we walked to class; I couldn't believe it myself.

During class, he found every little excuse to touch me, pointing to my notes, making sure our fingers brushed. He tapped his toe lightly on mine a few times and every time I would look over to see him smiling. I liked the smiling Dane over the arrogant one; it looked really nice on him.

We walked to the Student Center for lunch after class

was over. Jade was sitting at our usual table with the lunch boys and grinned from ear to ear when she saw us walking toward them. She may have been even more excited about my new relationship than I was. For the moment, I was enjoying Dane and all the happiness he was giving me.

Everyone was staring at us as we sat down. It was like I had something written on my forehead with an arrow pointing to Dane as eyes found me and then moved to him. "You guys know Dane, right?" No one spoke, but I did get a few nods. "What? Do I have something on my face?" I asked, drawing their attention back to me.

"You guys are, like, together? I mean, you're eating lunch together by choice?" Chris asked, searching my face.

Jade laughed as she answered for me. "Wow, you really are a genius." Now everyone was laughing as the tension dissipated.

"And you're smiling. I don't know if I have ever seen you smile and believed it," Chris added. I smiled even bigger as Dane leaned in to place a kiss on my cheek.

I shrugged. "Thanks."

We talked about a band that was playing at Loft 10 on Friday night. Dane had to work, but he said we should all come and he would save us a table. I was happy that this part of my life was meshing well with my new boyfriend. It was nice to have someone to hang out with besides Jade. I hadn't spent much time getting to know anyone besides her since I arrived at school, so much of my time was spent studying, but I had to admit it was nice to have a balance.

Later that night, Dane took me to his favorite pizza place for dinner. It was a small place that sold pizza by the slice. We took a seat at one of the small tables adorned with a red and white, checkered table cloth. The place was cute and perfect for a date; the fact that he wasn't trying too hard to impress me put a smile on my face. Dane was real; what you saw was what you got.

"How was class this afternoon?" he asked, as he sprinkled red pepper flakes on his slice.

"It was okay."

"Why do you do it? Why do you continue to take classes in something you have no interest in?" He stared into my eyes and I knew my only option was to tell the truth.

"My parents have very strong opinions and going against their wishes would cost me everything. It may be hard to understand now, but if you met them you would totally get it. My life is good as long as I don't rock the boat." I peeled the cheese off my pizza and placed it in my mouth.

"Is your life really that good?" he challenged me. His eyes hadn't left my face during this whole exchange.

"It is at this moment." I winked and realized that I, Alexandra Riley, was flirting.

"That isn't what I meant. You could be working toward your art degree right now, but instead you're wasting your time in Pre-Med just to keep your parents happy. What are you going to do when you are done with Pre-Med? Go on to Med school? Do you have any intention of pursuing an art career?" His line of questioning frustrated me, but then again my life in general was frustrating.

The thought of having to go to Med School and work as a doctor the rest of my life was depressing. When I was in elementary school, my art teacher showered me with kind words and encouragement. She was like sunshine on my pale skin. She was everything that my mother wasn't. As a little girl, you want your mother to do things with you. You want to share moments full of laughter, creating memories, and I didn't have that. My mom was always working on this charity or that, worrying about who had RSVP'd to the next big event or who her tennis partner was for the day. She had a hair appointment on Monday, manicure and pedicure on Wednesday, and massage on Thursday. Tuesdays were spent shopping with her friends and Fridays were spent getting ready for the weekend's events. I had nannies who were nice, but I really wanted, and needed, my mom.

Dad wasn't much better. He worked a lot and even when he wasn't supposed to be working, he got called in. If I didn't know better, I would say he wanted to avoid my mother just as much as I wished she would spend some more time with me. I never saw them kiss or hug in private, but if they were at an event Dad would place a hand on her back and she would smile at him. Her smile was as plastic as a Hollywood housewife's face and I wondered if I was the only one who noticed.

"Earth to Alex," Dane said, waving a hand in front of me. I startled, breaking my thoughts.

"Sorry, I was just thinking. I, uh, actually haven't decided what I'm going to do." I took my eyes off him, focusing them on my plate. "I mean, I know what I want to do obviously, but I haven't decided what I'm going to do. Can we just leave it at that for now?"

"I'll leave it alone for now, but I'm not going to let this go." His hands were fisted on top of the table and I could feel the frustration rolling off his body. It was time for a subject change.

"What about you? What does your mom want you to

do?"

He laughed. "Oh, Baby, my mom was just surprised that I finished high school. Nolan didn't get that accomplished so, at this point, I'm the golden child."

"Didn't she have anything she wanted you to become when you were growing up?" I leaned forward in my chair in an effort to take in every word. There was so much about him I still didn't know.

"That would be a no. My mom was drunk most of the time. In fact, she's only been sober these last couple years. I practically raised Nolan; I didn't do a very good job of it, but I did what I could." He avoided my eyes as he popped the last piece of crust into his mouth.

"So what does Nolan do now?" I asked, my voice soft. He talked about Nolan just enough that I knew he was his brother, but the rest was a mystery.

His lips pressed tight as his eyes focused back on me. "Last I checked, he was earning money selling drugs. I don't think it's his dream job, but it supports his own habit."

His words pulled at my heart as I reached across the table to take his hand in mine. "I'm sorry."

"Don't be," he said, rubbing his thumb over the top of my hand.

"Do you see your mom often?"

"She has dinner at her house once a month. I try to make it and Nolan shows up when he can."

"That's good." I guess it doesn't matter if you have money or not. Dane and I are just people when you strip away all the material things. We have the same issues; we just sleep in different houses and drive in separate cars.

I could tell from the look on his face that he was ready to

end this conversation and he reached for my hand. "Ready to go?"

"Yes, I have a paper to write." I could feel the tension radiating off of him and reached up to place a soft kiss on his lips. He seemed surprised for a moment before reaching behind my back with our clasped hands to pull me closer. This kiss was full of so much need and hunger that I forgot I was standing in the middle of a pizza shop. He finally broke away just enough to smile against my lips before kissing the top of my nose.

"Are you sure you want to go back and write that paper?" he whispered, his face only inches from mine.

I could feel my face flushing. "Yes, I need to write that paper."

He placed another soft kiss on my lips. "If you say so."

He walked me back to my dorm and gave me a proper goodnight kiss. I decided that if I died at this moment I would be happy because I now knew what a body-melting kiss felt like.

As I settled into bed later that night, my phone beeped.

Dane: Sweet dreams, Baby.

How can you not go to bed happy when your day ends like that?

CHAPTER TEN

We fell into a nice pattern for the remainder of the week. Dane came to my dorm room every morning with coffee and walked me to class. Some nights we grabbed a bite to eat together and quietly studied afterward. He picked up a shift at the bar on Wednesday night and I had to admit I missed him. He texted me every night before bed to tell me goodnight and then texted me every morning to say good morning. The guy I once thought of as cocky and arrogant was turning out to be sweet and thoughtful.

It was now Friday. It sucked having a boyfriend who worked every Friday and Saturday night, but Jade agreed to go to Loft 10 with me so I could see him. Dane said they had a live band playing and he would save us a table. I decided to wear my light grey skinny jeans with my black boots and a fitted black tank top and to let my hair fall down my back with natural waves. Jade approved and that meant I would pass anyone's inspection.

The club was crowded when we arrived. We walked up to the bar and placed our orders with Jay. Jade ordered her regular vodka and grapefruit juice while I decided to stick with beer; after what happened last time, whiskey shots were off the table for tonight. When Dane saw us, he pointed to a small round top in the corner with a reserved sign placed on top. Tyler joined us soon after. I wondered how serious things were between them; it was hard to tell because Jade was so tight lipped about her love life.

The band started to play and Jade and I made our way out to the dance floor. It felt good to be out there and after a few songs, I was completely relaxed. After a week of classes and studying, it was nice to let loose. Tyler eventually joined us and was all over Jade; she was enjoying herself according to the huge grin on her face. There was definitely something going on there as I watched their hands exploring each other's bodies. I was a little jealous; I desperately wanted to dance with Dane.

I saw Kevin and Chris walk in a short while later; I was a little nervous because of what happened last time we were at a bar together drinking and dancing, but I waved them over anyway. I'd seen Kevin a few times since the incident a couple weeks ago, but we hadn't talked. I had resolved that what happened between Kevin and I that night was due to alcohol consumption and that it wouldn't be happening again.

"Hi guys, you can put your drinks on our table if you want to dance," I said as they approached. Chris shrugged and headed toward the table. Kevin stood in front of me, arms crossed and staring me down like he was going to confront me. He was making me uncomfortable. "Kevin, I don't care what you were trying to accomplish the other night; I think you know it was a mistake. We both had too much to drink so can we just forget it ever happened?"

He let out a breath he had been holding in. "I'm really sorry for being an asshole."

"Yes you were, but I won't be dancing with you tonight," I said, giving him a teasing smile.

"I completely understand. If anyone attempts that with

Dane in the building, they're freaking stupid," he said, before he walked over to the table to set his drink down.

We were all laughing and having a good time as the band played song after song. Chris was actually a great dancer so I decided to move with him; dancing with a partner was always better than dancing alone. He was a nice guy and I was confident he wouldn't pull a Kevin since we'd only had one drink each. Besides, if I danced with Chris I wouldn't have to worry about other hands finding there way onto my body. He placed a hand on my hip as I wrapped my arm around his shoulder making sure our bodies weren't pressed too close. The band played songs with an upbeat tempo and I completely lost myself in the music.

After a few minutes I watched Dane walk up behind Chris, tapping him on the shoulder until Chris turned to face him. I wasn't sure what was said, but Chris stepped back with both hands raised in the air; he didn't even bother to look in my direction before he walked away. The scowl on Dane's face made my stomach drop as his eyes locked on mine. I stood motionless before he pulled me close, wrapping both arms around my lower back. I didn't know what to do; he looked so angry one minute and the next he had me wrapped up in his arms. I buried my face into his chest, feeling his rapid heartbeat on my cheek. The band wasn't playing a slow song, but we stood locked together on the dance floor like we were dancing to one. I needed to be close to him and help wash the anger away.

When the band announced a break, I looked up to see he still had his eyebrows pulled in and a frown played on his beautiful lips "Hey, what's wrong?"

He remained silent as he pulled me closer, burying his

nose in my hair. "You only dance with me," he said, touching his forehead to mine.

I couldn't think of anything to say, so I nodded. Jealousy may be offensive or annoying to some people, but Dane's possessiveness sent heat through my whole body. He kissed the top of my nose. "I'll be at the bar, Baby. Come find me in a bit." And just like that he walked back to the bar, not waiting for my response. I was left stunned and speechless as I headed back to our table. I needed another drink.

We were all having a good time, laughing and joking, but I noticed that Chris wouldn't even look in my direction. "What did Dane say to you?" I finally asked.

He scanned the bar before he turned to me. "He said I shouldn't touch what's his."

His words sent shivers down my back. I liked feeling wanted, but hearing I was his sends electricity down my entire body. "Seriously?"

"Trust me, I'm not joking about anything Dane Wright." I knew he wasn't joking because I got the exact same message. "Be careful with that one," he continued while taking a swig of his beer.

"What do you mean?" I pulled my brows together as I thought of one million different answers he could give me that I didn't want to hear. I had to know, though.

"He has a reputation. I've never known him to do the relationship thing." I tilted my head to the side while I waited for him to continue. "I'm not saying you're not relationship worthy because believe me, you are, but he's far from innocent."

"What do you mean by that?" I searched Chris's eyes for any bit of truth, but all I saw was nervousness.

He seemed to consider what to say before he replied. "That's for him to tell you, not me."

For the first time all week, I wondered if I really knew Dane at all and decided to get to the bottom of it after his shift ended tonight. We each came from a different place and the last thing I wanted to do was hold his background against him. I wasn't sure where this thing between us was going, but if there was something I needed to know, I would rather know it now before things got too complicated.

I caught a glimpse of Dane behind the bar and couldn't help but smile. The man was beautiful on the outside, and over the last few weeks I was starting to see the beauty he held on the inside. He was a little rough around the edges, but that only increased his appeal. I knew there were some girls who were extremely attracted to bad boys, but I had never considered myself to be that way.

My attraction to Dane was about passion. I saw a passion in him that I didn't often see in people our age. There was mystery around him and every day I felt like I was peeling back a little bit of him. He was true to himself, my complete opposite in every way.

I turned back to join the conversation when I saw Jade glance behind me, lines forming between her eyes. What I saw when I turned around to see what caught her attention caught me completely off guard. A tall brunette in a very short black dress had her hand on Dane's chest as he whispered something in her ear. She said something back to him before throwing her head back in laughter.

I felt sick to my stomach as I turned back around, not wanting to see anymore. Jade gave me a weak smile and exchanged a look with Chris who had also witnessed the scene behind the bar. I could tell she was thinking the same thing I was. Her face dropped when she looked behind me again, causing me to spin around. When I did, I saw Dane and the brunette had disappeared. The anger building in me, combined with the sinking feeling in my stomach, was too much. He wouldn't let me dance with Chris, but it was okay for some other woman to have her hands all over him? Maybe this was what Chris warned me about.

"I think I'm going to head home. It's been a long week and I'm really tired," I said. Not the full truth but what was I supposed to say, "The boy who is sweeping me off my feet is flirting with another girl right in front of me and I don't want to witness another minute of it"?

"Oh, sweetie, do you want me to go with you?" Jade asked as I stood to put my coat on. My whole body was shaking, making it difficult to get my arms in the sleeves. I gave up and threw it over my arm. The anger rolling off my body should be enough to keep me warm.

I shook my head. I didn't want to ruin her night. "No, you stay. I'll be fine."

"It probably isn't what you think," she said, but I could see in her eyes that she didn't believe her own words.

She mouthed sorry to me before I turned and walked out of the bar. The night was chilly, but I didn't care. I just wanted to go home, put on my sweats and bury my face in a pillow. How could I be so stupid? More importantly, why was I letting this man I'd only known for a few weeks affect me so much? I had let my guard down just this once and look where it got me, alone on a cold Friday night.

It only took me a few minutes to get settled into bed before the tears started to fall. I wanted Dane to be different.

I wanted to prove to my mother that her opinions and ideals were wrong, but once again she was right. Men like Dane Wright would only break my heart.

I must have drifted off to sleep because some time later I heard a loud knock on my door. "Alex, please open the door. I need to see you." It was Dane. I rolled over and looked at the clock; it was just after two in the morning.

I remained silent as he continued to pound on the door, begging me to open it. I was concerned that he would wake up others in the building, or even worse the police would be called. "Go away. I have nothing to say to you." My voice quivered as I tried to hold back my emotions.

"I'm not leaving until you talk to me! Open.the.door!" he yelled, causing me to jump out of bed and head toward the door. I was pissed about what happened earlier and I was even more upset now because he was causing a scene when I wasn't ready to talk to him.

He was about to pound on the door again when I opened it, stopping him in his tracks. I ignored the pained, tired look on his face. "Please leave. You need to go home and leave me alone," I said without my voice breaking which surprised me.

"Not until you tell me why you left so quickly. I thought you were staying until I got off work and when I noticed you were gone, Jade wouldn't tell me anything. Please tell me what I did wrong." He pulled his hands through his hair, almost as if he was trying to pull it.

"You're kidding me, right? You stopped me from dancing with a friend, yet you had your hands all over some chick while I was sitting less than 20 feet away. Then you disappeared! I don't play games, Dane, so why don't you go find your bar tramp?" He winced at my words, rubbing his hands over his face.

"Can I come in?"

Is he crazy? "No." I exclaimed, crossing my arms over my chest.

"Please, I can explain." Standing my ground while looking into his amazing eyes was getting more and more difficult. "Alex, please." I quietly opened the door to let him in. "Thank you."

I laughed. I'm not sure why, but hearing him say thank you for letting him in was almost too much. I had friends who had been cheated on, but looked the other way because they didn't want to lose their boyfriends. My parents had numerous friends whose relationships had been rocked by infidelity, but yet they stayed together. I always told myself that I didn't want to resort to that level of pathetic sadness.

Would I hold my breath waiting for Prince Charming? No. Would I hold my breath waiting for someone who was kind, respectful and honest? Hell, yes.

"What's so funny?" he asked, glancing around the room.

"You. Say what you need to say and leave. I want to go back to bed." Detached Alex was back and she felt completely numb.

"Nothing is going on between me and Bree. We had a thing once, but it meant nothing. She needed some help tonight and I gave it to her. End of story."

I swallowed down any hint of emotion. "Did she need help getting out of her dress? Did she need help memorizing every part of the male body? What was it, tell me."

"Fuck! I thought you were different. I thought you wouldn't look at me and think the worst," he yelled, pacing the room with his hands on his hips.

His words cut right through me, but I know what I saw. "I don't think the worst, Dane, I saw it. And don't you dare tell me I'm like everyone else."

"And what did you see to make you think I did anything even remotely like you think I did?" He moved forward with every word standing a foot away from me.

"What would you think if you saw me whispering in some guy's ear with his hands on my body?"

He was silent and I see understanding flash across his face. "You saw all that?"

"Yes," I whispered.

"I'm sorry. I should have taken her hands off me, but I honestly wasn't thinking. I only have eyes for you, Alex, only you." He slowly reached up, rubbing his thumb across my cheek. I stopped him by grabbing his wrist.

"What did she want?"

He looked up at the ceiling. "I dated her for a while in high school and she knew I worked at the bar. She was out with some friends and her car wouldn't start. I went out to take a look at it for her. That's all it was, I promise you." I'd always been convinced that when someone was lying they wouldn't look into your eyes and he was looking right at me.

"You can't tell me who I can and can't dance with and then allow someone else to touch you. This isn't going to work that way."

"I know. I was being a jealous ass and I'm sorry." We stood there silently staring into each other's eyes.

"Alex," he reached up, cupping my cheeks in his hands, "are we okay?" His voice was soft and unsure.

"You need to be open with me. That is the only way this

will work." I said, looking into those glassy green eyes for the truth.

He put his forehead to mine, still holding my cheeks in his hands. "I'll do everything in my power to do right by you, but you need to give me a chance before you run. Just please be patient with me and for God sakes, talk to me," he whispered. I answered him by pressing my lips to his. He groaned before wrapping me tightly in his arms. He held me in place for several minutes; I could feel his desperation and sincerity with every kiss, every movement of his fingers on my back. Falling for him could easily turn my heart to glass and shatter it into a million little pieces, but I couldn't stop myself. This thing I was feeling had me so wrapped up in him and I may never be able to release myself from the tangles.

"Can I stay with you tonight?" he asked, causing me to tense. I'd known him for just a few weeks and we had only been dating for a week.

"I'm not ready for that. Did you walk? Do you need a ride home?"

"No, you go back to bed. I can walk." He grabbed my chin with his index finger and pressed his lips to mine. "So we're good?"

"We're good," I whispered and after one more kiss, he was gone.

I fell asleep thinking about Dane and all the things that could be, all the things I wanted, and all the things that could never be. Tonight was a wake up call; I now knew what it would feel like to lose Dane. I knew what it would feel like to see him with someone else and I never wanted to feel that again.

CHAPTER ELEVEN

I'd never had a boyfriend on Valentine's Day. It never bothered me because there are expectations that came with it and I'd rather not deal with them. For instance, what do you get a guy for Valentine's Day? Do you get him a shirt representing his favorite sports team? Do you get him a watch? I never wanted to deal with those types of decisions, but that had changed this year. Dane and I had talked about our plans yesterday after class.

"Valentine's Day is Wednesday and I was hoping we could do something, you know, different than studying and eating dinner in the student center." I could hear a little bit of nervousness in his voice. Dane was the poster child for confidence and it was very interesting that this one holiday had caused him so much anxiety. It was actually kind of cute.

"What did you have in mind?" I bumped his shoulder with mine in an attempt to calm his nerves.

He smiled. "I want to take you to dinner at the Italian restaurant we went to on our first date."

"That was our first date, huh?"

"It was."

"Sounds perfect. What time?" I asked, leaning into him.

"6:45, I have reservations for 7," he said, grabbing my hand and placing a gentle kiss on my lips. I loved the taste of mint that always seemed to be on them.

Our lips lost contact, but our foreheads still touched.

"You got yourself a date," I whispered. This time it was me who leaned in for a kiss. If I could, I would stay attached to those lips forever. My first Valentine's Day would be celebrated with Dane; everything was easier with him.

Now we're one day before the big holiday and I was trying to decide what I should get him. I thought about asking Jade, but I doubted she had ever had a boyfriend on Valentines. Fling yes, boyfriend no. I was dating Ryan at Christmas time. He gave me a diamond bracelet. It was beautiful and must have cost a fortune, but if he had known me a little better, he would know I wasn't a huge fan of shiny things that scream, "I have money".

I remembered Dane talking about this Warped Tour Music Festival he wanted to attend this summer and decided to get him two tickets. I knew he liked music and hoped it would mean more to him than any material thing ever could. I also got him a gift certificate to his favorite tattoo parlor, a little something he could use now and keep forever.

When I told Jade what I got him, she told me I did good. When Gwen called, I got a different reaction. She knew I'd been dating a guy named Dane, but she hadn't met him and, though I told her he was different than my past boyfriends, I don't think she understood what I meant by that exactly.

"Any plans with the new guy tomorrow?" she asked. I told her our plans for tomorrow night and she seemed impressed.

"What did you get him? You know you have to get him something, right?"

I rolled my eyes. "I'm not stupid!"

"Okay, okay, sorry. What did you get him?"

I played with the bottom of my t-shirt while I talked,

bracing myself for what she would say when I told her what I got him. She reacted pretty much as I expected she would.

"You got him a gift certificate for a tattoo? Why on earth would you do that? I understand the concert tickets, but a tattoo?" She spoke rapidly, not allowing me to get a word in.

I lay back in my bed and covered my eyes with my arm. "He likes tattoos."

"He already has some? Mom and Dad are going to flip. I mean flip." She wasn't telling me something that I didn't already know. I knew things would not go well if they ever met Dane. They would never take the time to get to know the guy inside, but would take one look at him and make my life miserable. I didn't plan for him to meet my parents today or ever, to be honest.

I calmed her down by telling her I was just enjoying my college years. She didn't necessarily agree with my logic, but she let it go. She was planning to visit me this coming weekend and while I was excited to see my sister, part of me was already thinking of ways to keep her away from Dane. I wasn't ashamed of him, but I knew if the life I was supposed to live and the life I was currently living ever met, the result would be disastrous.

💔 💔 💔

I put on my long sleeved red shirtdress with a black belt, black knit tights and stilettos for our date and drove to Dane's apartment. I was nervous as I drove closer to his building. I wasn't sure if I should go in and get him or if he was watching for me, but as soon as I pulled up to the curb, he came out looking absolutely edible in grey slacks, a black button up and, of course, his signature leather jacket.

He leaned in and gave me a kiss on the cheek before grabbing my hand in his. He stared at me for a while without speaking. "You look beautiful."

I smiled. "You look good yourself."

Dinner was even better than the first night we were here. You always hear about couples that have a restaurant they go to on every anniversary because it was their place and I imagined if Dane and I got married, this would be our place. Marriage may never be in the cards for us, but for a moment I imagined how nice it would be if it was.

I was so nervous about the gifts I had picked out for him that I could barely concentrate on what he was saying. Should I give them to him now or wait? What if he didn't get me anything and I made him feel bad? I decided to keep it in my purse until later, hoping for the right opportunity.

He paid for dinner and we walked back to my car, hand in hand. I'd never had such a desire to touch a man. Usually it was something I felt inclined to do because I was in a relationship, but with Dane I couldn't get enough. I think I surprised him when I turned and wrapped my arms around him, nuzzling my face in the crook of his neck. I felt safe and comfortable; I could stay in this moment forever. When he cupped my face and kissed me on the forehead, I felt like the only girl in the whole city. There was so much care in his touch; he made me feel appreciated. I finally let him go as we drove back to his apartment in silence.

I wasn't ready for the evening to be over and I hadn't given him his gift. "Do you want me to come up?" I asked. I couldn't believe these words were coming out of my mouth. A couple weeks ago, they would have petrified me, but every day I felt more comfortable around Dane.

"I assumed you would. I have something for you," he said with mischief in his eyes. He jumped out of the car and ran around to open my door, offering me his hand. I think I swooned a little bit; this was the type of thing movies were made from.

His apartment was just like I remembered it the first time I was here: very clean and organized. "Do you want something to drink?" he asked.

"I better stick to water. I have class tomorrow." I learned my lesson the last time I drank and wound up in Dane's apartment.

He brought me a bottle of water and a beer for himself. I didn't say anything as I watched him take sips from his beer. He looked at me with a knowing grin; Dane Wright knew how sexy he was and how to use it to his advantage.

I cleared my throat. "I have something for you too." My hand trembled as I reached in my bag and handed him his gift.

"You didn't have to get me anything." His smile absolutely melted me. I wondered if he'd received gifts when he was younger since his parents weren't really around. I could picture Dane giving his brother Christmas presents while getting nothing for himself; he was as unselfish as they come.

"I wanted to. Open it."

I waited nervously, ringing my hands together as he opened the envelope. I had carefully picked out a card that didn't say, "I love you", but didn't sound too impersonal either. I settled on one that talked about happy moments shared in the past and those yet to come. Dane smiled as he read it before lifting his eyes to mine. I smiled back, motioning for him to look in the envelope. He removed the two music festival tickets, grinning like a child in an ice cream shop. "I can't believe you got these. You remembered. I know who's getting the second ticket."

"Who?" I asked, genuinely perplexed.

"You. Who else would I give it to?" He cocked his head to the side and looked at me like I had just called him by the wrong name.

"We'll see." It probably wasn't the right time to tell him that I didn't think we would be together then. I would be back in Greenwich and he would be living his life in the city. I motioned back toward the envelope. "There's more."

He reached behind the tickets and pulled out the gift certificate to the tattoo parlor. Now he was grinning like a five year old on Christmas. "Thank you, Baby. You have to come with me when I use this. Maybe you can get one, too."

"Well, I'm glad you like it, but a big no to the tattoo for me. My parents would disown me." This might be an exaggeration when some people say it, but for me it's the absolute truth. My mother in particular would flip out if I marked my skin.

"You're an adult and you can do whatever you want to do. If you want a tattoo, get one."

"We'll see," I said, glancing around the room for any hint of my gift.

"But really, this is great. You don't know how much this means to me. No one has ever actually bought me anything besides of my mother, and that was only when she was sober." He gave me a soft kiss on the lips followed by another on the tip of my nose. "Let me go get your gift."

He disappeared into his bedroom and I felt a dozen

butterflies in my stomach. The anticipation was killing me. He returned with a large box wrapped with a red bow around it. "I'm sorry. I can't wrap to save my life," he said, handing me the box.

"It's okay." I nervously untied the bow and opened the box. Inside was one very new, very real, dark purple leather bomber jacket. "Dane, this is too much!" I ran my finger over the nice smooth leather before bringing it to my nose. I loved the smell of real leather.

"You're worth it," he said, stepping closer to me.

I lunged at him, wrapping my arms tightly around his neck as I planted kisses all over his cheek. "I love it," I said before pressing my lips to his neck.

"I can't wait to see it on you," he whispered as he kissed me below my ear. When his lips finally met mine again, his tongue pressed against them and I opened to allow us to taste each other with the kiss. He kissed like his life depended on our connection, like it was his first kiss and his last kiss and the only kiss that had ever really mattered.

Before I realized what had happened, my back was on the couch and he was nestled between my legs, my skirt working itself up my thigh. He slowly unbuttoned the top three buttons of my shirtdress, exposing my bra and cupped one breast in his hand while the other worked its way through my hair, his lips never leaving mine. All I could think about was him: his scent, his taste and his body pressed against mine. When he pulled one side of my bra down and teased my nipple between his fingers I thought about stopping him, but I couldn't. My body had never felt so aware, or so hungry. I wanted Dane; his touch and his kisses made me feel everything. He started to kiss his way down so his mouth was where his fingers had been, rolling my nipple with his tongue. I could feel his excitement pressed against my leg and something inside propelled me to touch him, running my hand over his slacks. He ran his hand up my leg before pushing my panties aside, settling it between my legs as he started moving his fingers against me, shooting electricity through my whole body. It was like nothing I had ever felt before.

For a few minutes I forgot my name, my life; all I felt was the gorgeous man on top of me, sending jolts of lust through places I didn't even know existed. I never let myself feel this way: so free, so open, so willing to do new things. Dane made me want more. I finally came undone, saying his name before he captured my mouth with his again. He lifted himself up and started pulling my panties down, but I grabbed his hands, freezing him in place. "I don't want to go any further, okay?" My body was singing for me to experience everything with Dane, but my mind wasn't quite ready to take that step.

He gave me a questioning look before climbing back up my body, cupping my face in his hands. I could smell my arousal on him and it shot more warmth through me. "Do you want to stop?"

"I don't want to go any further, not now." I gave him a kiss on the tip of his chin while running my hands through his hair.

He sighed, but a sated smile touched his lips. "I might need to go take a cold shower."

"I should probably tell you something." I bit my lower lip, trying to work up the courage to have "the talk". This was a conversation I'd had with other guys, but they were easy to deny. Dane was different; I could see myself giving this part of me to him and it made me really nervous.

"You can tell me anything, Gorgeous." His eyes were looking right into mine and the warmth behind them helped me relax.

"I'm a virgin." The words came out so quickly and quietly that I was not even sure if he understood what I said, but his body went completely still.

He finally blinked. "What?"

I closed my eyes and took a deep breath. "I've never had sex before."

He pushed up so he was supporting himself with an arm on either side of me. "What? Why?"

"I guess I've never found the guy who deserves all of me yet. I want it to be special and really, I would like it to be the guy I'll be with for the rest of my life." My voice was shaking as I thought about the meaning behind what I said. I was talking about forevers and happily ever afters.

"I've never been anyone's first. I can't," he said, shaking his head.

"What are you talking about, Dane?" He was making me nervous; I hoped my little admission wasn't a deal breaker. I knew I wasn't the type of girl Dane was used to, but he was certainly not the type of guy I was used to either.

He tilted his head to the side. "I've had my share of girls, but I've never had anything serious. I would hate it if my sister lost her virginity to some prick like me. I don't deserve it." His words ripped through me. I hated that he thought of himself like that; if he could only see what I see.

"What if you're the one I want to give it to?" I cupped his face in my hands and ran my thumbs over his cheekbones.

"I've never felt this way about anyone before. I still can't believe you're mine. When the time comes, if you're sure-"

I cut him off. "If I do anything, it's because I'm sure. I won't do anything I don't want to do. I'm just not ready now."

"I can wait, especially if I can do a little of this." He laid back down on top of me and started to kiss my neck again. We continued like this for at least an hour before we fell asleep, wrapped in each other's arms. He felt so warm and safe; I could sleep like this every night.

CHAPTER TWELVE

I was woken the next morning by Dane's warm kisses across my face. This was better than an alarm clock any day. "Good morning," I whispered, curling into him.

"Good morning, Gorgeous. Did you sleep well?" I slept better than I had slept in forever.

"Yes, I had this amazing human blanket keeping me warm and cozy all night." I wrapped my arms around his neck, halting his kisses. As he looked in my eyes, I felt something new inside of me. It was a feeling I had never felt towards a man before; it made butterflies multiply in my stomach, but at the same time scared me to death. Looking up at Dane, I realized I was falling for him; that realization caused me to freeze and panic.

The part of me that doubts everything made a sudden appearance. I saw my parent's disappointed faces flash before me. I thought of the times I wasn't enough. Dane didn't tell me what to do or what I needed to change. He was lying here beside me, calling me Gorgeous, kissing me like he meant it and for once I felt complete. Dane was the half that makes me whole.

Dane lifted my chin, bringing my eyes back up to his, "Are you okay? You have a weird look on your face," he said, brushing the hair out of my eyes with his free hand. The softness of his touch made me close my eyes and take a deep breath; he had a way of relaxing me.

"Yeah, I'm sorry. I was just thinking about something I have to do this morning before class. I should probably get going." I needed time to think about what the feeling in my chest meant. "And I should probably change out of the clothes I wore last night."

His face broke out in a smile. "Yeah, you don't want anyone to know you just spent the night wrapped in your boyfriend's arms."

"Come on, time to get up," I said, lightly smacking him on the shoulder.

He stood as I began to button my dress, pulling everything back into place. Fortunately, I'd worn my long pea coat which would help me cover the wrinkled state of my dress.

He reached for my hand, kissing my palm before wrapping his arms around me, pulling me in for a lingering kiss. We said our goodbyes and I had to hold back the words that wanted to escape my lips. I wanted to be honest and tell him that being with him scared me. My heart ached because I wanted to tell him everything about my parents and the conflict they caused within me. Most of all, I wanted to tell him he made me happy and made me feel things I'd never felt before. I was already broken, but he had the ability to break me into a million more pieces if I let myself fall for him.

Jade wasn't in our room when I got back. She didn't have class this early on Thursday so I could only assume that she didn't come home last night. No surprise there. This happened a lot since she had started hanging out with Tyler.

I'd been stuck inside my own head since I left Dane's apartment. What I felt this morning after waking up next to him terrified me. For one thing, it was too soon to feel this strongly about someone. This was not supposed to be happening and I let it. Was I ready for this?

I showered and dressed for class, not expecting Dane to come over with coffee; I had just left him an hour ago, but once again he surprised me. I was trying on the leather jacket he gave me when I heard the knock at the door and when I opened it, he noticed the jacket right away. "I knew it would look great on you. It looked great hanging in the store, but on you..there are no words," he said, biting his lip and running his eyes down the length of my body.

"I love it. It's not something I would have picked out for myself, but you have great taste."

He walked closer to me. "I've never seen anything sexier than you in that jacket." I blushed before reaching up to kiss him. We didn't have Art class so most of the day would be spent apart. I was going to my much-hated medical classes while he was enjoying his other Art classes. Every day I spent with Dane increased my desire to follow my heart because I watched him follow his without reservations. I didn't know if I'd ever act on my desires, but they were growing like a weed.

After a few minutes of kisses, I looked at the clock. "I have to get to class. Some hot guy had me wrapped up all night and I'm already running late." I winked as I pulled my black ankle boots on over my jeans.

"Sorry, Gorgeous. Next time, I'm not letting you go," he said with a sly grin on his face. He grabbed me for one more kiss.

"Is that a promise?" I asked, breathing heavier than normal. Within seconds, he was behind me, pressing against my back. I felt exactly what I did to him.

"You better be careful what you ask for," he whispered, pushing against me one more time. "I may have to show you." His voice was breathy and I would have been lying if I said I wasn't aroused by what he was doing to me. I'd never been with someone so intense and didn't realize how much it would turn me on.

I turned, trying my hardest to hide the blush on my face. I placed my finger over his lips. "Hold that thought. I have to go to class." He eyes burned with desire as he turned to open the door for me. He certainly made things interesting and fun. I hoped it would stay that way when Gwen arrived on Saturday.

Gwen was in the city to meet her florist and we had made plans to have dinner. I was a little surprised when she suggested I bring Dane. I wanted them to meet, but I was nervous about it. If Gwen couldn't accept him, there was no way my parents would accept him. I was happier than I had ever been in my life and I didn't want anything to ruin it.

A knock at the door pulled me away from my thoughts. I didn't even have to look to know who it was. As I opened the door, Dane pulled me in for a kiss with one hand while holding a carrier with two coffees in the other. He broke away long enough to whisper, "Good morning, Gorgeous", against my lips before capturing them for one more kiss. If this was my future, I would be a very happy girl.

"Good morning. Thanks for the coffee," I said, smiling up at him. I opened the door to let him in and watched as he took his usual seat on my bed. We hadn't spent the night together since that one night; I think Dane knew that moving too fast scared me and had decided to give me my space. I appreciated how considerate he was, especially since I was pretty sure he was not used to being so patient. He continued to surprise me on a daily basis.

He watched me as I pulled my hair into a loose knot at the top of my head and applied makeup. I would have thought he'd be bored just watching me do this day after day, but he never complained. "Are you excited for Gwen to get here?"

"Yeah, I'm a little nervous though," I said, honestly. We'd talked about this throughout the week. I told him my family was a little judgmental, but Gwen was the least evil of the three. If we could get through today, I would be one step closer to meshing my two lives. I never thought this was possible a month ago, but being with Dane changed me.

"Baby, it'll be fine. I'll be right there with you and I promise to be on my best behavior," he said, taking a drink from his coffee cup.

I took a deep breath. "I know. You don't have to do this, you know."

"Quit saying that. I want to meet your family," he said, grabbing my hand in his.

I sat on his lap, wrapping my arms around his neck. "Thank you," I whispered.

"Wouldn't miss it, especially if it's the only time I'm going to see you this weekend." He gave me a quick kiss. "You should come over on Sunday. I'll cook you dinner."

"You cook?" I raised an eyebrow.

"For you, Gorgeous, I can do anything." How did this guy always know what to say? He could melt a thousand hearts with his words and he didn't even realize it.

"Sounds like a plan. No hot dogs or macaroni and cheese, though." He laughed.

"Don't worry, you are worth at least a hamburger," he winked. I replied by tickling him on both his sides until he was laughing uncontrollably. I knew from previous experience that this would drive him mad and he would be begging me to stop. It worked. "Okay, okay, steak? Pork chops? You name it, Baby, and it's yours." Yep, I had Dane Wright wrapped around my finger.

Dane left right after coffee to run a few errands and I went to the library to get a few hours of studying in before Gwen arrived. I had a hard time concentrating on my notes because I couldn't stop thinking about tonight and how everything would play out. Would Gwen like Dane? Would she see what I saw in him? What if she hated him and ran right to Mom? I prayed she would see him through my eyes and give him the benefit of the doubt. Hopefully she would see how happy I was and give him credit for his part in that.

I finally gave up on my attempt to get some studying in and walked back to my dorm. It wouldn't be much longer until Gwen was here. When I opened the door to our room, Jade was standing there in a tight black cocktail dress and four inch heels. "Wow, Jade, where are you guys going tonight?"

I invited Jade to have dinner with us, but she had said she had plans. I didn't press her, but I thought her and Tyler were getting kind of serious. She seemed happy, but guarded, and I hoped he had good intentions. I didn't want to see her heart broken.

She looked at me, a huge smile pulling at both sides of her mouth. "Tyler's company is throwing a cocktail party at Keen tonight to celebrate the completion of a big project. He should be here any minute." She was absolutely beaming and I knew that look; I'd seen it in the mirror numerous times over the past few weeks.

There was a soft knock at the door. Jade moved as fast as she could in her killer heels to open it, only to find Gwen standing there. The two had met before and while they got along, I doubted they would ever hit friend status; they were two very different people. "A little happy to see me, Jade?"

"Sorry, Gwen, I thought you were someone else."

Gwen completely ignored Jade, walking past her to give me a big hug. "I missed you, Alexandra. I feel like we haven't seen each other in forever."

"Doesn't absence make the heart grow fonder or some weird crap like that?" Jade piped in from across the room.

I gave her a warning look before turning back to Gwen. She was a little shorter than me, but had the same shade of blonde hair that she kept shoulder length and pin straight. She wore black dress pants with a crisp, light blue button down. In some ways, she looked older than she was; more mature, actually. "I missed you, too. Are you ready to head to dinner? Dane is going to meet us there."

"God, yes. I have been waiting for this all week," Gwen said enthusiastically.

Jade stared at us from across the room and an awkward silence fell over all of us. Tyler couldn't get here soon enough. I could deal with Jade and I could deal with Gwen, but the two of them together was almost too much for me.

Jade grabbed her long black coat and glanced at her phone. "Tyler should be here any minute. I'm going to go wait downstairs so he doesn't have to come all the way up here to get me. Gwen, it was nice to see you again. You girls have a good night and don't wait up for me." She winked before disappearing through the door.

Gwen stood there with a confused look on her face. "Won't she be cold in that dress? It's freezing outside."

I rolled my eyes. "Believe it or not that type of outfit's pretty standard, even this time of year."

"Hmmm" was all she said in reply before we left to head to restaurant. It was a cold night and snow had just begun to fall. I was happy I was able to dress in a sweater and jeans with a warm beanie covering the top of my head and my favorite white mittens. Something about this weather combined with the lightness in my heart put an extra bounce in my step. Gwen looked at me and laughed; she may be a little prudish at times, but she had this other side that only I saw. She needed someone to bring it out of her.

"So how are you and Dane?" she asked, tucking her hands into the pockets of her tan pea coat.

"Really good. I can't wait for you to meet him." Just talking about him made me smile.

"Oh my God, you're in love." Her eyes were huge as she waited for my response.

"No, I'm not," I said, blushing.

She hugged me. "Oh, Alexandra, you are. I can see it in your eyes."

"Being in love scares me. I don't know if I can handle it," I said honestly. I thought about all the ways I had changed recently and how my heart changed pace when I talked to, or looked at, Dane. Just thinking about him made my pulse pick up. But I wasn't ready to admit to the "L" word, much less say it.

When I saw Dane standing on the street in front of the café we had agreed to meet at for dinner, I jumped into his arms and wasted no time finding his lips with mine. Any hour spent away from him was too much and I hadn't seen him since this morning.

After we finished our greeting, he started to run his fingers over a loose strand of hair that had fallen across my forehead. "Did someone miss me?"

I tapped his nose with my index finger. "Just a little. Come on, I want you to meet Gwen."

I had left Gwen standing a few feet away when I ran to greet Dane. She looked a little uncomfortable seeing this affectionate side of me. She offered a small wave as we approached her. "Hi, I'm Gwen."

Dane extended his hand to her. "I'm Dane. I've heard a lot about you."

She accepted his hand. "All good I hope."

He laughed. "Of course."

"Why don't we go inside? It's freezing out here," I said as the cold wind blew in my face. It was particularly unpleasant today.

"Good call," Dane said, throwing an arm around my shoulder.

As we took our seats and ordered, I stole glances at both Gwen and Dane. Gwen was quite literally staring at Dane and he was oblivious because his eyes were glued on me. He removed his leather jacket, revealing his long-sleeve grey t-shirt, with sleeves rolled up to his elbows showcasing his tattoos. I didn't even notice them, but Gwen couldn't seem to stop staring.

I cleared my throat, hoping to gain her attention. She lifted her eyes to mine and then looked over at Dane. "So, Dane, did you grow up in the city?"

"Yep, I have lived here all my life and I don't ever see myself moving away." He glanced at me and the side of his mouth turned up. We had talked about our mutual love for the city and our desire to stay here forever a few times since we had been together.

"That's cool. What are you going to school for?"

"Art. I do sculptures and sell them at local shows," he replied.

"Do you make a lot of money doing that?" I glared at her in an attempt to send a warning signal; she caught my eye and quickly worked to fix her mistake. "I mean, it must be expensive to live in the city."

He shrugged, "I do alright. I wish I didn't have to work tonight so I could hang out with you ladies longer," he said sticking out his lower lip. I loved his attempt at a subject change.

"Where do you work?" Gwen asked. So I guess we weren't done with the personal stuff.

"Loft 10. I'm a bartender." Her eyes shot to me and I knew what she was thinking; our parents were going to hate this guy. I couldn't wait for the one hundred questions that would come my way once we left this place.

The rest of lunch went pretty much the same way. Gwen's inquiring mind kept working and I kept trying to change the subject. I didn't mind her curiosity, but at times I felt like she was judging Dane and, in turn, judging me. At one point she got up to use the restroom and Dane leaned into me, kissing me below the ear. "I think I'm under investigation," he whispered.

I turned to face him, planting a quick kiss on his lips. "She is just watching out for me."

"Does she do this with all your boyfriends?" he asked.

"No. You're the first boyfriend I've had that she didn't know for years before we started dating." I saw her coming out of the bathroom and placed one more kiss on his lips before returning my attention to my food.

When we were done, Dane insisted that he pay for our lunch. Gwen's face registered surprise before she thanked him over and over.

Dane had to leave for work so Gwen and I headed back toward my dorm. "So what did you think?" I asked, taking in the city lights as we walked through the hustle and bustle of downtown.

"He's really cute and nice," she said, but I could tell she was holding something back.

"But?" I inquired.

"Our parents would hate him," she finally blurted out.

I let out the air I had been holding in my lungs. "I know, but I'm doing this for me. It may not last forever, but I want to experience this. I need this."

"Are you bringing him to my wedding next month?"

"No. I mean, I don't think so." I hadn't given it much thought, but my gut reaction was that it would not be a good idea. Just the thought of asking my mom for permission to bring him made me sick to my stomach. I didn't want to think about what would happen if I actually brought him. "I mean, you know Mom. It's not a good idea, right?"

"I agree, but that doesn't mean you can't continue to see him." She gave me a sympathetic smile. "Oh, Honey, I hope this works out for you. You guys are really cute together."

"I hope so, too."

After Gwen left, I settled into my pajamas and grabbed my kindle to read my latest contemporary romance find. I missed Dane and wished he didn't have to work every weekend night. I would love to be cuddled in bed with him, watching a movie or just talking. I couldn't help myself when I picked up my phone to text him.

Alex: I miss you

It didn't take more than one minute to get a reply.

Dane: I miss you too. I can't wait for tomorrow night.

My skin tingled when I thought about watching his lips as he said those words to me. I missed his lips.

Alex: What time tomorrow?

Dane: How about 6?

Alex: Sounds great.

I fell asleep that night thinking and dreaming about Dane.

When I woke up Sunday, I threw on some comfortable

sweats and walked down to the coffee shop to grab my morning latte. Sunday was the one-day I didn't expect to see Dane because he slept until at least noon. I didn't blame him; I would be tired, too, if I worked until the early morning hours two days in a row.

When I returned to my dorm, I laid in my bed with my iPod for some much needed thinking time. Today's playlist consisted of Pink and the Kings of Leon. I let the words work into my head as I thought about how well the weekend went and how much I was looking forward to seeing Dane. I was about to drift to sleep when my phone buzzed.

Dane: Dinner's at Mom's tonight. Want to go?

Was he asking me if I wanted to meet his mother?

Alex: You're not cooking?

Dane: I can, but I forgot it's Sunday dinner.

It was only one night and as much as it scared me, I wanted to meet his family to help me understand him better.

Alex: Dinner with your mom sounds great.

Dane: Can't wait to see you.

I decided I had better get moving and make myself look nice if I was meeting his mom. My stomach was in knots as I went through my closet, picking out a cashmere winter white turtleneck and a pair of dark blue skinny jeans. I wanted to look good, but not too overdone. I carefully curled my hair, making sure that every piece was perfectly in place, and pulled on my brown knee high riding boots. I eyed myself in the mirror before throwing on a coat and heading out the door.

Chapter Thirteen

I was nervous as I drove to Dane's apartment to pick
him up for dinner. It was just another thing that was going to
take me out of my comfort zone. I spent so much of my life
only knowing one way to live and now I was becoming
accustomed to learning new things. Change used to scare the
hell out of me, but now I welcomed it because the more
things that changed, the better I felt about myself.

Dane had a very unusually serious look on his face when
he got into my car. Maybe I wasn't the only one nervous
about tonight. I wondered if me meeting his mom was as
frightening for him as him meeting mine was to me. He
seemed nervous and fidgety as we made our way to his
mom's apartment.

"Will Nolan be there tonight?" I asked, trying to ease the
tension in the car.

"Who knows. I guess we'll find out when we get there,"
he said, biting his thumbnail.

"Hey, are you okay?"

He dropped his hands back into his lap. "Yeah, just a
little nervous, I guess. You're the first girl I've ever brought
home." My stomach fluttered; I liked hearing those words.
There were some firsts I could still have with Dane.

"It'll be fine. I'm sure I'll love your mom." I glanced
over at him and watched for a second as he worked his
bottom lip between his teeth. I wished I wasn't driving so I

could lean over and kiss him. He looked good, even when he was nervous.

"It's not you I'm worried about." He turned his attention to the window as we drove the rest of the way in silence. I wondered what he was talking about, but I didn't ask. His body language told me he didn't want to talk about it.

His mother lived in a rough part of the city. Dane had mentioned that she struggled with minimum wage jobs and didn't have a lot of money. She lived in an old brick building with a torn canopy and barred windows. A few of the railings around the fire escape were covered with clothes and blankets left out to dry. There were two kids playing on the front step and I pictured a young Dane sitting there. "Is this where you grew up?"

"After my dad left, yeah. I know it's not much, but-"

"Dane, stop. It doesn't matter what the building looks like. We're here so I can meet your family." I placed my hand on top of his. He was worrying too much and I had to calm him down.

He closed his eyes and took a cleansing breath. "Let's do this." I cupped his face in my hands and pressed light kisses on his forehead, cheeks and finally along his jaw line in an attempt to wipe away his worries.

He grasped my hand tightly in his as we made our way into the building. The walls were yellow and the tan carpet had seen better days, but it was clean. I noticed an overwhelming mixture of smells, like each renter was cooking a different item for dinner and their scents had married in the hallway. It reminded me of a mall food court.

His mom's apartment was on the second floor, all the way down the hall to the right. He turned to me with fire in his eyes; something was still bothering him. "Look, if my brother is here don't let him get to you, please." I wanted to ask for more information, but he knocked on the door instead, halting my question. My hand was sweating as I waited for the door to open. I didn't know what to expect, but the woman standing on the other side of the door was short, maybe five foot two, with a thin figure and long blond hair. It was easy to see she had once been beautiful, but stress and alcohol must have done a number on her.

She held her hand out to me. "Nice to meet you," she said. I recognized her eyes; they were the same exact green color as Dane's. There was no denying they were related.

"Nice to meet you, too," I said as I shook her hand.

"Call me Janet. And you are?"

"Alex," I said, pulling my hand back.

Dane gave his mom a quick kiss on the cheek, never letting go of my hand. "Hi, Mom."

"How have you been?" she asked, her eyebrows squeezing together.

"Same as last week. Everything is going well at school and in life," he said, looking down at me as he finished the last part. I could feel my face heating up.

"Good. Come in. Make yourselves comfortable." She stared at us, rubbing her hand over her collarbone, as we made our way into the living area. She seemed nervous or distant; I couldn't quite put my finger on it.

"Your brother will be here shortly." I heard Dane scoff before sitting down on the sofa, pulling me with him. "I'm going to get supper ready," she said, disappearing into the kitchen.

I glanced around the apartment, noting it had the same

worn carpet as the hallways, but with white walls. The furniture was older, but well maintained. There were several photos of small children on the wall, but no recent photos of Dane or his brother. "Is that you?" I asked, pointing to a picture of three little kids. The boys were almost identical, but the little girl had short curly blond hair and big blue eyes.

"Yeah, I was eight, Nolan was five, and my sister was four. That is actually the last picture of us together before the accident. After my sister died and my dad left no one took pictures anymore." His voice was full of sadness, especially when he mentioned his sister. My heart clenched as I reached up to squeeze his shoulder.

"She was adorable," I whispered.

"Dinner's ready!" his mom yelled from the kitchen. I looked up at Dane who had unshed tears in his eyes. He simply nodded before he stood, pulling me up with him. I wished we had more time to talk. He seemed to hold so much inside and I wanted to break in and take it all out to ease his pain.

His mood shifted as we sat down at the small round table in the kitchen. Dane was just as good of an actor as I was; I had to give him that. His mom sat at one end of the table while Dane and I took seats across from each other. He winked at me, leaning in to help his mom cut the pot roast. My mouth watered as I eyed all the delicious foods that I didn't usually eat. There was roast, potatoes, carrots, corn, rolls and a layered chocolate cake. Maybe I shouldn't have worn jeans.

"Well, dig in. I can't eat all this myself," his mom said as she spooned potatoes on her plate. I took just a little bit of everything in an attempt to save room for cake. Dane had mentioned his mom took up baking after she went through recovery. It was something to keep her busy when she got a craving.

I was about to take my first bite when the door slammed in the other room, startling all of us. I noticed Dane and his mom both seemed tense while staring at the doorway. I assumed that Nolan was about to join us and their reaction was making me nervous. What was it about him that made them react this way? A few seconds later, a man who looked just like Dane came into the kitchen. He was a little taller and his light brown hair was longer, but they had identical eyes and lips. He didn't say anything as he sat down and filled his plate until there wasn't room for anything else. I looked around the table and noticed I wasn't the only one staring.

"What are you fuckers looking at?" he asked, looking up from his plate. "And who is this sexy bitch?" he added, staring at me with his mouth turned up on one side.

Dane shot out of his chair, grabbing Nolan by the shirt until their faces were inches apart. "Don't you ever call her that again. Do you hear me?" I could see the veins in Danes neck and every bit of exposed skin had turned beet red.

Nolan didn't seem the least bit intimidated. "Chill, dude. I'm just trying to have a friendly conversation." I looked over at Dane's mom who wasn't looking at her boys, but instead running her fork through her potatoes over and over while using her other hand to rub her collarbone.

"I mean it, Nolan, don't fucking talk about her like that," Dane said, letting go of his shirt.

Nolan didn't waste any time before returning his attention back to me. "Does he treat you like that?"

"No one gets treated like you Nolan because no one acts

like you," Dane answered for me.

Nolan laughed. "Yeah, I bet you are nice to her as long as she's warming your dick every night."

"Nolan, stop!" Dane yelled, slamming his fist on the table. It was quiet for a couple minutes while everyone picked through their food. I didn't have much of an appetite anymore, but I managed a few bites of vegetables, never taking my eyes off my plate. This whole dinner had left me feeling uncomfortable. It was easy to see why Dane was so nervous on the ride over.

"Nolan, I'm glad you came tonight. How are things going?" Janet asked, smiling at her youngest son. He had been nothing but rude since he walked in, but his mother acted like she hadn't heard a thing.

"I've got a fucking mess. I'm short on rent this month and if I don't come up with $100 by the end of this week, I'm out. Can I borrow some money? I'll pay you back as soon as I get paid," Nolan said, pleading with his eyes as he stared at his mother.

"Sure, Baby, I'll give you some before you leave."

"Don't give him a fucking penny!" Dane yelled, interrupting their conversation. "He is just going to turn around and buy drugs. How can he pay you back when he doesn't have a job?"

This whole conversation was getting to be too much. All they were doing was yelling and arguing and I needed a moment to collect my thoughts. My family dinners were always focused on accomplishments and goals; I loathed them for years, but now that I'd seen this I kind of missed them.

"Where is the bathroom?" I asked. I wasn't even sure

they remembered I was sitting there during this whole exchange.

"Go through the living room and down the hall to the left, sweetie," Janet offered.

Dane quickly stood up, but I motioned for him to stay. It looked like they needed some family time without me. My legs were shaking as I made my way toward the bathroom. I'd never felt more out of my element, but I needed to do this for Dane. The problem was, it didn't seem like his element either. The bathroom was small with a pink toilet and bathtub and an old, gold and white marbled sink. I sat on the edge of the tub, putting my head in my hands; I wanted to leave, but I couldn't do that to Dane. He had given me so much over the last few weeks and it was my chance to return the favor.

After a few minutes and many deep breaths, I made my way out of the bathroom. As soon as I walked into the kitchen, Dane stood up, "Are you okay?" His face showed concern and I wondered if he said anything to Nolan while I was in the bathroom. Nolan's demeanor hadn't changed as he sat back in his chair with his arm resting over the top. Janet sat in her seat, smiling up at me like this was some sort of pleasant experience.

"I'm fine. I just needed to freshen up," I replied, offering my best smile. Dane glared at Nolan before sitting back in his seat. I'd lost my appetite completely, but I sat down and made myself take one bite of everything. I didn't want to seem rude because his mother has obviously spent a lot of time preparing it.

"So, what have you been up to, Nolan?" Janet asked.

"Just working and going to school. That reminds me, Mom, I need you to put some money in my account for school this term."

Dane dropped his fork on his plate. "You don't work and I know you haven't stepped inside a school for almost two years. Stop the bullshit." I looked over at Dane's mom who just sat there with a blank expression on her face. Maybe she had spent so many years out of her mom role that she was trying to make it up by feeding her son's habit. I wondered how it would feel if your children were young one day and the next time you could really see things clearly, they were adults, all grown with their own issues.

"Oh, is that the game you want to play big brother? Fine." Nolan focused his eyes back on me. "Did Dane tell you he fucked half the girls in high school? What makes you think you're so special?" His eyes burned through me and I felt my throat close. This wasn't what I expected when I came here tonight. He eyed me quietly before his lips turned up. "Oh, I get it, you haven't fucked him yet. That's why you're here. You're one of those chicks who want everything. Well, let me tell you, sweetheart, this ass can't give you that. If it doesn't work out, I'm single." The look on his face made me cringe, but his words made my chest burn with anger. When I looked up, Dane was standing beside my chair, offering me his hand. I grabbed it, using his body to hold me up on my wobbly knees. I didn't know what to think anymore.

"We're going. I'm not wasting my time here anymore," Dane said in a controlled voice. He was done fighting.

Dane's mom finally stood up from her chair. "Don't go. We haven't even had cake yet."

"I don't care about the cake," Dane said as he moved us toward the door, holding me tight to his side. As we reached the door, he turned us back around where his mom was standing in the kitchen doorway. "Mom, I know you're trying hard to make up for all those years you weren't around, but why don't you focus on helping him instead of feeding his addiction? You of all people should know what it takes to break it. I'm not going to sit here for another minute and let him tear apart my girlfriend while you pretend everything is fine. Everything is not fine; it hasn't been for thirteen years."

She grabbed her throat as she began to sob. "Dane, I'm sorry. I'm so sorry. Please don't go. I just wanted us to have a nice family dinner." My heart broke for the woman who had lost her way when her daughter died.

He placed his hand on the knob. "It may be a little too late for that. Sorry, Mom, I can't do this," he said as we exited through the door. I didn't remember the walk from the apartment to the car. I was in such a haze. I felt bad for Dane, but at the same time Nolan's words cut me. Would Dane leave me as soon as I had sex with him? He wasn't like that, was he? One hour ago, I had myself convinced that Dane was all I needed and now I was so confused.

Dane opened the passenger door and helped me in before reaching across to buckle my seatbelt. There was question in his eyes as he stared at me. I had to look away because I was scared of what I would see. Was everything his brother said true? It all brought me back to some of the things Chris said that night at the club.

"Baby, please look at me." I squeezed my eyes shut and silently counted to ten before looking back in his direction. "I'm so sorry. I knew this was a bad idea, but I didn't think it would turn out like this."

"Can you just take me home? I'm tired and I need some time to think," I said, taking a deep breath to hold back the tears that threatened. I felt so lost and confused. I needed time to myself.

"Fuck, I knew it was a bad idea to bring you here," he said, running his hand through his hair. "Alex, please. Don't let what happened in there come between us." He reached up to rub his thumb over my cheek.

I closed my eyes. "What Nolan said, is it true?" I opened my eyes again to see him as he answered. I needed to know the truth.

"I'm not going to lie. I've been with a lot of girls, but not like he said. You're special, Alex. The other girls don't matter to me and I can't see anyone in my future besides you. Don't you see that, Baby?" I wanted to cry. This whole night had been so exhausting. I hated doubt, but I wasn't immune to it.

I took a deep breath. I knew Dane better than to let Nolan's words get in my head. If Dane wanted only one thing from me, he wouldn't be spending all his time getting to know me. "He just said all this stuff and, God, I've never heard anyone talk like that."

"I'm sorry, Baby. You have to trust me. I'm not like that anymore," he said, cupping my face in his hands. I felt myself softening under his touch. He hadn't done anything to deserve my mistrust.

I leaned into his hand. "I do trust you. Is that what all your family dinners are like?"

"If Nolan is there, they can get like that. When he doesn't show up, they are much quieter. I promise I won't make you go to one again. When I've calmed down enough to have dinner with my mom again, she can come to my place. No Nolan, I promise." His eyes were full of sadness. I wanted to show him that we were okay. I ran my hands through his hair before bringing his mouth to mine. When our lips finally met, I became lost in the feelings he drew out of me. His tongue moved to part my lips and I quickly gave him what he wanted, allowing him complete control. We stayed like that for several minutes, healing each other, and when he moved away I wanted more. I always wanted more with Dane.

CHAPTER FOURTEEN

Dane had a few pieces of art in a show the following Sunday and invited me to go with him. We didn't talk about his mom or brother again. Not because I didn't want to, but because he tended to avoid it. He seemed a little out of it all week and I knew today would lift his spirits. This was his element; the thing that made him happy. I envied him because he had nothing standing in his way. His reality was my dream.

He had to be there early so I told him I would meet him and invited Jade to come with me. There were supposed to be a few up and coming photographers at the show that she was dying to meet. It was scheduled to begin at two in the afternoon so I told her it began at one. Lying isn't bad if it's necessary and I wanted to be on time so I could see Dane in his element before the place was overrun with people.

"Where did you say this show was at?" she asked, trying on her third outfit.

"The Modern." She looked up at me, tapping her index finger on her chin. "Wear something hip, yet sophisticated. We're not going to a nightclub, we're going to an art show."

I dressed in an emerald green sweater dress with black tights and my black ankle books, but left my hair in a loose, messy knot at the top of my head. I was adapting to Dane's philosophy of looking good without too much effort.

I wasn't sure how many things Jade pulled out of her

142

closet before deciding on a black velvet shift dress, but it was ridiculous. She chose a pair of black tights with some killer black heels. It was quarter to two when she finally declared that she was ready. Did I know this girl or what?

We hailed a cab and gave the driver directions to The Modern. When we arrived, an older gentleman took our coats and handed us a program. I couldn't even begin to tell you the feelings that went through me as we entered the gallery. I put my whole heart into my work and as I glanced around, I could see the heart of others displayed on the wall. I could walk around for hours, dissecting what the artist was thinking or experiencing when the art piece was created. I could look back at every piece of art I'd ever completed and tell you what was going through my head at that moment. Major life events always triggered something in me that lead me to art. I have a painting representing my first day of high school, my first kiss, my first break-up. A lot of the things in between are dark, a symbol of the girl trapped inside me who can't get out.

Although Dane and I hadn't talked about why or when he began to sculpt, I wondered if he did it to let out some of his feelings and frustrations over his childhood. I pictured the little boy who had lost his sister and then had to watch his family fall apart. I wished I'd known him back then so I could have been there for him. I wasn't the type of girl who needed to save every broken man she encountered, but Dane was worth saving. I wasn't sure if I'd ever have children, but if I did I wanted to make sure they had a better childhood than Dane and I had experienced. I may have had everything material, but I felt like I had nothing. Dane really had nothing. Every time I thought about him, I felt my chest tighten. He was everything I didn't think I could have and somehow, he'd become everything I needed. There was a part of me that knew I would never recover if this fell apart, but what I felt now was worth it.

I walked around a little bit before I spotted Dane standing in the center of the gallery, pedestals displaying sculptures surrounding him. The moment he saw me, his face broke out in a smile that lit up the room...and my heart. He looked smashing in his icy blue button down tucked into charcoal dress pants.

When I reached him he wrapped his arms around me, hugging me close to his chest. He kissed me right below my right ear before joining his mouth with mine. His kisses were always full of passion and yearning, but this one remained soft. He reluctantly broke away, pressing his forehead to mine. "I'm glad you came. I missed you."

I smiled. "You saw me last night."

"Last night was a long time ago," he whispered. I heard Jade clear her throat behind me. I turned around, narrowing my eyes at her. She just ruined my perfect moment.

"Okay, lovebirds, you all are really cute. But if you continue to do that, this might turn into something a little dirtier than an art show."

"Don't be jealous, Jade. You're the one who said I should go after him."

She laughed. "And that you did."

I stared at her until she finished her girly rant. "Do you want to check out some exhibits with me? We better let Dane get back to work." I glanced back at him one more time before walking toward Jade. He didn't let me get far before he grabbed my hand and pulled me back. "Don't go too far,

Baby."

Jade and I walked around looking at paintings, photos and sculptures. All the artists were very talented, but one painting in particular grabbed my attention. It was a creature with eight arms, each one being pulled in a different direction. The look on the painted creature's face was one of pain and confusion; it haunted me because it was my own face in the mirror. I felt like I had two hands pulling at me all the time and I wished I could take a paint brush and make them go away, but I couldn't get rid of them that easily.

When we made our way back to Dane, he was talking to an older woman about buying one of his sculptures. I loved how confidant and professional he was during his shows. He gave me a quick glance before returning to his work. Today his sculptures were not of people, but rather hearts molded with different colored metals to show in various colors. They were so simple, but so beautiful.

Dane ended up selling a sculpture while Jade and I eyed his latest creations. I was excited for him because I knew it meant he could breathe a little easier financially. "Good job, Baby, I'm proud of you," I said after the lady left. He gave me a shy grin, one I rarely saw.

"I should be thanking you."

"Me?" I asked, drawing my brows together.

"Yes, you inspired all of these. With every sculpture here today, I thought of you." Did he really just tell me I inspired all of this? Part of me felt like he had told me too much and another part wanted to reach up and kiss him until I could no longer breathe.

My chest tightened with anxiety. I knew what he was trying to say because I think I felt it to. Once it was said, we couldn't go back. So I did what any girl who was about to hear I love you from their completely sexy and sweet boyfriend would do; I raised my finger to his lips. He looked confused, but it didn't stop me. "Don't," I whispered. I gave him a kiss on the cheek before turning back to Jade. "What are we doing after the show?" I asked.

Dane didn't give Jade time to reply. "Actually, some friends of mine are having a get together and invited us to go." I turned around and saw something that looked like defeat written all over his face. I felt bad for making him hold back. After all, that was what everyone did to me growing up.

Jade broke me out of my haze. "That sounds great. Is Tyler going to be there?" I found it kind of strange that she didn't know if he was going to be there or not.

"He was invited," Dane replied.

"I'm in. What do you say, Alex?"

"Yeah, sounds fun."

"All right, ladies. Let me get everything put away here and then we can go." Dane didn't even look in my direction before we walked away to retrieve our coats.

As soon as we were ten steps away from Dane, Jade began to question me. "Okay, what happened between the moment when you guys were creating a soft porn movie in the middle of the gallery and now? Dane looks like you just killed his puppy." I bit my lower lip and contemplated if I should tell Jade about my "I love you" diversion.

"I'm pretty sure he was going to tell me he loves me," I said quietly.

She stared at me like I had grown another head. "He looks sad because he was going to tell you he loves you?

146

What am I missing?"

I blew out all the air I was holding in my lungs. "I stopped him."

"You what?"

"He was telling me he thought about me while making all the heart sculptures and I could see it in his eyes. There was so much more he wanted to say, but I stopped him."

"Are you freaking kidding me? Alex, I can see in your eyes that you feel the same way about him. You have to stop this bullshit. Quit running and let him catch you," she said, grabbing onto my arm.

"I can't. This wasn't supposed to be more than just two people having a good time," I whispered.

"But it is."

"Yes," I finally agreed. "Look, can we just drop it for now?" She had no reply for me. Instead, she put her coat on and started walking back over to Dane who was almost done wrapping his sculptures and putting them in boxes.

I hated that I had to bottle all this up. I hated that I couldn't just tell him exactly how I felt and take in his words, locking them in my heart where I could hold them forever. I hated that I couldn't be honest and instead opted for this semi-reality I had been living in for years.

When I made my way back over to Dane, I decided I needed to smooth things over before we left. I didn't want to spend all night in awkward silence. I wrapped my arms tightly around him. He tensed up before clasping his hands on top of mine. "I'm sorry," I whispered just loud enough for him to hear me.

He turned around, bringing his lips to my forehead. "We're not done with that conversation," he said. Before I

could reply, he led me over to Jade who was in deep
conversation with one of the photographers. "Ready to go?"
he asked.

"I'm always ready to drink. Let's go," she said, eyeing
me curiously as she stepped behind Dane and I.

The party we were going to was only a few blocks from
the gallery. The walk was relatively quiet unless you count
Jade's comments here and there about clothing in storefronts
or people who passed us on the street. Dane held my hand,
but said nothing as we entered a brick apartment complex.

There were at least twelve people in the apartment when
we arrived. It was a small loft space with a seating area
where two guys sat playing some type of video game. On the
other side, near a small kitchenette, were two card tables.
Dane seemed to know almost everyone as he introduced us to
Blake and Carter, who lived in the apartment, as well as
Gavin, Jack, Andrew, Brandon, Kyle, Sara and Taylor.

The only one in the room I recognized was Tyler who
was sitting next to Taylor, a scantily clad blond with Bambi
eyes. His hand was resting on her knee and as soon as she
spotted us coming through the door, she smiled and laid her
head on his shoulder. When I looked at Jade I knew I wasn't
the only one who noticed. Her face fell as she looked at me
and nodded toward the door before disappearing through it. I
looked up at Dane who shook his head. "Let him go after
her," he whispered. Tyler was eyeing the closed door with a
deer in the headlights look on his face. After a few seconds,
he got up from the couch and ran out after her. I didn't want
to see Jade go through this. She guarded her heart so much,
but she had seemed to be opening up to Tyler.

"What was that all about?" I asked, nodding toward the

door.

He shrugged. "Tyler didn't know she was coming, I guess. He usually doesn't date one girl. I think he likes her, but doesn't know what to do about it."

"Who's the girl?"

"You mean Taylor? They see each other off and on, but I thought they were off. He isn't usually this much of an ass."

"Well, he better make it right," I said, frowning up at him.

He pulled me in for a hug and I felt myself relax again. "Come on, let's have some fun."

I walked toward the card table because video games and I do not get along. I ended up on Dane's lap because there weren't enough chairs for everyone. Personally, I thought this was more comfortable than a folding chair anyway. Blake, Andrew, Sara, Carter and Gavin were in the middle of a game so we sat back and watched. I studied the game and quickly learned the rules so when it was time for us to join, I felt like I had a good handle on it.

My studying paid off, like it always did, and I ended up winning the first game. Was I excited? Just a little. "Oh, my god, I won!" I jumped up off Dane's lap and through my arms in the air.

"That's my girl." Dane picked me up and twirled me around in his arms. I didn't care that everyone was watching because in that moment it felt like just the two of us.

"When are you taking me to Vegas? I'm feeling lucky."

"Vegas, huh?" he asked, nuzzling his face in my neck.

"Yeah, I think you may have a gambler on your hands," I replied, working my bottom lip between my teeth.

"I would take you anywhere as long as you stop biting

that lower lip. You don't even know how sexy you are." My pulse picked up, but I couldn't think of anything to say in reply. "Come out to the rooftop deck with me," he whispered before putting me down. He wanted to talk; I knew it and I owed it to him. The game and my recent victory had relaxed me enough that I didn't hesitate to follow him, knowing I was going to have to open up at least a little to make this better.

"Let me grab my coat." Jade and Tyler hadn't returned yet. I hoped for her sake that they were working their issues out. Maybe it was time for them to throw caution to the wind and become something a little more official. I get that they were both guarding themselves, but it might backfire in a big way if one of them didn't step it up.

As we made our way up to the deck, I realized what a bad idea this was. It was February in New York City and we were on a rooftop deck. It seemed like others shared my thoughts because ours were the only footprints in the snow and any furniture that may have been up here had been removed. We headed toward the edge, overlooking the night sky. Dane pulled me in front of him and held me tight against his chest in an attempt to chase away the cold. I could see my breath mixing with his as we looked out over at the flashing city lights. The city at night was amazing and it was moments like this that solidified my desire to leave Greenwich behind forever. It was a nice, safe place to grow up, but New York City was where my heart was. I loved the mix of people and culture, the solitude of living somewhere so big, it was easy to disappear.

By the time Dane finally spoke, I almost forgot why we were out here. "Why did you close up on me earlier, Baby?"

I closed my eyes and thought for a moment. I could either be honest with him or run like I had been for the last nineteen years. I decided to be honest, to take the fall and let him catch me. "I'm scared, Dane. I'm scared of how you make me feel," I whispered.

He didn't waste any time before turning me in his arms, pulling me so close that our chests were touching. "Look at me." When I didn't meet his gaze, he placed his finger under my chin, lifting my head until I had no choice but to look in his eyes. Even in the night, illuminated by the city lights, I could see the passion and desire burning in his eyes. "What are you afraid of?"

It took me a moment to answer and when I did my voice was shaking. "I'm afraid of falling in love. I'm afraid of loving someone so much that if it ends; there will be nothing left of me. There would be nothing that could put me back together if something came between us." I couldn't hold my emotions back any longer as a tear rolled down my face. Dane used his thumb to wipe it away.

"Alex, I love you. From the moment I saw you in the club, I knew there was something different about you. Then, when we ended up in the same Art class, it was like fate had intervened and brought you to me again. I love everything about you. Why would that ever stop? I can't think of one thing you could do to make me stop loving you." His words coated my heart and I knew without a doubt what I was feeling. Was there really any difference between feeling it and saying it?

I cupped his cheeks in my hands and pulled him down so our foreheads touched. "I love you, too." His lips met mine, softly at first then as his tongue pressed into my mouth as he moved to deepen the kiss. His kiss was hungry and passionate; it reached my heart it a way I didn't even know was possible. A kiss had never meant this much; kissing someone I loved was ten times better than any kiss I had ever experienced in my life. It might have been cold outside, but everything in me was on fire and I wanted to stay like this forever.

When the kiss finally broke, my lips were numb and swollen. Dane smiled down at me, rubbing his thumb over my bottom lip. "I could kiss these lips forever and never get tired of them." I returned his smile and placed a kiss on his chin. "I can't wait." And I didn't have to wait as he leaned down and met my lips with his again.

When you find someone you truly love, nothing else matters. I finally realized that being in love was worth the heartbreak that may follow. Nothing compared to how he made me feel and I was ready to feel more and try everything with him.

CHAPTER FIFTEEN

If someone asked me for money and I loaned it to them, I could get that back. If I loaned a textbook, I could get it back. Hell, in some instances when you gave your heart away, you could still get it back. But this was different. Virginity was the one thing that once you gave it away, you couldn't get it back.

All through my childhood, I felt like every decision was made for me. I'd even gone as far as to pursue a career that others had chosen for me. I knew with every ounce of my being that my parents would not choose Dane as the man I gave my virginity up to, but this was my decision to make. They couldn't take this from me. They couldn't control it. I knew I loved Dane, a deep in my heart, consuming type of love, and it was hard to imagine having this with anyone else. I couldn't imagine feeling comfortable giving it to anyone else.

My nerves kicked into high gear as I got ready to head over to Dane's for dinner. I chose black lace lingerie for the special occasion and threw on a pair of jeans, a fitted grey tee with my purple leather jacket and topped it off with my black knee high boots. I was comfortable and Dane loved it when I wore the leather jacket he bought me.

I took deep breaths as I walked from my dorm to his apartment. Just because I made this decision and felt good about it, didn't mean I wasn't scared out of my mind. I'd been thinking about it for days, and with each one that passed I felt more confident in my decision. I'd never been one to live for today, but everything in me wanted to do this one thing I had one hundred percent control over. This was mine.

I buzzed his apartment and he quickly let me in, pulling me into his arms and showering me with soft butterfly kisses. The love and tenderness he gave me made me feel like all was right and everything would be okay. I stopped his soft eyelash kisses by attacking his lips with mine. I kissed him often, but tonight I really kissed him. I kissed him with everything I had and thought about everything I would give him.

"Whoa, what was that about? I like it, but we have to eat first, Baby." He gave me a sexy hooded smile as I bit my lip to stop myself from kissing him again. He groaned, capturing my lips with his again, and pulling my bottom lip between his teeth. When he finally pulled away, we were both breathless.

"Nothing, I'm just really happy to see you."

"I'm happy to see you, too. Come on, let's eat." He took my hand and led me to his small dining table. He had gone all out with candles and a vase of flowers; I wondered who was trying to seduce whom tonight. I hadn't told him I was thinking about this, but for the last week it had consumed my thoughts more often than not. I had never felt this close to someone and I knew it would go to a whole new level once we had sex. I was ready for more.

"What are we having?" I asked. The apartment smelt like garlic and fresh bread.

"Spaghetti and meatballs with garlic bread; it's something I used to cook for my brother all the time." He retreated to his small kitchen and started pulling plates from the cupboard.

"Do you need any help?" I asked.

"No, sit. Tonight is all me." He came out carrying a basket of bread that smelled out of this world followed by two huge plates of spaghetti.

"This looks great. Thank you." We ate and talked about our current classes, Dane's upcoming art show, and our plans for the weekend. We had grown into this comfortable routine that I loved and he genuinely made me feel like someone cared about me. He listened. There was a part in both of us that missed this as children. Neither one of us had the type of parents who sat with us during a meal and asked about our day or how we were feeling. We had two completely different backgrounds, but had experienced some of the same things.

After dinner, he insisted on cleaning up on his own and I retreated to his living space to turn on some Ed Sheeran, who we were both fans of. I stood there, looking out the window and taking in the breathtaking city view. My mind was working overtime thinking about what was going to happen tonight. Would Dane be ready? What if I couldn't go through with it? How would I feel when it was over? I had always wondered if having sex really changes a person or not. I remembered where I was emotionally before I met Dane and then I thought about how I felt now and there was no comparison. Even if things went incredibly wrong, I didn't think I would ever regret him. Ever.

I felt Dane wrap his arms around me before he kissed my neck. In this moment, I felt so calm, like everything was right. "Dane".

"Hmm"

"I'm ready," I whispered, my body shaking with anticipation. His body tensed around me as his mouth stopped its exploration of my neck.

"For what?" I knew he knew what I meant.

I turned around in his arms, looking him squarely in the eye. "Make love to me."

He stared into my eyes, searching for something. "Are you sure?"

"Yes." My response was breathy and I followed it with a kiss that said everything I wanted to say, but couldn't. He slowly inched my jacket off my arms and threw it on the couch, pulling back from the kiss just enough to whisper bedroom against my lips before backing me in that direction. I instinctively jumped up, wrapping my legs and arms around him. My whole body was on fire from the heat of his kiss; I had never wanted anything as much as I wanted this. When we reached his room, he sat me on the edge of the bed before unzipping my boots and pulling them off slowly. I could see his Adam's apple move as he swallowed and looked into my eyes. "I love you, Alex, only you." His words only solidified my feelings; there would be no doubts or regrets.

"I love you, too."

He stood and pulled me up with him, lifting my shirt above my head. He wrapped his arms around my waist and kissed me softly before pulling away. "God, you're beautiful. Are you sure about this? I don't want to go any further if you aren't sure." I nodded, sending him back into motion. He slowly ran his hands down my shoulders, over my breasts then down my stomach before unbuttoning my jeans and carefully working them down my legs. I heard him whisper the words beautiful and mine as he took my body in with his eyes. Everything Dane said and did sent warmth through my body and all that mattered in this moment was us. After tugging his shirt above his head, I began to plant kisses on his chest, working my way over every tattoo and paying special attention to the angel. He gasped as I ran my trembling hands over his abs and pulled on the top of his jeans to bring him forward for a kiss. Somewhere along the way, he unclasped my bra and slid it down my arms. I was completely exposed in a way I had never been before but everything about this moment felt so right.

My heart was beating rapidly as I undid his jeans and slid them down his hips. I wanted to touch him so badly. I pulled down his boxers and grasped him in my hand as he groaned and pulled my hand away. "Not yet, Baby."

He stopped kissing me and looked into my eyes. "Are you absolutely sure? We don't have to do this now."

"I have never wanted anything more in my life." And just like that my back was on the bed and he was nestled between my legs. I reached up to kiss his chin and ran my thumbs over his brows as he reached between my legs and rubbed slow circles on my sensitive spot. I wasn't thinking of anything but the two of us, together. He had the power to make me forget. I was already close when he entered me with one finger, then two. "You feel so good; I can't believe you are giving me this," he whispered in my ear. "God, Baby, you feel so good." The combination of his slow circles and the in and out motions of his fingers and sweet words slowly wound my body up and I came undone around his fingers, panting and saying his name. It was better than any orgasm I'd ever experienced.

Brushing soft kisses across my face, he whispered, "I'm going to go really slow, okay? Let me know if you want to stop." His kisses put me on a cloud, but I needed more. As if he could read my mind, he reached into his nightstand drawer and pulled out a foil packet, quickly opening it and rolling it on. He positioned himself between my legs and whispered I love you one more time before I felt him ready to enter me. He looked right into my eyes as he moved in slowly. It burned as he continued to slowly push inside, but his tenderness was drowning all those negative feelings away. Once he was all the way in, he stopped. I could feel tears running down my face. They were tears caused by love, passion and pain. I felt love for Dane before, but as our naked bodies joined together I felt something so deep and pure that I knew I could never go back to life before this. I always wondered if this moment would change me and it had; I felt everything in my heart and wanted nothing, but for this moment to never end.

He wiped his thumb across each side of my face and winced. "I'm sorry," he whispered, tenderly kissing my lips.

I said the only thing that I felt in my heart at that moment. "I love you." With that he kissed me, and began to move in and out slowly as my body adjusted to him. I ran my hands through his short hair then down his shoulders to his back. I felt consumed by him, the way he felt on me and inside of me. I had always imagined having sex with someone I loved, but never imagined the intensity of the moment when I would give away this part of me. The pain was replaced by pleasure as our eyes locked. After several minutes of slow motions, his pace quickened before he found his release, putting his lips to mine.

"I love you," he said, kissing my forehead.

"I love you, too." We laid still for a couple of minutes, catching our breath and holding each other close. He moved away only to remove the condom, tying it and throwing it in a trash can near the bed. He was only gone for seconds, but I missed him. I didn't know if I would ever be able to spend another minute away from him again.

He returned to the bed wrapping me in his arms. "Did it hurt?" he asked, brushing the hair from my face.

"It was amazing." I reached up to plant a reassuring kiss on his lips. I couldn't imagine doing this with anyone I didn't truly love. Doing this with love in my heart made the whole experience beautiful, rather than painful.

"That was my first time," he whispered a few minutes later. I propped my head up on my hand and looked him in the eyes. They were glistening as I reached up to trace the line on his forehead. I knew I was the first virgin he had ever been with. I wondered if it was painful for him and how it had compared to his other experiences.

"I know."

"I mean it was my first time making love to anyone." My eyes grew big and all I could do was kiss him. At that moment, he was everything I wanted and everything I needed. I fell asleep in his arms that night feeling content and loved. I didn't care that I didn't have clothes for class in the morning or even that I had class in the morning. Living in the moment was far better than living by a script.

I woke up the next morning, wrapped in Dane's arms. I felt happy and content, but a little shy as I lay next to him, still completely naked from the night before. I always feared I'd regret my first time; that I would wake up the morning after and wish it never happened. That was a big reason it had taken me so long to get to that point; I let fear and regret rule my life. With Dane, there was no regret or fear. I was relieved that I had waited for him because I couldn't imagine sharing that experience with anyone else. I couldn't imagine ever doing that with anyone else.

A smile spread across my face as I thought about the night before and how tender and sweet he was. Dane may have some rough edges, but I always saw the good. I wished others could see what I saw inside him. I wished my family could meet him and not draw opinions simply by looking at him. All I knew was that I'd never felt this happy and the man lying next to me had everything to do with that.

I felt warm lips on my shoulder and smiled. I worried things would be awkward between us this morning, but his kiss was all it took to calm me. He worked his way up my neck until his mouth was right above my ear. "How are you feeling this morning?"

I shivered as his breath hit the side of my face. Everything inside me wanted a repeat of last night. I didn't know what this man did to me, but suddenly I felt like I could never get enough of him. I turned in his arms. "I've never been better."

He kissed my lips with a certain tenderness that I usually did not get from his kiss; this one was full of love and contentment. I broke away and looked right into those green eyes, which I could now see every time I closed mine. "I love you."

I could feel him smile against my lips. "I love you too." I

didn't waste another minute before I assaulted his lips with mine. I'd had enough of his soft kisses and all I wanted now was hungry, passionate Dane. He seemed to get the idea and used his tongue against my lips to deepen the kiss. My hands began to move down his arm and over his stomach while he pressed his hand on my lower back. I could feel him harden against me and, like a child with candy being dangled in front of me, I moved my hand down and gripped him. He tensed before grabbing my hand. "Alex, not today. You need to wait a day or two."

Sighing, I removed my hand. "Please."

He didn't hesitate in his response, "No, but we can continue to do what we were doing with our lips. I kind of liked that." I didn't bother to reply with anything, but my lips.

Dane and I stayed in bed all morning, kissing until my lips were swollen and numb. He heard my stomach growl and insisted that we get up and have some breakfast. I thought what I was eating for breakfast was good enough, but he didn't quite agree. "Eggs? Pancakes? Toast? What do you want?" he asked.

"Surprise me. I usually just have a latte."

His brows furrowed. "You need to eat breakfast."

I rolled out of bed and began looking for some clothes. "Okay, boss."

I heard him get up from the bed and felt his arms wrap around me. "I like the sound of that. Say it again."

"Okay, Dane," I laughed.

He pulled me in closer to him. "That isn't what you said."

"Really? I can't remember what I said."

He trailed kisses along my jaw line. "I think you do."

His kisses left me in a daze; I didn't know that anything could feel that good. "I don't remember," I finally said.

He stopped kissing me and loosened his grip. "Okay, then go get dressed. You can borrow a pair of pants and a t-shirt, second and third drawer."

"Okay, boss," I replied, smiling up at him. His eyes shined with mischief as he grabbed me and threw me on the bed where he began to tickle me everywhere and anywhere with his long fingers. I hadn't laughed so hard, well, ever and I regretted not using the bathroom before deciding to play games with my super sexy tickle monster boyfriend. "Dane, stop! I need to go to the bathroom."

He smiled down at me. "Say it again and I'll let you go."

I relented, "Okay, boss, now can I please go to the bathroom?"

He stopped tickling me, grabbed my hands and pulled me up so I was standing right in front of him. He quickly kissed my forehead and stepped to the side so I could walk past; I realized he wasn't done with me yet when he lightly smacked my ass as I walked past. I picked up my pace and quickly closed the door to the bathroom.

After using the bathroom, I decided a shower was in order. Dane was right; my body ached from the newness of last night's activities. I started the water, letting it run a little hotter than I usually would. It felt amazing as it washed over my body. I used Dane's soap and it made me happy to think I would get to smell like him for the remainder of the day.

I dressed in Dane's clothes, which were a few sizes too big, and walked out to the main living area where I was greeted by the smell of bacon, coffee and maple syrup. Dane was standing over the stove with his back to me wearing grey sweat pants and a fitted white tee. I could spend hours...days staring at him, taking in every inch of his body and never get bored. He was kind, protective, decisive and more than anything he was mine and I didn't have to be anyone but me when I was around him.

Walking up behind him, just loud enough not to scare him, I wrapped my arms around his stomach and rested my head between his shoulders. He was warm and I felt safe just being near him. When I finally lifted my head to see what he was cooking, I saw pancakes, eggs, bacon and hash browns. "Who's going to eat all this?"

"You," he said, placing his hand over mine.

I laughed. "I hope you have a doggy bag."

He put down his spatula and turned, wrapping his arms around me tightly. "I love that sound."

"What sound?" I asked. I could hear the bacon crackling in the background.

"Your laugh. You didn't do that often when we first met. I like hearing it," he said, leaning down to kiss the corner of my mouth.

Pulling his head to mine, I looked right into his eyes. "You make me feel things I have never felt before, you know that? I didn't laugh because I had very little to laugh about." I moved my hands to the back of his head and kissed him. If I could, I would spend the rest of my life showing Dane how much I appreciated him. That very thought broke me from the kiss. This was too good to be true for a reason; it couldn't be my forever. My forever was somewhere between Hell and misery and this was just a stop in what I wanted and couldn't have.

Dane must have sensed that I was pulling away. "Hey, stay with me. What are you thinking about?" At some point I needed to talk to him about my parents, but not today. He helped me make my life better, but this was one area that even he couldn't fix.

"Nothing, I guess I'm just tired. Do you realize we missed class? I have never, and I mean never, missed class. What are you doing to me?" I said, smiling up at him.

His eyes bore into mine and I could tell that he was trying to read me. "I hope I'm turning you into Mrs. Wright." It felt like all the air I had in my lungs escaped me and I couldn't breathe. He didn't just bring up marriage. No, I wasn't hearing him right. It was too soon and I needed things to remain simple. Okay, we said I love you and we had sex but I needed this to remain where it was. "Hey, calm down. I was just kidding...sort of."

I took a deep breath. "Yeah, I knew that."

"Come on, over-thinker, let's eat."

As we ate breakfast, I thought about Dane and what it might do to him if this had to end. I spent so much time thinking about myself and what my parents were going to say that I hadn't thought about Dane and his part in all of this. There had to be a way to make this work. I could have Dane and make my parents happy. There had to be a way.

Chapter Sixteen

I woke up this morning and felt complete. I couldn't tell you what it was like to walk through life from day to day living someone else's dream. There were no words to describe what it was like to be a puppet with someone else holding the string. The big house, nice cars, country club membership, and last name affiliations may be important to my parents, but they were never what defined me, never who I was on the inside. When people thought of Alexandra Riley, they thought of money; I wanted them to see Alex Riley and think of the person. I could never get that at home, but college was like my second birth. I began to live my life the way I wanted to.

It has been a week since Dane and I were together for the first time and it had done nothing but bring us closer. We had continued our nightly study sessions during the week, but now we usually ended up at his apartment and studying often turned into something else. He treated me like I was a piece of fine china and I wanted to tell him how right he was. My mind constantly drifted to the future and he sensed it. He could read me like no one else could and I was having a hard time letting him in completely. The best way to drown out those thoughts was with his kiss; it had become my drug of choice.

He was always caring and attentive, nothing like I thought sex would be, but I think it had a lot to do with the guy I was with. I wondered if my mom ever had this with my dad or if things were always so robotic between them. I wondered if my sister had this with her fiancé, but I knew the answer to that one. Their lives were about appearances and parties and I couldn't remember a time where I ever looked at them and thought, "They look so happy". A part of me felt sorry for them because they have never experienced this. But then again, they didn't really know any better.

My sister's wedding was two weeks away and I hadn't brought Dane up to my parents or the wedding up to Dane. If I told my mom about Dane, she would ask a bunch of questions that I wouldn't want to answer or I would lie about everything. Either way, it was not going to be easy. If I told Dane about the wedding, he would expect to attend with me. That was what couples did, right? My solution was to wait and tell Dane about the wedding a few days beforehand. That way he wouldn't be able to get off work and I wouldn't have to introduce him to the parents. I didn't feel good about doing it, but it was what was easiest for all of us. It was a way for me to stay in my own little world a little while longer.

Jade thought I was being stupid and selfish and I was. I wanted Dane to go with me and help relieve some of the stress my family created, but I knew it would only cause new stress. Gwen agreed with my decision to keep my new relationship on the down low; she knew the fall out it would cause if my parents knew about Dane. The difference between Jade and Gwen's advice was just another game of tug of war playing in my mind, but Gwen knew what I was facing more than Jade did.

I was also starting to think about what would happen over the summer when I returned to Greenwich and Dane remained in the city. I spent hours one night looking at summer internships, but they really did not exist for someone who had just completed her first year of Pre-Med. Getting a real job was out of the question; my parents would never let me work over the summer. The only thing I could hope for was a few weekend trips to the city to see Dane because it wasn't like I could have him come to my house.

On top of everything, midterms were coming up and I needed to do some serious studying so I could maintain the grade point average I was expected to have. I was well aware that study sessions at Dane's apartment were not very productive so I opted to study in the library today. I did invite him to join me; I couldn't imagine spending the whole evening without him, but here we would be focused and monitored. He couldn't distract me with his sweet kisses and beautiful body.

I wandered into the library and found a quiet table in the corner. It appeared I wasn't the only one trying to find a quiet place to study; there were groups of students at almost every table with their noses buried deep in a book. I pulled out my Calculus book and got to work. Dane was supposed to meet me here after his last class. This was not a place he would usually go, he had reminded me of this over and over, but said he would go anywhere that I was.

Just like I knew he would, he walked in a little after four and put his bag down on the chair across from me before kissing my cheek. He smelled so good, like soap and mint; it took everything I had to not grab his head and kiss him senseless. That kind of kissing was definitely not meant for the library. "Hey, Gorgeous, have you been waiting long?"

"No, not really. I was just studying for my Calculus midterm."

"That sounds exciting." He sat across from me and started pulling his laptop and notebook from his bag. "I need to write a paper for art history. I thought it was a punishment until you mentioned Calculus."

"Well, Calculus is the one subject I'm not very good at so let's get some studying done. Let me study until seven and then you can take me out for pizza. Deal?" I knew this would work. He liked to buy me things and take me places, but I always fought him on it. This was my compromise of sorts.

He leaned over the table so we were less than a foot apart. "Anywhere you are, remember that."

I swore my toes just curled in my brown UGG boots. Dane was every girl's dream and I was his only dream. I leaned in to kiss him on the lips quickly before sitting back in my seat and reading through my Calculus notes. After an hour or so, my eyes started to blur and I reached into my bag for my reading glasses. They were large and dark rimmed; my mother had hated them when I picked them out which made me love them even more.

I heard Dane clear his throat from across the table and looked up to find him staring at me. "Do you need help with something?"

He had a glint in his eyes...those beautiful green eyes. "Actually, yes. Can you see if you can find a book on Salvador Dali? I suck at finding books in the library; it's like the road less traveled without a map."

"But they have a whole system," I said. I thought that learning the Dewey Decimal System was a pretty standard part of elementary school education. Maybe it wasn't in New York.

"I know, I just don't have time to learn it today. Please. I'm buying you a pizza later," he said before sticking his lower lip out at me. How could I say no to that?

"Fine, I'll be right back." I walked through a few aisles to the back of the library. This was definitely a less utilized area of the library. The books all looked and smelled old. When I was younger, I used to go into my grandparent's library and pull books from the shelf to smell them. Some people liked the smell of gasoline or rubber cement, but for me it was always the smell of old books. The old leather bound ones smelled the best. I couldn't help myself when I grabbed a black leather Art History 1800-1899 book from the shelf and inhaled its scent.

I had completely lost touch with all reality, when I felt big strong arms wrap around my waist. Turning around quickly, I saw Dane standing in front of me with a huge grin on his face. "What are you doing over here? I thought you didn't know your way around the library?" There was a bit more annoyance in my voice than I had intended, but he had just taken me away from my 'moment'.

"I know my way around the library; we learned that back in elementary school." He was still grinning at me and I was not seeing the humor in this. He definitely had other things on his mind. They weren't the smartest, considering the circumstances.

"But-"

He placed a finger on my lips and moved us back so I was up against the bookcase. He replaced his finger with his lips and I was temporarily frozen in place. I couldn't believe my boyfriend was kissing me in the library in the middle of the day. Alexandra Riley did not do this, but after thinking about if for a split second I realized that Alex Riley would so do this and I wrapped my arms around his neck. The electricity between us was uncontrollable and I felt like I'd combust at any moment.

He walked us into a dark corner where he began to move his hands up to my breasts. "Dane!" A light chuckle escaped his mouth, but he didn't stop and God knows I really didn't want him to. I felt all self-control and self-consciousness leave my body as I wrapped my legs around his waist. I was not sure who started it, but our bodies began to move slightly and it created a friction between my legs that had me biting his shoulder a few minutes later. A week ago I hadn't even had sex, and now I was having orgasms in the library.

When I had calmed down, Dane stood me on my feet and helped me straighten out my clothes. I laughed as he worked to adjust himself. I felt bad that he hadn't got as much out of our little exchange as I had, but I wasn't quite ready to take care of that problem in the library.

I started to walk back to our table when Dane said my name. I turned around; he looked serious, but he was biting his lip to hold back an obvious smile. "Did you find that book?"

I walked toward him, stopping when our lips were only inches apart, "You seem to know your way around the library just fine". I ran my eyes down his body before returning them to meet his. He wanted me to kiss him; his eyes were hooded and bore into me with enough passion for the both of us.

When I turned to walk toward the table, he grabbed my wrist. "It was the glasses."

"What?"

"The glasses," he repeated, pointing at them where they

rested on top of my head. "They are sexy as hell and if you wear them to the library or anywhere else again, I'm going to..."

"Going to what?"

He pulled me close and whispered in my ear. "I'm going to fuck you and I won't care who's watching." He released me and I walked back to the table in stunned silence. His words sent another shot of warmth through my body and a red tint to my face. He sat down with a big grin; part of me wanted to smack it off his face and part of me wanted to return it.

We sat there studying quietly for a few hours as the library started to empty out. I glanced over at Dane and he must have sensed it because his eyes met mine before he looked down at my book and then back at me. I knew what he was asking; he wanted to know if I was done with my studies, but he wouldn't say it out loud. He knew how important this was to me. I smiled at him and turned my attention back to my textbook. I was ready to go, but making him sweat for a few more minutes sounded more fun.

He cleared his throat. "Alex."

I looked up at him again, taking the glasses from the top of my head and placing them on my face. His eyes grew big and I could see his jaw working back and forth. I loved that I could do this to him. "Yes, babe."

He quickly closed his book and shoved it into his bag before turning his attention back to me. The quiet, patient Dane had left the building. He abruptly got up from his chair and walked around the table, reaching from behind me to grab my book and put it into my own bag. He did the same with my notebook and pen. I didn't say anything. I knew he was telling me that it was time to leave. He zipped my bag and placed it on the table in front of me.

"What did I tell you about those glasses?" I could feel his warm breath on my ear and it sent a bolt of electricity through my body.

"You said-"

He didn't let me finish before pulling my chair back slightly and offering his hand to me. I stood and grabbed my backpack, watching Dane do the same before he led us out of the library.

"Let's go. We'll grab some dinner on the way back to my place." He didn't wait for any sort of confirmation from me. This level of spontaneity and excitement was something I would have to get used to. It was doing things to me that I didn't know were possible.

We stopped at a deli between campus and his apartment to grab sandwiches. Dane never once stopped touching me; he had his hand in mine or on my back the whole time. I knew exactly what was going to happen the minute we got into his apartment; I could see it in his eyes. I was happy he didn't keep his original promise to make it happen on the spot. Alex Riley wasn't ready for that...yet.

We entered his building and Dane took the steps two at a time as I tried to keep up. I had little choice since my hand was clasped in his. He let go of my hand just long enough to unlock the door before pulling me forward again. As soon as we were inside, he released his backpack and set the deli bag on the counter. He came back toward me, not wasting a single second before removing my coat. My heart was beating out of my chest as he backed me up to the door and placed an arm on either side of my head. God, if he didn't kiss me soon I was going to scream.

He grazed his lips up and down my neck, making me absolutely crazy with need. I'd never wanted anything more than I wanted him right now. The tension in the library, combined with our activities between the shelves and his constant touching, excited me more than I thought was possible. I thought he knew what he was doing and I wasn't far away from begging. He finally brushed his lips over mine, teasing at first, not quite giving me all the contact I needed. "Please," I said, bringing my head forward so my lips could meet his. He pulled back, grinning at me with his all too sexy grin.

"Don't you like being teased, Baby? I thought you liked playing games." He was making me insane with need. The look on his face just made me want him even more.

"Dane, please. I need you now." I was breathless and desperate.

"Let me think about it for a minute." He moved closer to me again, putting my body on full alert. "Do you want me to kiss you here?" He kissed me below my ear before pulling back to look at my face again. I shook my head. "Do you want me to kiss you here?" He placed another soft kiss on my collarbone. God, he was making me freaking crazy. I shook my head again. "Do you want me to kiss you here?" He leaned in close and I swore he was going to kiss my lips, but he kissed my chin instead. I was done playing his game; it was time to play mine. When he moved back to look at me again, I put my bottom lip between my teeth, glancing up at him through my eyelids. I knew that drove him crazy.

"Fuck" was all he said before his kissed me where I needed him to kiss me most. We were both so wound up that it didn't take long before we were completely naked against the wall, and on the bed, before finally ending in the shower. It was different from the other times; I felt crazy and free. It was just another piece in the puzzle of Alex that Dane was continually piecing together.

It was well after midnight when we finally sat down to eat our sandwiches. I was wearing one of Dane's t-shirts and he was in a pair of black athletic shorts; he looked good and it was hard not to reach out and touch his chest. The evening's activities had left me tired and hungry, but it didn't stop me from smiling. Dane rested his hand on my knee while we ate in silence, both too tired to talk.

When we were both finished eating, he pulled out my chair and picked me up in his arms, putting one arm under my knees and another behind my back. "What are you doing?" I asked.

"Taking my girl to bed," he replied, placing a kiss on my forehead.

"Dane, I'm tired." There was no way I was going to go another round. I had a midterm in the morning and I had already lost enough sleep. Not to mention that I didn't think my body could handle it.

"Shhh," he said softly near my ear, "no more talking."

He laid me in the middle of the bed before crawling in behind me, curling his body around mine. It wasn't long before his breathing slowed. I whispered, "I love you," before falling asleep in Dane's arms.

CHAPTER SEVENTEEN

Dane woke me up by rubbing his hand up and down my leg; he had proven himself to be the best alarm clock a girl could ask for. I thought about the night before and all the things I did that I'd never done before. Dane had led me through so many firsts. Each one seemed to open me up a little more and I couldn't wait to see what he still had in store for me. I turned around to face him, kissing his lips as he brushed my hair off my face.

We just looked at each other for the longest time, neither of us speaking. "I love you, too," he finally whispered. I pulled my brows together, confused. "Last night, before you fell asleep, I heard you. I love you, too." Where on Earth did I find this guy? He seemed more perfect with every day that past and I felt myself waiting for the other shoe to drop. He had to have a flaw or a secret, didn't he? Even I had my secrets.

We kissed for a few minutes before getting up to dress for class. I had my Biology midterm this morning and then I had a lunch date with Jade before spending another evening in the library getting ready for my Calculus midterm tomorrow. Jade and I hadn't seen much of each other since I had started to sleep at Dane's most nights. I wanted to know how things were going in her life; I missed her.

Dane and I walked to campus together, stopping to get our morning coffee on the way. While I missed his early morning texts and visits to my dorm room, this was so much better. He had a midterm this morning and a project due this afternoon, but he didn't seem nearly as nervous as I was. Just one of the many ways he balanced me.

He walked me to the door of my Biology class and wrapped me in a tight hug. "I will see you at lunch, okay? And stop stressing, you're going to do great."

"Good luck on your test," I said before I kissed his cheek and walked into class. I wished that I had every class with him so I could sneak looks at him when I was stressed. Just being with him made me calmer.

I finished my midterm a little earlier than I intended and handed it to my professor before starting toward the student center. It felt good having the first one under my belt; there were only a few questions I had to guess on.

I grabbed my usual grilled chicken salad and sat down at a small table in the corner. Dane was always late for lunch on Tuesdays and Thursdays; his morning class was all the way across campus. I wanted Jade all to myself today. We were long overdue for some girl talk and I wanted to tell her all about my nights with Dane; I needed her advice on a few things. This was all so new to me and I had no one else to talk to. I could picture the smile on her face already; she had experienced so many things that I hadn't and now we were on more even playing ground. I understood her a little better.

My phone beeped from my purse. As I reached in to grab it, I noticed I had a new text from Dane.

Dane: I am not going to make lunch. I forgot my project at home.

Alex: Miss you! Meet me in the library again tonight?

My heart flip-flopped a little when I looked back down at the word library. I would never think of that place the same way again.

Dane: Library again?

Alex: To study!

Dane: Whatever you want, Baby. See you at 4?

I wanted to see him now but I wouldn't be selfish.

Alex: Sounds good. Luv u!

Dane: Love U 2, Baby!

Those words never got old coming from him. My heart did a happy dance every time I heard them. I threw my phone back in my purse and waited for Jade. If I couldn't have lunch with Dane, at least I would have more time for girly gossip.

I saw her cross the room with a tray in hand. I waved to let her know where I was and couldn't help but notice the serious look on her face. I expected the smile that usually greeted me. Maybe she and Tyler were having problems again or maybe her midterms weren't going very well. Whatever it was, I wanted to cheer her up like she had done for me so many times. She sat down and wasted no time before beginning the grilling I wasn't quite expecting.

"Where's Dane?" she asked, taking a bite of pizza.

"He forgot a project at home so he isn't going to make it today," I replied, taking another bite of my salad.

"Have you talked to him yet?" My stomach fell as I realized why she was so angry. She had been pushing me to talk to my parents about Dane and invite him to the wedding. She had no idea how badly I wanted him to go; I really did. He would be there for me and give me a little piece of contentment when I usually felt nothing of the sort at home. I couldn't bring myself to face the consequences of the old and new colliding.

"About what?" I asked, trying to sound every bit of the blonde I am.

She sighed and dropped her pizza, looking right at me. "About the wedding, Alex. You can't hide your boyfriend from your parents forever."

"I'm not hiding him. I'm just not ready for them to meet him yet," I said, returning my attention to my salad.

"Alex, you can't keep doing this. Either you introduce everyone and deal with the consequences or one day you are going to have to choose. The longer you let this go on, the harder it will be." Her words ripped through me, causing emotional pain to be felt in my chest. They were a reminder of everything I already know, but to hear her say it tore my heart in two.

I felt tears pooling in my eyes at the thought of ever having to choose. It should be so easy, but it wasn't. I couldn't look at her so I kept my eyes on the table. "You don't get it! You don't get what it is like to have parents who treat you like their little Barbie doll, ready to marry the perfect Ken. My parents would hate Dane. They wouldn't even give him a second glance after seeing him. Hell, they probably wouldn't even let him speak one word before passing judgment on him." I took a deep breath to hold back the tears.

"You can't keep doing this. Look what it's doing to you. This is going to tear you apart," she said as she rubbed slow circles on my back. It was tearing me up every time I thought about it. I was just avoiding having any thoughts relating to the eventual consequences. If I pushed it away long enough, it was almost as if it doesn't exist.

"I can't do it right now. I can't. I'm going to go to that wedding without Dane and when I get back, I will have a couple more months of peace before I have to start to make choices. Please don't push me. Everyone's always pushing me. Don't tell him about the wedding, please?"

I heard a tray hit the table and looked up to see Dane. His face was red with anger and his shoulders were tense. He opened his mouth to say something, but just shook his head and turned on his heel toward the door. The hurt expression on his face was too much to take in as I sat there completely confused and shocked. What had just happened?

"Aren't you going to go see what that's about?" Jade finally asked.

I nodded as I got up from the table and ran for the door, bumping into a couple students along the way. As soon as I was outside, my heart fell into my stomach as I spotted him sitting on a bench with his head in his hands. Still confused, I started to walk toward him slowly, hoping he would look up and this, whatever it was, would all go away.

When I reached him, I sat down next to him and put my hand on his back. He looked up at me with sadness in his eyes. "Don't touch me." I quickly removed my hand. His voice was completely cold and detached. I didn't like where this was going.

I wasn't good at confrontation. I avoided it whenever I could. "I thought you went back to your apartment to get your art project. What's wrong?"

"Don't give me that shit, Alex. You know exactly what's wrong. I'm not good enough to go to a wedding with you, huh? I'm not good enough to meet your perfect little family? Tell me, Alex, why are we doing this? Is this some of bad boy experiment to piss your parents off?"

It took me a little bit to process his words and when realization hit, I felt sick. He had heard us. He had heard everything that Jade and I had talked about at lunch and he was mad. He had every right to be. In my mind I thought I was protecting him, but all I was doing was hiding him because I was afraid. "I'm sorry. It isn't like that. You're not an experiment. I tried not to fall for you, I really did. I knew I shouldn't have you, but I couldn't stop myself. It has nothing to do with pissing my parents off, Dane. I love you and need you. Don't you see it?" My voice started off as whisper, but quickly elevated as my frustration grew.

He just shook his head at me before staring forward with a hurt, confused expression. "You tried not to fall for me? What the hell are you talking about?" he asked, running his hands through his hair. I think I pissed him off even more. Good going, Alex.

I couldn't hold the tears that had been held in my eyes any longer. I wiped them away with my sleeves. Usually I would care that people were around me, watching me cry, but today I didn't. I'd hurt Dane and I needed to find a way to repair this. "Dane, my family is difficult. You know all the pressures I have to become a doctor and, well, I have the same pressures on most other aspects of my life. They wouldn't understand us and I was trying to protect you. When I first met you, I thought you were wrong for me, but you have been nothing but right. I didn't want to fall for you because I was scared. You're almost too good for me. You live your life like no one is watching and I live mine to make others happy."

"That's a bunch of crap and you know it. You can't hide behind your fear. Everyone has choices, Alex," he said through clenched teeth.

"I'm sorry, Dane. I'm so sorry. Please," I cried, placing my hand on his thigh.

He looked down at my hand. "I'm not going to be anyone's little secret. I'm too old for that shit."

"I'm sorry. What more do you want me to say?" I asked, removing my hand from his leg to cover my face.

Dane sat silent for a moment. He still hadn't looked at me or touched me. "Alex, you're an adult now. You have to start taking control of your own life or you're going to be miserable. You should make choices that make you happy," he said, finally looking up as he ran his thumb under my eyes. He was right. Dane was always right. I was a coward and I was making myself unhappy. I couldn't blame my parents for everything.

"I'm so sorry, Dane, I just don't know what to do. I want you to come with me; you're the only person who makes me feel like everything is going to be okay, but my parents…" More tears fell down my face as I tried to finish, "my parents will pick you apart. I can't do that to you. I can't make you go through what I've been going through. I love you with everything I have and you've done more for me in the short time that I've known you than anyone else has ever done. You've showed me a side of myself I didn't know existed."

Dane grabbed my face in his hands, looking right into my eyes. "Baby, we can do it together. I can be there for you. Let me be there for you." I rested my forehead on his and for the first time since I sat on this bench, I know I haven't lost him. He was still mine. It was the first time in my life that I felt secure with someone. I was showing him the worst side of me and he was still mine.

I thought about it briefly. What was the worst that could happen? My parents wouldn't like him, I was sure of that, but I could make them understand, right? I could do this. He had given me so much and now all I had to give him was a chance. "Okay," I finally whispered. "Dane, will you come to my sister's wedding with me? It's the weekend after next?" I smiled before adding, "I would really like it if you could come."

He kissed me like we weren't sitting outside on a bench for everyone to see. He kissed me with his heart, telling me without words that he loved me and would be there for me. His kiss was full of forgiveness and I met him with my own kiss that said I was sorry and I loved him right back. I needed him more than anything else in this world.

"Is that a yes?" I asked, after we finally separated.

He just smiled and bit his lower lip. "Anywhere you are, remember that," he said, melting me from head to toe. How did he always know what to say? This man was trouble, but not the type I expected. "But, Alex, you have to start opening up. You can't hold all of this in. I need you to talk to me. Promise?"

"Promise," I whispered, looking him in the eyes. I was really going to try. This exchange had left me feeling lighter and I could only assume letting him in, all the way in, would be what was best for me. I spent so many years holding things in that I wasn't quite sure how to let them out.

"Why don't we go back inside and eat?" he asked. He stood up and waited for me to join him, wrapping his arm around my shoulders.

"I thought you had to go get your project," I said, still curious as to why he was in the student center to start with.

He pulled open the door. "I came to see you. You said you missed me and I couldn't let my girl feel that way all afternoon." I swear my heart stopped for a few seconds. That might have been one of the sweetest things anyone had ever said to me. There were no words that could describe how he made me feel.

When we reached the table, Jade was still sitting there with our three trays. She looked weary at first, but when she looked at our joined hands she smiled. I knew I had Jade on my side and that made things a little easier.

"Looks like you kids kissed and made up. Thank God! I didn't want to share my room every night again," she said with a hint of sarcasm in her voice. I loved Jade and her ability to lighten the mood.

"You can keep the room; Dane's bed is much more comfortable than the one in the dorm anyway," I said as I smiled up at Dane. I could tell she wanted to know more, but I wasn't going to mention it while we were all sitting here and she wasn't going to ask. "Dane's going to Gwen's wedding with me."

Jade's face gave way to a surprised expression. "Oh good. You guys are going to have so much fun! I love weddings."

Jade and I started talking about weddings after she mentioned her love for them. I had to admit I was also a sucker for a beautiful wedding, but I could tell the subject didn't thrill Dane. Men only seemed concerned with the type of food that would be served and if there would be alcohol. Still, he sat and listened before leaving to go get his project from his apartment. I was really beginning to notice how well he fit into all aspects of my life.

I filled Jade in on what had happened outside before we left to go to our respective afternoon classes. She didn't seem surprised and even though she didn't say it, her expression said, "I told you so." She suggested I call my mom to move the whole thing forward and I agreed that I should start preparing my parents now. I didn't know what I would say, but it wasn't right to just show up with the guy I was in love with and not give them some warning. And for the first time, I felt like this might all work out. There may be a way to be with Dane and still keep my old world in place. Maybe they would have no choice but to love him.

Chapter Eighteen

I didn't want to put off talking to my mom any longer than I had to so I told Dane I needed to sleep in my own room tonight after we left the library. I didn't tell him why exactly, but blamed the exams I had to take tomorrow and my need for sleep. That part wasn't a lie because I hadn't been sleeping much at Dane's.

I was relieved that Jade had gone out for the night: I didn't want her to be my audience. This was something I needed to do on my own.

I paced back and forth, trying to slow my heart and quiet the screaming voices in my head. I tried to decide exactly what to say. I wanted to tell her enough of the truth that Dane wouldn't be a complete surprise, but I didn't want to say so much that she would already have her mind made up to like him or not before we got there. I had to walk a fine line.

I almost couldn't breath as I dialed the number to the house. Part of me hoped that she wouldn't pick up, but just like every other time the phone only rang twice. "Hello, Riley residence."

"Hi, Mom," I said. My hands and voice were shaking.

"Alexandra, how are your midterms going?" she asked. Never "how are you?". That would be too much to ask.

"Fine. I have two more to go and then I'm done. Biology went well and I turned in a paper for Art. I only have

Anatomy and Calculus left," I replied, closing my eyes and taking a deep breath.

"I don't know why you waste your time in Art. All it does is take up time you should be using to study for things that matter." And make me happy, I thought.

"Mom, listen, I called to tell you I'm bringing a date to the wedding. His name is Dane and we have been dating for a while now." I bit my cheek as I waited for her response.

"Dane who? What do his parents do?" My heart rate picked up again because I knew my answer wouldn't satisfy her.

"Well, his name is Dane Wright. His mother works in the restaurant industry and his dad is no longer in the picture. He's so sweet; I can't wait for you to meet him." I closed my eyes again as I braced myself for her response. She didn't care about the last part, but I hoped to make her forget about the other things I mentioned. I didn't care where Dane came from because I was wrapped up in who he was now. Why couldn't she see things that way?

I heard her sigh on the other end. "What about Ryan?"

"Mom, I will always love Ryan, but we didn't work in that way. He is a friend and nothing else."

"I can't stop you from bringing him, but we're going to talk about this. Ever since college started, you've done nothing but make poor choices. You need to get control of your life again, Alexandra." I let out all the air I had been holding in my lungs. This was going better than I expected. She didn't say I couldn't bring him and I was used to her threats. What she really meant to say was that she needed to get control of my life again.

"Is it okay if he stays at our house? If not, we can get a hotel," I asked, biting the inside of my cheek again.

"You're not staying at a hotel with some boy. You can both stay at the house, but he is not sleeping in your room. He can have one of the guest rooms." I did a fist pump; this was a small victory. Before I picked up the phone tonight, I didn't think I would get her to even agree to Dane attending and now I had her setting up a guest room for him. Maybe I was overreacting. Maybe everything would be okay.

"Thanks, Mom. I should probably let you go. I need to study before I go to bed," I said, trying to hold back some of the excitement in my voice.

"Yes, you do. But, Alexandra, we really are going to have a talk when you get home," she said, leaving no room in her voice for argument.

"Okay, well I will see you in a couple weeks then. Good night."

"Good night," she said before quickly hanging up the phone. As soon as I put the phone down, I did a silent dance around the room. I had just done something I never thought I would do and I made it through. I felt like I was swimming.

While I thought it went well, I wouldn't know for sure until we get there. Hopefully my mother would be so busy that she won't have the time to pay attention to me and my love life. We would be leaving that Friday after class, arriving just in time for rehearsal and dinner, have wedding festivities all day Saturday and gift opening and brunch on Sunday before heading back to school. I just had to make sure we didn't spend too much alone time with my parents. This might just work after all.

I pulled out my Calculus book and studied until my eyelids felt heavy. It was only 11pm when I threw on my pajama pants and tank top. A good solid eight hours of sleep was exactly what I needed to get through my Calculus test. This whole night had gone much better than expected and I had no doubt that I would sleep well tonight.

My phone buzzed as I started to drift asleep. Dane. Whenever we are apart, he always texted me right at 11pm.

Dane: I love you. Sweet dreams.

It only took me seconds to respond.

Alex: Love you too.

I hugged my phone to my chest as I closed my eyes and drifted to sleep.

For once, I was taking a chance for myself and I didn't want to ever regret it because if I did, there wouldn't be any more chances. I wanted this one to pay off.

The next two weeks flew by and it was now the Friday of rehearsal dinner. My relationship with Dane was on strong footing since our argument over his attendance at the wedding and I had only spent that one night apart from him.

Last night he'd had me help him pack. He usually didn't care much about how he looked, but he really wanted to make the right impression. We stayed away from jeans and t-shirts, opting instead for dress pants, polos and button ups.

The wedding tomorrow was black tie so we rented a tux for that; I couldn't wait to see it on him. I loved him exactly how he was, but didn't every girl dream of seeing the man she loved in a tux?

After Dane had fallen asleep last night, I laid there thinking about all the things that could go wrong. What if my parents, Mom especially, said something completely inappropriate? How would Dane react? What if Dane hated my life and wanted to go home? It all spun in my head as I thought about what my reaction would be to each and it all ended in me having a complete breakdown. I just needed to get through this weekend, stay close to Dane, and hope everyone else was too busy to pay much attention to anything but the wedding.

I wasn't looking forward to being Alexandra for the next two days, but I went into it knowing I could fit back into my comfortable self on Sunday. I wasn't a natural actress and the more I got to know the real me and understood where and what I wanted to be, the harder the act became. Eventually I would either have to accept it or take it on headfirst. I couldn't do either at this point.

I placed my bags in the trunk and headed to Dane's apartment. I knew it bothered him that I was driving, but taking his motorcycle to Greenwich in March with two huge suitcases was not an option.

As I pulled up to his apartment building, I noticed him sitting on his suitcase on the sidewalk. He wore a beanie and his signature leather jacket, but he opted for grey dress pants instead of his usual jeans. My heart clenched at the realization of how much he cared for me. There was nothing he wouldn't do for me.

I popped the trunk so Dane could throw his suitcase in with mine and waited for him to join me in the car. I hadn't seen him since this morning and I craved one of his calming kisses. As soon as he was comfortable in his seat, I grabbed his jacket and pulled his face to mine. I could feel the smile on his lips as I completely took control of the kiss. "Did you miss me?" he asked when I finally pulled away.

"I always miss you," I replied before pulling him in for one more kiss. "Are you ready to meet the parents?" I asked as I pulled out into the street. I glanced at him out of the side of my eye and noticed that Dane Wright actually looked a little nervous.

"Of course, I can handle meeting the parents," he said before reaching for my hand and kissing the tips of my fingers. "I should probably warn you, though. This is the first time I have ever met the parents; I hope I pass the test."

"Well, if it makes you feel better, this is the first time I have brought someone home they didn't already know. I guess, in a way, that this is my first time bringing someone to meet my parents." We both laughed.

"I guess it's just another first we are experiencing together," he said. I looked over at him and he gave me one of his sexy signature winks. "How about a little game to pass the time? Ten questions?"

Playing a game sounded a little silly, but I was down for anything if it would relieve the anxiety I felt. "How does that work?"

"We take turns asking each other questions and no matter what, you have to answer it. No passes," he explained. His eyes showed a hint of mischief; this could be fun, actually.

"Okay, can I go first?" I asked. I wanted to set the stage for this game; it might be the last piece of control I got for a couple days.

"Go for it."

"Okay, how old were you when you lost your virginity?" I asked. I'd been curious about that for a long time, but hadn't known how to ask.

I expected him to answer right away, but he looked hesitant. "Bringing out the big questions already. Are you sure you want to know?" I nodded. "I was 14; the girl was a little older than me and things progressed faster than they should have."

There was a heavy feeling in my stomach; I was a little surprised that he was so young. I didn't even get to go on my first date until I was 16 and Dane had been having sex for two years before that. I again reminded myself that the past was the past and I only needed to concern myself in the now. "I think it's your turn to ask me a question now."

He sighed. "Okay, the night I first met you at the club you were with another guy. What happened to him?"

"Ryan and I have been friends for years and when he asked me out last year, it sounded like a great idea. His parents and my parents are friends and he's a great guy. I tried, I really did, but that spark was missing. Our relationship was more like a friendship and I needed more; it just didn't feel right. I broke up with him that night I met you in the club and haven't spoken to him since." I stopped for a second before adding, "He's going to be at the wedding this weekend and don't be surprised if my mother brings him up a time or two. She is completely obsessed with the idea of him and she wasn't all that pleased I had moved on." His jaw was clenched and his fingers were wrapped tightly on the door handle. I grabbed his left hand in my right to calm his fears; he had nothing to worry about where Ryan was concerned.

"How many boyfriends did you have before Ryan?" he asked, turning his eyes toward me.

I looked over at him quickly before returning my attention back to the road. "It wasn't your turn to ask a question which means I get 2 now. I have had two serious long-term relationships and several short lived ones." There were several times I went out with someone who my mother or sister set me up with only to find out after a date or two we were not compatible at all.

He seemed to think for a few seconds. "And your parents knew all of them?"

I worked my lower lip between my teeth, trying to decide how to answer this without sounding meek. "Yes, my mom actually set me up with a couple of them and she knew the others through her social circle. My parents are very controlling of my life and when I say that, I mean every aspect. They are good at telling me what to wear, what to be, who to date, what to eat and where to go. You're my one exception."

"You can't do that anymore, you know? You can't walk through life using someone else's plan." His face was serious and his jaw had taken a hard line again. He wasn't telling me anything I didn't already know, but he was telling me something that seemed impossible.

"I know. It just takes time to break out of it. It's harder than it seems, trust me." I looked in his direction as we sat at a red light. "I think it's my turn to ask you a question."

"Yeah, it probably is," he said as he glanced out the front window. He was thinking about something, I could always tell, but this time I didn't really want to know what it was. He was thinking I was a coward and weak and I didn't want to hear it.

"Okay, then, tell me something about yourself that I don't already know," I said, as I quickly looked over at him again. I could tell he was thinking.

He looked over at me with a sad expression. "Are you sure you want to hear this?" I nodded. "I was addicted to drugs from the time I was 15 until I was 19. That's the main reason I didn't start school until this year." I leaned forward in my seat, gripping my steering wheel with both hands. I wasn't expecting that, not at all, and if we hadn't been sandwiched in a stream of cars, I might have run right off the road. Never in my dreams did I think Dane was an addict; I knew he'd had a troubled past, but not this.

"What? Why?" I asked when I finally found my voice again.

He had a pained expression in his eyes and I would have done anything to wash it away. I knew what it was like to be broken and all I wanted to do was find all of his pieces and put them back together. "I had just started high school and I had all this pressure. My mother was busy getting drunk every day and I was full-time Mom and Dad for my brother; it was too much and one night something inside me snapped. One of my new friends said it would make me feel better and I was too stupid to think beyond that night. I've regretted it ever since. I was addicted and it took me years to break it." My throat tightened as I listened closely to every word he said. His admission shocked me, but more than that I felt sad for him. He must have felt so lonely and desperate and I could imagine that the drugs would have temporarily made him feel better. I couldn't imagine what it was like for him to have all the pressures of an adult, to go through so many things alone and then need someone, but have no one to help him.

"What were you addicted to?" I asked, when I regained my voice.

"Just ecstasy at first. It made me feel good and gave me all this energy to get the things done that I needed to get done. It's hard to raise someone when you're 15. I started to do cocaine my senior year and that's when things really spiraled out of control. I started to forget lots of things."

"How did you kick the habit?"

He sighed, focusing his eyes back on me. "One weekend I was partying with some friends and I realized the following Monday that I didn't remember anything that happened that weekend. There were so many things that could have gone wrong. I was out of control. I was no better than her." I could understand why he was giving his mom a chance. He knew what it was like to become overcome by a substance. "I checked into a 30 day program and haven't looked back since."

"Are you still tempted?" I knew Dane still had a lot of stress in his life.

"Sometimes. Life's hard and when you know there are ways to drown it out, it's hard to stay on the right path. It's a constant struggle. For a long time, I did it by myself."

As soon as traffic allowed, I pulled over in a small parking lot, unbuckled my seatbelt and leaned over the console, taking him in my arms. I needed him to know that everything was okay; he had me and could tell me anything. He held me so tight against his chest that I could feel his heart beating fast against mine. "You have me and I'm not going anywhere, okay? I'm here for you." I pulled back and placed a kiss on his nose then his lips; his eyes were both glossed over when I finally looked up at his face. "I love you," I whispered, touching my forehead to his.

He grabbed my face in both hands. "This doesn't change anything, does it? I didn't mean to bring it up on the way to meet your parents, but you asked that question and I have been meaning to tell you for awhile," he said, his voice cracking with every word. I placed my finger over his mouth to quiet him. I loved him and nothing he did in the past was going to change that.

"We all make mistakes and do things we wish we could take back, but it is what we do after that truly matters...and I like your after."

"Thank you."

"For what?"

"For letting me be me. For not judging everything I've ever done." I thought back to some of the things Dane's friends had said about him being trouble or having a past. It still followed him around and I was dismissing it. He had as many things to work through as I did.

"I'm here for you. Always. We should get back on the road unless you want to meet the bad side of my parents when we're late for rehearsal. You will get to know my parents a little too well if we're late." I crawled back to my side seat and buckled my seatbelt. This had not been what I had in mind when I agreed to play Ten Questions, but it had helped take my mind off my family.

We drove in silence the rest of the way, with only a few glances here and there. We were both much more subdued than we had been leaving the city. I hoped that things would be smooth and easy tonight.

Chapter Nineteen

I didn't think about where I would be going for the weekend, or whom I would be spending it with, again until we pulled up to the long driveway to my childhood home. It was a large two-story brick home with white trimmed windows and black shutters. Even the circle drive in front of the house was brick up to the point where it led to the large wooden front door. It wasn't the type of house you could just sneak into, expecting to bypass anyone; I had tried too many times and always failed.

I turned to Dane whose eyes were stuck on the large house in front of us. "We're here," I said, raising my arm in the direction of the house. I had to admit that every time I hadn't seen it in awhile and drove up the driveway that it looked obscenely large. I hated what it stood for. I knew my mother loved the house, but it was for all the wrong reasons. It didn't feel like a home, but it got her to her desired status level.

I parked in front of the door so we could bring our bags in as I waited for Dane to say something. I needed to know that everything was okay before we entered the house because, if anything, the atmosphere in there was just going to bring us down even further.

He finally opened his door and climbed out, stretching his arms above his head. "Holy shit, you didn't tell me you lived in a freaking mansion." He looked at me before looking back over to the house. "I've never seen a house this big in person."

I popped the trunk and climbed out of the car to grab our bags, but Dane grabbed them before I had a chance. "There is more to life than big houses and fancy cars. You pay a price for them and it isn't always monetary."

He just shrugged. We grew up on two different ends of the economic spectrum, but we were both lonely and starving for attention. Anyone who thought money would solve all their problems was just asking for trouble.

We walked up two steps to the large door before Dane grabbed my hand. "We're okay, right? I mean, what I told you in the car earlier hasn't changed anything?" He had a concerned look in eyes. This damaged man was looking for reassurance of my love for him; I hated what his childhood had done to him.

"The past doesn't matter to me. I love you," I said, giving his hand a reassuring squeeze.

He used our joined hands to pull me toward him. "I love you, too. Now let's go meet the parents." He gave me a squeeze before turning me toward the door. Here goes nothing, I thought. I held my breath and opened the door. It was now or never.

The foyer had white marble floors, high ceilings and a grand wrap around wooden staircase. A wooden table stood in the center with a large vase of fresh cut flowers, which just happened to match my sister's wedding colors. How very festive of my mother.

"Alexandra, is that you?" a familiar voice yelled from the kitchen. It was impossible for anyone to sneak into this house. When I was a kid, I used to wish I was invisible. I didn't know the impossibility of it at the time, but it seemed like it would solve all my problems.

"Yes, we're just going to bring our bags upstairs and then we'll be ready to go to rehearsal." I pulled off my coat and placed it in the coat closet before reaching out to take Dane's. He had a white button down shirt on, tucked into his grey slacks and accented with a thick black belt. He looked incredible and every part of me wanted to come up with an excuse to skip rehearsal and stay home with Dane in my bed.

I heard heels on the marble before my mom came into view. "Oh no you don't. You can't just sneak upstairs the minute you get home without introducing me to your friend," she said with her signature fake smile. I panicked. My two worlds were about to meet: I just hoped they wouldn't collide.

"Mom, this is Dane. Dane, this is Catherine Riley." I watched Dane extended his hand toward my mother. She lifted her arm to meet his before her fake smile fell slightly and her eyes doubled in size. I hadn't noticed when Dane took off his coat, but his sleeves were rolled up to his elbows, exposing some of his tattoos. Whatever came of this, it was not going to be good. I watched as my mom seemed to regain her composure and shook Dane's hand.

"It's nice to meet you, Mrs. Riley." Dane was nothing but polite and charming in my element.

My mom had her fake smile back on. "Well, yes, it is nice meeting you, too." She didn't like him; I could tell. That was the exact same tone she used at her fundraisers and country club functions when she greeted a woman only to turn around five seconds later and complain to her friend Lori that she couldn't stand her. Watching her at these functions made me want to be anything but her.

She turned her attention to me, wrapping me into a tight hug. She never hugged me. Never. Her intention was fully noted a few seconds later when she whispered in my ear, "Please make sure he covers up those tattoos before going to the church. Don't embarrass me, Alexandra." She released me before continuing. "I set Dane up in the green guest room. Let me know if you need anything." I gave her a tight smile before heading up the steps, pulling Dane behind me.

We hadn't even been here five minutes and my mother was already passing judgment. She didn't like him; I could see it and I hated how she compartmentalized people into good or bad so quickly. She was everything I didn't want to be. I wanted to live with hope; I wanted to love with my heart and turn my dreams into reality. I wanted to.

I just didn't.

As soon as we reached the top of the stairs, Dane pulled me back into his chest. "Are you okay? You seem really tense all of a sudden." I didn't want to lie, but I couldn't exactly tell him that my mom doesn't like him without making the rest of the weekend really awkward.

"I'll be fine. She just unnerves me sometimes, you know? I just need to get out of this house; it suffocates me," I confessed. I wanted to get out of this house and get this whole weekend over with.

Putting his forehead to mine, he said, "Baby, just remember you don't have to do anything you don't want to do. And always remember I'm here for you. You have to let me in."

I took a deep breath. "My mom would like you to cover up your tattoos before we head to the church." I didn't want to suppress who Dane was. I had been suppressed my whole life and I hated every minute of it.

"I can do that if it will keep her off your back." He kissed the tip of my nose before grabbing my hand and leading me down the extensive hallway. "So, which one is mine?"

"Third door on the left," I said, before turning the knob on my own door. "This one is mine, in case you need to find me or something."

He swatted my behind as he walked past to his room. "You know I'll need something." I walked into my room, taking it all in. Sleeping alone in my bed was going to be hard, especially knowing Dane was right across the hall. I grimaced as I looked around; it was the same as it has been for the last twelve years.

I remembered the day before my seventh birthday when my mom said they were going to redecorate my bedroom as part of my birthday gift. I was so excited and had visions of green and blue polka dots; they had always been my favorite colors. My mom had a decorator come over and I didn't get to speak one word; it was the Catherine Riley show. Two weeks later my room was splashed with various shades of pink and purple and I absolutely hated it. I hated everything about it, but I just smiled and said thank you because that's what I was expected to do.

A couple of years ago, I had replaced the pink comforter for a white down comforter; it was the one piece of me that was in this room. In fact, I liked it so much I bought the exact same one to take to college with me. I glanced at the pin board above my desk; it was covered with photos of Ryan and I. I hadn't been home since I broke up with him so they were still on full display. I put my bag on the floor and started to pull the old photos down when Dane walked in. He had rolled his sleeves down to his wrist, covering all his tattoos. I loved that he did that for me without saying too much; I didn't need another person telling me what to do.

I continued to pull pictures off the pin board as Dane came behind me and wrapped his arms around my waist, hugging my body close to him. It felt uncomfortable having my current boyfriend stand behind me while I took down pictures of my ex-boyfriend. Dane didn't say anything about the pictures as I took them down one by one, but I could tell he wasn't looking at them as he moved his lips up my neck and to my earlobe.

When I was done, I placed them in a box I kept on top of my desk. I may not be with Ryan anymore, but memories never fad; they are just kept where we can no longer see them.

"I was just thinking, we don't have a picture of the two of us." I could feel Dane's warm breath on my ear as he spoke. We didn't. I had known him for almost two months and we had not taken one single picture of the two of us together.

"We could fix that right now," I said, tilting my head to give him better access to my neck.

I felt his lips leave my skin. "I think we should. Your board looks kind of bare now." I left Dane's arms long enough to grab my purse and pull my iPhone out of the front pocket.

I stood beside him, wrapping one arm around his waist and pressing the top of my head to his. "Ready? Smile." I snapped a couple pictures and then instructed him to kiss me. When I was done, I did the typical girl thing and went through the pictures to make sure our eyes were open and we looked okay. My smile was different than any other picture I had seen of myself; it was real.

"You look beautiful, Baby," Dane said from behind me.

I tucked my phone back into my purse and gave him a kiss on his cheek. "We should get going. Rehearsal starts soon."

He nodded. "Are you sure you're okay?" I wasn't okay, but there wasn't much Dane could do to make my nerves go away. He couldn't change my parents and as much as he wanted to, he couldn't change my reaction to them.

"I'm fine. Come on, we need to go because if we're late, I will not be fine." My mother would have my ass.

We rode to the church in silence as I worked through all the emotions that were going through me. I was nervous about tonight, but more than that I was scared of what could happen. I didn't want to leave Dane alone, even for a minute. We would need each other tonight.

I took a few breaths before entering the church I had grown up in. It was a beautiful Catholic church with pastel colored murals painted on the ceilings and gold accents; it took my breath away every time I stepped inside. My sister had chosen light pink, gold, and ivory as her wedding colors and the flowers looked amazing with the church as a backdrop. Though I didn't think she was marrying the love of her life, I had to admit she was going to be a gorgeous bride and her wedding would be one the town would be talking about forever.

Since I was maid of honor, I was needed in the bride's room to prep for rehearsal. I never understood why we had to practice with fake bouquets and all. It really doesn't take that much skill to hold some flowers in front of you while walking down the aisle.

I walked Dane to a pew in the back of the church, hoping no one would bother him while I was hanging out with the bride. My dad hadn't met him yet and I wasn't sure what his reaction would be. I didn't want Dane to be alone when it finally happened.

I walked into the bride's room where Gwen was having a meltdown because her rehearsal dress wasn't the same shade of pink as the flowers in the test bouquet the floral shop had sent over. For one, I couldn't believe my sister had real flowers sent over for rehearsal and two, was it really that big of deal? They were maybe a shade off. As soon as she noticed me standing inside the door, she ran over to me and wrapped me into a hug. "Oh, Alexandra, I'm so glad you're here. Don't these flowers look hideous with my dress? Tell them."

Seriously, this was the least of my worries this weekend. I patted her on the back. "I think you look really pretty. The two different shades look stylish. I personally love it." I didn't want to see what would happen tomorrow if things weren't exactly how she imagined them.

She sniffled. "Really?"

"Yes, no one is going to be looking at anything but you," I replied. I meant it; everyone stares at the bride.

"Thanks, Alexandra," I squeezed her once before pulling back. "We should probably get going; the guys won't be happy if we make them wait to eat."

Rehearsal went as smooth as it could go with a wedding planner, as well as my mom and sister running the show. After three run throughs, we knew exactly how we were to walk down the aisle and how quickly. My mom was worried that the wedding guests wouldn't be able to see the front of my sister's dress. I made a quick mental note to get eloped if I ever decided to get married. This would put me straight into a psychiatric hospital.

I glanced at Dane every few minutes. He had his arms on the back of the pew; he looked very comfortable and relaxed, exactly what I was not. His eyes never left me; every time I looked he was staring right at me. I tried to smile at him, but it would have been a Catherine Riley smile and he deserved more.

When the priest announced that we were done for the evening, I was relieved. As soon as we were locked in the car alone, he pulled my face to his and kissed me like a man who hadn't eaten in days. His hands locked into my hair as he slipped his tongue into my mouth. For a moment, I forgot everything. I forgot where we were, forgot the nerves in my stomach and forgot the weight on my heart. Dane was my first and only addiction. I understood what he meant about drugs making him forget.

I was feeling a little more relaxed as we drove to the club for the rehearsal dinner. Maybe this wouldn't be so bad since my sister was the focus of the weekend. I couldn't let myself get too comfortable, though. When we pulled into the parking lot, I noticed it was almost full. As long as we didn't miss the toasts, we should be fine. Dane grabbed my hand and walked me inside.

The banquet room was decorated with gold table clothes and pink and white roses. It probably cost more than most couple's wedding receptions. Most of the chairs were taken and I noticed the bridal party and their significant others were seated at a large rectangular table at the front of room. I didn't want to eat in front of all the guests, but it didn't look like there was any other option. "It looks like we are up there," I said pointing to the front of the room. Dane nodded before following me across the room.

My heart sank when I realized there was only one chair left at the table and the nameplate said Miss Alexandra Riley. Where was Dane's chair? My eyes met my sisters before she looked over at my mom who was seated right in front of the main table. The expression on my sister's face was pained; she may not resist my mom as much as I did, but I know she didn't agree with half the stuff she does either.

When I glanced in my mom's direction, she seemed to read my mind because she stood and started to move in my direction. I was seething. I told her I was bringing Dane; why would she do this to me? I felt uncomfortable and I couldn't imagine how it was going to make him feel. I didn't want to confront her in front of him. "Wait here. I'll be right back," I said, motioning my mother to meet me outside the door.

I had enough time to take a couple deep breaths before she reached my side. "Is something wrong, dear? You don't look so good." She was smiling at me. I wanted to rip that smile off her face, but just like all the other times, I did nothing.

"Why doesn't Dane have a seat at the head table? You knew he was coming," I said with the calmest voice I could manage.

She set her lips in a firm line. "You and Dane aren't married."

I laughed. It was fake, but I laughed. "Neither are Tim and Rebecca or Anna and Reed, but they are sitting together at the table."

"Well, there must be some mistake," she replied before turning her lips back into a smile.

I was mad. There wasn't any mistake; it was my mom being my mom. "Where did you expect Dane to sit?" I finally asked.

"I arranged for him to have a spot with your cousins from your father's side." She hated the cousins on my dad's side. She did this all on purpose.

This was my chance to take a stand. To stand up for myself and tell her I was not okay with the way she treated me but I couldn't. I just froze. Confronting her now meant confronting everything. I couldn't do it; not now when it was my sister's special day. So I simply walked away from her. It was my way of telling her I didn't agree with what she was doing, but I wasn't strong enough to fight her either.

Dane had a puzzled look on his face when I approached. He didn't know these people and wouldn't realize that he was the only significant other not at the table. I grabbed his hand and led him to the back of the room. "Since I gave my mom such short notice that you were coming, she put you with my cousins." I watched as his face fell slightly. "I'm sorry. As soon as we are done eating, we can leave." My parents would be the perfect hosts and stay until the last guest left. With any luck, I could have some alone time with him before the chaos of tomorrow began.

I liked my cousins on my dad's side; they were down to earth and funny. While my mom saw this as a punishment, it may be better than sitting at the head table. I gave him a kiss on the side of his mouth before turning toward the head table. It was time to eat and get out of here.

Things never happen as I expect them to when I'm around my family. Tonight was no different. After finishing my dinner, I stood from the table to get Dane and leave, but my mom stopped me to introduce me to a bunch of random people. When she was not done with her introductions several minutes later, my frustration hit a new high. "Mom, I need to go talk to Dane," I finally said in an attempt to break free from the fake pleasantries.

She grabbed my elbow, moving me to the left. "There are people I still want you to meet. You're not home very often so I don't want to hear you complain when you are." I pulled my elbow out of her grasp, but followed her.

I glanced over at Dane who was watching me as I followed her across the room. I watched him laugh a few times during dinner, but now he looked impatient and concerned. When I turned back around, I was face to face with Ryan and his mother. I hadn't called him before this weekend like I intended to; I was too busy with finals and Dane. I wished I had now, to ease the awkwardness of this moment.

My mom was saying something to Ryan's mom. I didn't say anything; I just stared at him while he did the same to me. I wanted to say something, but words wouldn't form. As if in the middle of some choreographed move, the two older women dismissed themselves to talk to the caterer, leaving only Ryan and I. He looked like he wanted to say something, but was stuck in the same place I was.

"How are you?" My voice was so soft I didn't think he heard me.

He cleared his throat, still looking right at me. Before I could react, he wrapped his arms around me, pulling me against his body. "I'm sorry I left the way I did that day. I'm sorry I didn't call," he murmured into my hair.

"Ryan, I'm the one who should be saying sorry," I replied, wrapping my arms around his back.

He lifted his head just enough to look back down at me again. "Are you saying you're sorry you ended it?" His eyes showed so much hope and I hated to take that away again.

"That's not what I'm saying. I'm sorry about how things ended that morning, but I'm not sorry I did it." He loosened his grip on me and took a step back. He had a pained look on his face. I wanted him to find what I had with Dane. He may have loved me, but I don't think I would've been his happily ever after. I was just as comfortable for him as he was for me. He let out a breath and I continued, "Do you think we can be friends again? I miss my friend and I regret everything that happened between us that ruined that friendship."

"I miss you, too. Just give me more time." He stepped forward again speaking in a low voice, "I've got to go help our moms with some stuff. I'll see you around okay." I nodded as he placed a light kiss on my forehead before walking away.

I stood frozen for a minute before turning toward Dane's table. I immediately began to panic because he wasn't there. I looked over at the bar area and he wasn't there either. Had my mom gotten to him? What had she done this time? I needed to find him before it was too late. I had a pain in my chest as I walked over toward my cousins. I asked if they knew where he went and they hadn't seen him leave either. I felt sick to my stomach after one more glance around the room confirmed that he wasn't here. I headed toward the lobby hoping he was there, but he wasn't. Maybe he needed a breather. Yeah, that's it. Maybe he just needed to step outside to get some fresh air.

I hurried through the double wood doors and didn't see him anywhere. I walked toward my car; I needed a minute to myself. I needed to decompress. I wanted all this pressure in my heart to go away. I wanted Dane. Where was he?

I was almost to my car when I heard my name. I glanced to my left and saw him sitting on the curb. He had rolled his sleeves back up and unbuttoned the top two buttons on his shirt. When I looked at his face, I noticed his angry stare and clenched jaw.

I swallowed down my panic enough to approach him. "I was looking all over for you. What are you doing out here?"

He glared at me, "I was done watching my girlfriend and her ex hug and kiss. Sorry, I should have told you, but I didn't want to interrupt," he said, his voice rising with every word.

I sat down next to him on the curb, pursing my lips. "That was nothing. I hadn't seen him since the morning I broke it off and we had some things to discuss." I wrapped my fingers around his. "I'm sorry about this whole night." I would be lying if I said it hadn't been what I was expecting. This weekend wasn't going to be easy and I knew it going in. This was my life and I was used to it.

"Do you still have feeling for him?"

"Yes, but not like you're thinking. He's been my best friend since we were kids. He's always going to be a part of my life, Dane."

He sighed. "I don't like to watch any guy put their fucking hands on you."

I thought back to the night at the club when I saw the leggy brunette touching Dane and something registered within me. I knew how innocent my exchange with Ryan had been, but Dane had no way to know that. He needed reassurance just as I had that night. He needed to know that I was his and no one was going to take me away. "I'm sorry. I should've stepped back when he hugged me, but it all happened so fast. We had some things to say to each other, but I promise you it was nothing more. I love you. You have to know that by now."

He turned his hand, clasping my fingers in his. "I love you, too. I've never felt this way about anyone and it makes me feel so fucking crazy sometimes."

"Do you want to leave? I've had about as much as I can take for one day and we have to do it all over again tomorrow," I said, standing up and pulling him with me. This whole day needed a reset button.

"So, how long do we have before your parents get home?" he asked. I didn't miss the glimmer in his eyes.

"Probably a good couple hours, why?"

His sexy grin returned. "You are so tense and I know how to relieve that for you." Warmth flooded my belly just thinking about it.

He drove us back to my house going a little over the speed limit and stopping just long enough to be legal. As soon as we made it through the door, he picked me up in his arms and carried me upstairs. The excitement of having sex in my parent's house doubled my usual need for him.

As soon as the door to my bedroom closed, he set me down, pressing my back against the door. He began to kiss down my neck as I wrapped my legs around his waist to bring our bodies as close as possible. He worked at my skirt until it was wrapped around my hips as he nibbled on my earlobe. His lips were hard and punishing as they met mine. I could feel his erection pressed between my legs as I began to move up and down against him. I didn't let go as he walked backwards toward the bed. He knelt down, slowly moving us so my back was pressed against the mattress, and covered me with kisses. God, I wanted him. He was a sex God and I was his worshipper.

He gently lifted my body and pulled my dress over my head before working my underwear down my legs. When I laid back down on the mattress, he gently kissed a path down my chest and stomach until his lips and tongue connected in the one place they had never been. My body tensed; I wasn't sure I would like it, but it opened me up in a way I had never felt before and my body began to hum. I couldn't stop him; I had to have him. After a few minutes of pure bliss, I came harder than I had ever come before, grasping the sheets in my hands. I couldn't even describe how good it felt, but it sent shocks through my whole body. "You're so fucking beautiful," he said, kissing the inside of my thighs. His mouth worked its way back up my stomach, stopping at my chest. Desire flooded my body as he teased my nipples with his tongue and soon I was so wet with need that I couldn't see straight. His lips finally connected with mine again and I could taste myself on his kiss; it excited me even more. I loved that he did this to me.

I cupped his cheeks to break contact. "I need you inside now," I said, practically panting with need.

He smiled a lazy, sated smile. "I'm not done with you yet, Baby." I was breathless and couldn't take much more.

"Dane, please." I tried to unbutton his pants, but my fingers were shaking. He kept kissing my neck while rolling my nipples between his fingers. Finally, he sat back up and I saw the same lazy smile playing around his lips. Dane found my eagerness comical. He was stalling, teasing me and it was driving me insane.

I sat up, rubbing my hands over his chest. As they slowly traveled down his stomach, he grabbed my wrists and pushed me back down onto the mattress. Lifting my eyes to meet Dane's, I noticed that the smile was gone from his face. Instead, it was replaced with a savage look of desire. One that told me how much he wanted me. How much he needed me. A reflection of my own need for him.

He pulled his shirt off, followed by his pants, showing me exactly what I wanted. My heart was pounding and I felt breathless. If he wasn't inside me soon, I would die with need. He looked down into my eyes and with one thrust, he filled me completely, his mouth capturing mine. The sensation of his naked body against me was the most incredible thing I had ever felt in my life. We were made for each other. He moved slowly at first then quickened his motions until I could feel the tension building in my body. With one more quick push, my body finally let go with his. It was so intense that I couldn't stop the screams that left my body. It felt euphoric; I forgot where we were and I didn't really care.

We stayed in each other's arms that night. I didn't ask him to go back to his room because I needed him. I would deal with the rest later. For now, I was just high from the excitement of having sex under my parent's roof. In a small way, I had defied them, and it felt good.

CHAPTER TWENTY

I felt better after a full night's sleep, especially after
Dane had done as he promised and relieved some of my
tension. That was the first time I had even kissed a boy in my
bedroom and it had gone way past that. It felt incredible to be
a little rebellious and go against mother dearest's wishes.
Straying from her strict guidelines didn't feel so bad after
what she put me through yesterday. Today would be better, I
told myself. I felt a heavy arm wrap around me and pull me
close.

"Dane, you should probably go back to your room
before my mom comes looking for me. We have hair
appointments in less than an hour." His grip on me tightened
and I giggled into his hold; he wasn't going to make this
easy. "If you get caught, you're going to have to sleep in
your room tonight."

He groaned before rolling over and putting his pants
back on. I hated to see him go as much as he hated to leave.
When he was with me, everything felt lighter. "So, what
exactly is the plan today?" he asked, sitting back on the side
of the bed.

"Well, I have to go get my hair and makeup done with
the girls and then we are heading to the church to get the
bride dressed. The guys are going golfing so you can either
join them or you can take my car to do whatever. Just make
sure to be at the church a little before two," I said, pulling the

sheet up over my chest and climbing out of bed. I didn't make it far before the sheet was yanked from my hand.

I squealed. "Dane Wright, what are you doing?" I tried to pull the sheet up, but he had a firm grasp on it.

"I like you better this way," he said with a cocky grin.

I couldn't help but smile. "I'm sure you do, but I can't walk around like this all day. Plus, this is only for you to see, remember?"

He stood up, placing his hands on my hips. "Yes, you are. Only mine, now and always." My heart swelled in my chest.

"Always," I whispered against his lips. Our lips met and the moment my bare chest touched his, I knew I was in trouble. I never imagined I would have such an intense need for physical connection. I guess when your heart was wrapped up in someone, the physical need followed.

Before we could go any further, there was a knock at the door. I felt the tension seep back into my body. Only one person ever knocked on my door. "Alexandra, we are leaving in fifteen minutes. I suggest you get in the shower." It was the voice that played in some of my worst dreams. That voice had just broken me from my current dream. My mother always ruined my best moments, but never noticed the bad.

"I'll be down in a little bit!" I yelled back, still wrapped in Dane. The longer I stayed hidden in here with him, the better off I would be.

I kissed him one more time. "Let me put on some clothes and then I will make sure you get back to your room safe and sound." He hesitated before letting me go. I peeked out the door to make sure the hall was clear and held the door open for him to go across the hall. As soon as the door clicked behind him, my heart ached from the separation. I wondered if it was normal to miss someone this much?

Throughout the day, I didn't have time to text or call him because I was constantly being swept from one place to another. It was hard to focus on the wedding activities when I didn't know where he was or what he was doing. Had he gone golfing with my dad? I kind of hoped he hadn't. My father wasn't as bad as my mother, but he wasn't warm and fuzzy either. Dane didn't seem the type to be easily scared, but my father was a different breed of intimidation.

I had changed into my ivory and gold bridesmaid's dress with a sweetheart neckline. It was belted around the waist and had a layer of organza over top. It wasn't what I would have chosen, but it went perfectly with my sisters beautiful lace covered ivory dress. The deep v of her dress, coupled with the mermaid skirt, made her look absolutely gorgeous. I loved my sister and I wanted her to be happy; putting on her dress had done that for her. I wondered if it would last beyond the wedding day.

The wedding was beautiful. Ivory and pink flowers were everywhere with gold ribbon accents. The aisle was white and lined with flowers and candles and the church lights had been dimmed for a romantic feel. Something was missing though; the groom didn't shed a tear when he saw his bride and the bride came down the aisle with her eyes on the guests rather than on the groom. I didn't feel the connection that usually made me cry at weddings and my heart broke for my sister. I wondered if she even realized what she was doing or that she was walking down the same path our parents went down. I looked over to where Dane was sitting in the third row and smiled as I bit my lower lip. When you find someone you truly love, nothing else matters. I realized that being in love was worth the heartbreak that may follow. Nothing could compare to how that man made me feel. I knew what they were missing.

The recessional started, taking me away from my warm thoughts. After greeting the guests, we followed the bride and groom to where a huge pearl colored stretch limo was waiting. I searched for Dane in the crowd of people who waited patiently for us to leave. I motioned him over from where he was standing at the back of the crowd.

He approached me with a puzzled look on his face. "Is everything okay?"

"Yeah, everything's fine. I forgot we rented a limo to take to the reception. Just leave the car here and we'll take a cab back to my house and pick the car up in the morning."

"Limo ride, huh? Is there beer? I could really use one," he said sounding a little uncomfortable. This wasn't his element. I could see it all over his face, but I appreciated that he came for me.

"Champagne….and me," I said, tilting my head to the side and working my lower lip between my teeth.

"What are we waiting for then?" He put his hand on my lower back and guided me toward the limo door. I was about to climb in when I felt a small cold hand on my wrist. My heart dropped. I didn't have to even look up to know who the hand belonged to.

"Alexandra, limo is for wedding party only." Her tone left little room for argument, but I was seething. I brought Dane here to spend the weekend with me, not to be separated from him.

I gave her a fake smile, barely moving my lips as I found some rare confidence. "Dane is my guest. He goes with me this time." I couldn't see Dane's face, but I felt his hand press into my back.

She looked into the crowd and smiled. This was her discreet way of making sure no one was watching our exchange and if they were, she wanted them to think it was a happy one. So fake, just like everything else surrounding her. She was still smiling when she returned her attention to me, "I paid for this limo, my rules."

I wanted to slap her. I was not a violent person, but every muscle in my body was screaming for me to slap her. I didn't, of course, but I wanted to. She needed to control everything. I wondered if it is as exhausting for her as it was for me. I was not going to let her control me this time. It was time to score one point for Alex. I turned, grabbed Dane's hand and led him toward my car. A smile spread across my face and when I looked over at Dane he had a prideful smirk on his. I felt really good for once. Maybe this was why my mother liked control.

I heard her say my name once, but she didn't come after us. She can't make a scene here and I used it to my advantage. For once, I didn't think about the consequences and concentrated on how it made me feel now. Dane was the ultimate prize, but rebellion felt really good too.

As soon as we got to the car, Dane picked me up and twirled me in his arms. I laughed as he put my feet back on the ground and pressed my back into the side of the car. He was standing so close and my heart was pounding out of my chest; I could feel every part of his body against mine. One of his hands touched the side of my neck while the other rested on the top of the car. He tilted my head up and kissed me so long and deep that I forget about everything but him. His tongue worked against my lips until I opened to give him better access. It was hungry, yet sensual. I loved it when Dane kissed me like he might die if he didn't have me. I wanted him just as bad.

Raindrops started to fall from the sky, rolling down my make-up covered face and bare shoulders. I didn't care what it was doing to my seemingly perfect appearance. Nothing was going to break me away from him. I started to shake from the chill the rain had brought on a few minutes later. Dane pulled back, leaving me breathless and lonely, so he could pull his jacket over my shoulders. "Come on, let's get you in the car before you get sick," he said, practically setting me into the passenger seat. I rubbed my thumb over my lower lip, remembering the kiss he just gave me. He noticed what I was doing when he entered the car and reached for my thumb, kissing it softly. If a heart could smile, mine would be beaming right now.

"Are you cold?" he asked, rubbing my arms. He cranked the heat up as high as it would go.

"I'm feeling better," I replied. He made me warm in more ways than one.

Right before he put the car into gear, he turned to me. "What you did back there, Baby...I'm proud of you." I wanted to cry. He didn't know it, but that was the first time anyone had ever said they were proud of me. To me, saying I'm proud of you was almost as important as I love you. I entwined my fingers with his as we drove in silence to the reception. So much had happened in such a short amount of time today. I felt revived and happy.

The reception was a circus of wealth; wealthy people, rich décor, fancy suits, beautiful dresses and an extravagant feast. This time it was just wedding party at the head table and Dane sat with the other spouses and significant others. I hated being away from him, but at least this felt fair. One of my duties as maid of honor was to give a speech. My nerves were already working overtime in anticipation. Talking to a room of people made me uncomfortable and it was even worse that I didn't know these people in the literal sense. This was sad, considering I had been around them for years.

The best man gave his speech first and then it was my turn. I took a deep, cleansing breath and stood up. I grabbed the microphone with one hand and held note cards in the other as I looked at the crowd. I saw my parents first; my mother was smiling with her mouth, but glaring with her eyes. It sent a chill down the entire length of my body; I wasn't looking forward to being alone with her again this weekend. She was angry; her eyes said it all. The rain had altered my appearance from my earlier made up look; I was sure that had her spitting bullets. My father looked like he had somewhere else to be. He always looked that way, like something was more important than what I had going on. He hadn't said a word to me this weekend and I was starving for any sort of attention from him. Then I looked over at Dane who was grinning from ear to ear. It wasn't a mocking grin, but one meant to ease my tension. He mouthed, "You can do it" before winking at me. That was all I needed for my lips to start moving.

"First of all, thank you for coming. I am so happy that Gwen finally found someone who makes her happy and whole. Phillip is a great catch and I know he will make a wonderful husband. I think we all wish to find that special someone in our lives and now there are two less people searching. I remember when my sister brought Phillip home for the first time. She couldn't stop smiling and everything was Phillip this, Phillip that. I knew then that he was her forever man. To love, happiness and forever. I love you Gwen and Phillip." I felt guilty as I sat back down in my chair. The words in my speech didn't quite reach my heart; there wasn't enough truth to it. I glanced over at Gwen before taking my seat again. She was crying. Were they tears of realization or happiness? I wondered if she knew her relationship was not what it should be.

After the cake was cut and the couple had their first dance, Dane appeared at the head table. Dane in a suit made my heart pound. He was handsome. Not in a classic way, but an edgy sort of handsome. The moment I looked into his eyes, the glisten told me he knew what I was thinking. He smiled and reached his hand out. "Dance with me." The thought of dancing with Dane made my body tingle. Dancing with him was like having sex with your clothes on; our bodies said what our lips didn't.

We danced for most of the evening, only breaking for a quick drink. Even when slow songs would turn to fast ones we stayed close, our arms wrapped tightly around each other. He had his lips pressed against my cheek and when he spoke it felt like a soft warm kiss on my skin. "Are you having a good time?"

"I am now."

"Do you want to have a big wedding?" he asked. This wasn't the first time he had referenced marriage in some way and it always made me a mixture of nervousness and elation.

I was nervous, because a big part of me didn't think I could ever have this. My parents would never approve of Dane and give me their blessing. Anything I had with Dane beyond what we had now would be an uphill battle. I was elated, because he was thinking about it. He wouldn't be asking about weddings if he wanted to completely avoid them. Did he see me as his forever? "Baby?"

I shook my thoughts. "No, I don't want a big wedding. I want something simple and intimate. I don't know if I will get that if my mother's in charge." Just thinking about planning a wedding with her made me sick.

"Your wedding should be exactly like you picture it. I hope when the time comes, my badass Alex comes out like she did today. You should have seen your mother's face." I hadn't glanced back as we walked away from her. If I had, I would have broken down and did as she wanted. I had always been that weak.

"It isn't always that easy," I said, honestly. "Do you want a big wedding?"

He pulled back and looked right into my eyes. "I didn't want a wedding at all until this certain girl popped into my life. Now I want whatever she wants. I would do anything to make her happy." Swoon. It was a good thing he was holding me because my knees went weak before I kissed him.

"I love you." It was all I could say. It was honest, and in this moment my heart was full of it.

He kissed me again. "I love you, too."

We stayed on the dance floor until the music stopped and the lights came on. It was one of the best nights of my life. I should have known it was telling. Happy moments never lasted long for me.

Dane was lying on his back with me nestled in the crook of his arm. He looked so peaceful in his sleep. I rubbed my index finger over his face, memorizing all of it. His nose looked like it had been broken a time or two, but I loved how it looked on him. His eyelashes were thick and long, the type every girl dreamed of but often seemed to be wasted on men. His lips were perfect; I couldn't help but use a light kiss to explore that part of him. I was still on a cloud from the night before; nothing was going to stop me today.

I crawled out of bed, threw on a t-shirt and my robe, and headed downstairs to grab us some coffee. It was early and I wanted to beat everyone else to the kitchen. My plan was to "sleep" in my room until brunch and the gift opening at eleven then leave immediately after. I needed to stay away from my mother as much as possible.

The house was quiet as I stood waiting for my morning coffee to brew. I thought about all the events from the day before and it made me feel elated, yet a little nervous. Elated I finally stood up to my mother, even if it was a rather small issue, and nervous for the same. I knew my mother; she would hold a grudge. Even if I avoided her today, she would get me back somehow. I took two coffee cups out of the cupboard and began to poor coffee into them when I heard my mother's heels clicking on the marble in the foyer. I immediately started to panic; it was almost impossible to get enough air into my lungs. I couldn't avoid her today and I was alone.

She came into view with a wicked grin on her face. It wasn't fake, but rather evil; this was going to be bad.

"Alexandra, please join your father and I in the study." She didn't wait for any response; she knew I would follow her. I always did.

My legs shook as I went down the hall toward my father's study. I didn't associate his study with happy moments, but then again there wasn't one room in this house that I associated with happy moments. The door was open and as I entered, I saw my father sitting in his chair looking at papers on his desk. It was like a knife in the heart; I hadn't seen the man in months and he had yet to acknowledge me. My mother sat in one of the two leather chairs across from him and motioned for me to sit in the other. Every inch of my body was shaking as I sat down and looked at the tall, thin man before me. His hair was brown with grey along the sides. If we didn't have the same eyes, people would have doubted we were related.

She cleared her throat. "Alexandra, your father and I are concerned about you. We think you're making some very inappropriate decisions in your life and would like to help you get back on track." The way the word help rolled off her tongue made me cringe. This wasn't going to be about help or guidance; they were going to give me an ultimatum.

My father still hadn't looked up from his desk, but I could see his face was stone cold; he showed absolutely no emotion. I could never read whether he agreed with her or just went along for the ride, but it was easier to just agree with her. "Okay," I said, meekly. My chest felt tighter every moment I spent in here, but no one could save me from this one. I was stuck.

My mother pulled her lips into a firm straight line. "You will stop seeing that boy immediately. He has become an inconvenient distraction and you need to focus on your studies. Do you hear me, Alexandra?" I heard her. I heard her and I couldn't think straight. I processed the words in my head a few times and each time stung worse than the one before. Tears threatened to fall, but I wouldn't let them. I wouldn't give them the pleasure of seeing the affect they had on me.

Something inside me snapped. "I love him. I couldn't let him go even if I wanted to." Please let them listen to me this once. Please. I have given up so much for them, but this one would break me.

My mother laughed. I wanted to upset her. I wanted her to feel something, but she laughed. "You don't know what love is. That boy can't give you anything; he has nothing."

"He gives me more than anyone ever has. He gives…." I heard my father's fist come down hard on his desk and looked up to see his eyes blazing and his brows furrowed. His facial expression drained all the confidence out of me as my body began to shake again.

He leaned forward in his chair and pointed his index finger right at me, never taking his eyes off mine, "You will get rid of that boy. You will bring your focus back to your studies and you will show your mother more respect." I couldn't say anything. My lips and mind were frozen. He continued, "If you refuse to follow our rules, Alexandra, there will be serious consequences."

"Consequences," I whispered. Consequences to some people meant losing their car or allowance. My parents liked to cut deeper. I could never bleed enough for them.

"If you continue down this path, we will revoke your car, monthly allowance, tuition payments and your trust fund privileges," my father warned. My hands clenched the side of my chair until my knuckles were white. They wanted to completely cut me off because I was dating Dane. This was what I had been afraid would happen. I knew it would happen.

I decided to give rebellion on more shot. "I can get a job. Some students pay for their own tuition." I sat up in my chair, trying to show mock confidence.

"Please, Alexandra, do you know how much it costs to go to NYU?" my mother mocked. "Do you know how much it costs to feed and clothe you? Don't be stupid. Your father and I just want what is best for you and that isn't Dan."

"Dane," I corrected her as I slid down in my chair, swallowing back tears.

"Whatever. You have one week to make this right. Do you hear me? If you go against our wishes, things will change dramatically for you starting next week." I sat there, unmoving. I wanted to tell them they were wrong about Dane, but the words wouldn't form. I looked at my mother who had a pleased smile on her face before turning toward my father whose angered expression caused me to quickly look away.

"You have been nothing but a disappointment lately. We know this boy is the cause of that. You're different. You're talking back to your mother, you show up at your sister's reception looking like street trash and you aren't focused. Why can't you be more like Gwendolyn?" my father added. His words ripped through me. He rarely acknowledged my presence and the one time he did, this is what he had to say. He had said more in the last ten minutes than he had said in the last year. I needed to get out of here before they saw how much they affected me.

Why did they have to compare me to my sister all the time? She was like them. She lived her life doing what would make others happy, but inside I know she had to be miserable. Why couldn't they accept me? My mind circled as the panic and tears built. I always wondered what it would be like to be buried alive and this must be it. I was trapped and no one could save me. No one would hear me.

After a few minutes of silence, I stood up to leave. I had nothing else to say to them and I didn't want to hear anything else they had to say. Just as my hand hit the doorknob, my mother chimed in again. "You know, we had someone investigate Dane yesterday and they found some incriminating information. He is not someone that you want to associate yourself with. We can make his life difficult. You wouldn't want that, would you?" I looked back at her and this time I couldn't stop the tears that fell from my eyes. She just smiled; I hated her. I hated that my misery caused her so much enjoyment. I slammed the door and headed upstairs, locking myself in the bathroom. The tears continued as I fell to the floor, wrapping my arms around my legs. I was mad and confused; I just didn't know what to do. I shouldn't be forced to make this choice. I wanted to choose Dane, but the little voice in my head kept reminding me what that would cost. I didn't know if I could continue.

I was not sure how long I stayed locked in the bathroom, but when I returned to my bedroom Dane wasn't there. My heart fell into my stomach. Where did he go? I turned to the hallway and saw his bedroom light was on. Part of me thought I should go over to his room and the other part of me wanted more time to think. Thinking won out.

I closed the door and walked to the window. The sun had disappeared behind the dark clouds. It was amazing how quickly the weather could change. I touched my fingers to the glass; it was cold and felt good against my fingers. I always liked the chill against my fingers; it reminded me I was alive on days I felt I was anything but.

I used to sit in the window seat in my room and stare outside for hours. I wondered what the family in the house across the street was doing. Was that family like ours? Did the parents kiss and hug their children? I would sit and imagine a life like that. The ones I watched on the Brady Bunch or the Partridge Family. Those moments always made me feel unworthy. Why did everyone have what I didn't? What had I done to deserve this? I wanted love, but instead I had this. Life could be so unfair.

I was still deep in thought when I felt a hand cover mine where it rested on the window. I startled and looked behind me to see Dane standing there, eyebrows pulled in, concern all over his face. "How long have you been standing there?" I asked. His presence in front of me in nothing but pajama pants sent butterflies in motion throughout my stomach. I wondered if there would ever be a time when that didn't happen with Dane.

"I've been in here the whole time," he said, pointing to a chair in the darkest corner of the room. "You seemed to be thinking about something and I didn't want to disturb you. What were you thinking about?" I let out the air I had been holding in my lungs.

"I was just thinking about life in general, I guess," I said, not taking my attention away from the window.

"Do you care to elaborate? You looked pretty lost there for a minute." He removed his hand and wrapped both arms around my shoulders, resting his chin on my head. I relaxed back into him; he was my comfort.

"Do you ever wonder what it would have been like to grow up in a different family?" I asked. He seemed to contemplate that for a second.

"I have envied friends who grew up in happy families, but I also believe that my less than ideal upbringing made me who I am." I turned around with a confused look on my face. His face was serious as he continued, "Sometimes when life hits you with too much, it makes you stronger and you learn from it. I know where I want to go while some of my friends don't. Life has brought me maturity. I make my decisions based on who I don't want to be, rather than whom everyone else wants me to be. I always want to be better. It took me time to see this, but it's true." If I didn't completely love him before, this certainly sealed my fate. He was sexy, kind, and smart, wrapped up in one complete package.

I wrapped my arms around his waist as tight as I could without hurting him. I wanted to show him, to tell him I loved him in any way possible. It felt like there weren't enough ways to tell him what he meant to me. I looked up at him, kissing his chin. "I guess I could learn a thing or two from you."

His face lit up with a smile that could break one thousand hearts; I knew for damn sure it could break mine. "We're adults now, Baby. When you become an adult, you get to choose your path. You take all the things you learned while you were on everyone else's and use it to build your own, but it's about where your heart wants to go. It's all up to you." I digested his words for a minute. He was right, but I wondered how that changes when you still have a very demanding tour guide. My mother was the tour guide from hell.

"It's almost time for gift opening, I better get ready," I said. I needed a hot shower and more time to think.

Dane put his finger under my chin and kissed me lightly, almost like a feather touching my lips. It didn't stop there, though, as it continued to my heart, touching it only like Dane could. His body was tense when I left him. There was no doubt that he could read the shift in my mood. A part of me wanted to tell him everything, but it was easier to close down. It had always worked for me in the past.

I jumped in the shower while my head worked overtime, sorting through my crazy mess. Dane made more sense than anyone I had ever met, but my parent's voices still rang loudly in my head. Their threats were on automatic replay and every time I heard them, they cut me deeper. They could make my life hell; I knew they could. If it had been just a threat against me, I could have dealt with that. I knew now, more than ever, that money was not the most important thing in the world. I wasn't dealing with their threats against Dane as well. Did they know about his brother? The drugs? What would they do with the info? I didn't want to find out and I didn't want Dane to have to deal with it.

CHAPTER TWENTY-ONE

My head was spinning the whole way back to the city.
Dane volunteered to drive, pointing out that I looked tired.
All the crying had done a number on my eyes and I couldn't
stop the voices in my head telling me what I should and
shouldn't do. I needed them to stop. I wanted them to stop.
How could I make them stop?

The gift opening was awful. I sat next to Dane who held
my hand the whole time. I made the mistake of looking at my
mother at one point and all I could see in her eyes was
warning. My father, on the other hand, kept his attention off
me completely. He had said everything he wanted to say. I
hated it; I wanted to run out of the room, out of the house and
never look back, but I couldn't.

I was miserable before I met Dane, and our time together
at school had made me happier than I'd ever been. I was
starting to feel miserable again because reality had crept back
in. I felt like I had so much, but so little. I just wanted things
to go back to the way they were before this weekend, but
they couldn't.

I knew what I had to do to protect Dane. Staying with
him would only hurt him and me, and in the long run we
would both be miserable. My parents would never accept him
and they wouldn't let me back into the house as long as I was
with him. Who tells their child they are no longer welcome in
their own home because of who they're dating? Who does

that? I couldn't put any more weight on Dane's shoulders. He had been through enough in his lifetime.

My eyes wandered to Dane a few times during our drive. He was usually so good at reading me, but he wasn't able to see the glisten in my eyes and pain on my face through the darkness. This was the one time I didn't want him to read me. I realized a long time ago that Dane made me breakable; I just didn't know it would hurt this bad before I even shattered. I needed to let him go. I couldn't be selfish. It was what was best for everyone. I would get my parent's blessing and he would be safe from their wrath, something I could never be. We would no longer have each other, though, and the thought of living without him was killing me inside.

I needed to feel what we had one more time before I let it all go. This was the one selfish part of me and it may make everything worse, but I needed him one more time. I turned so I was facing him. "Are we going back to your place?"

"Yeah, unless you don't want to. Do you want to pick up something to eat first?" He looked concerned.

"No, I'm not really hungry," I said sadly, taking his hand in mine and settling both of them on my thigh. We rode the rest of the way in silence and by the time we arrived at his apartment, I was ready to explode. I had to put this negative energy somewhere. I needed Dane to drown it out, just for tonight. I had made a life changing decision on the short ride from Greenwich to New York City and the weight of it was too much. Alex, you can to do this, I told myself. I just needed to push past the pain like I always did.

"Want to watch a movie?" he asked as we worked our way up the stairs with our bags. My legs were shaking and it was hard to not just collapse on the steps.

"No, I just want to go to bed." He looked at me for a second, eyebrows knitted together. I gave him my best smile as he grabbed my hand and led me back to his bedroom.

"T-shirt?" he asked as he grabbed one out of the drawer for himself.

I nodded. Ever since I started to stay at Dane's on a regular basis, I'd been wearing his t-shirts to bed. They were comfortable and smelled like him. He handed me a plain white t-shirt and I headed to the bathroom to change, stealing a glance at myself in the mirror. Stress was plastered all over my face and I looked older than usual. I splashed cold water over it a few times and took several deep breaths before going out to face the man I loved, the man I would always love. But this would be the last time I would face him as my lover. Maybe what I was doing was wrong, selfish even, but I couldn't stop it.

I let my hand rest on the doorknob for a few seconds before joining him in the bedroom again. He was lying on the bed in nothing but his white boxer briefs. Gorgeous. Beautiful. My Dane. He looked up at me with a big grin on his face, the grin I was going to destroy in a few short hours. "Come here, Baby. What are you waiting for?"

I willed myself forward and tucked myself into his side, nuzzling my face in his neck. "Dane?" I whispered.

"Hmm?" He was using the tips of his fingers to rub small sensual circles on my back. My body was on full alert; I needed him. Even with pain flowing through my veins, I wanted him.

"I love you," I said, placing a kiss on his chest.

"I love you, too." He kissed the top of my head and brought both arms around me so we were on our sides, face to face. "Are you okay?" His voice was full of concern and love.

I answered by claiming his mouth in a long, slow kiss. I relished the familiar mint taste that was always on his tongue. I would never to able to taste or smell mint again without thinking of him; it would haunt me forever. He flipped me on my back and kissed every bare inch of my body. I memorized his lips, how they felt on me and what they did inside of me. No one else would ever make me feel this way. No one else could hold my body and heart at the same time like Dane could. I ran my fingers through his hair before lightly tugging on it to pull him forward, placing his lips back on mine.

We stayed connected forever; I didn't want him to pull away when he sat on his heels and began to slowly pull down my panties. Panic really started to set in as he pulled down his own boxers; this would be the last time he would enter my body. It was the last time we would have this connection. Dane was my first and I had always hoped he would be my last, but it just wasn't meant to be. I wondered if anything good was ever meant to be.

As if he knew what I needed, what I so desperately wanted, he began to slowly enter me. His motions remained slow and deliberate as he told me how beautiful I was, that he loved me, that I was his forever. Tears slowly began to roll down the side of my face and it took everything I had to compose myself enough to tell Dane I loved him too. I wiped my hand over my face to hide the tears. I thought back to the night in the club when we first met. I had never believed in fate, but I think fate put us there and then in the same Art class. I remembered the first time he kissed me in the art gallery; it was the first time I lived life like no one was watching me. I remembered the first time we ate at the little Italian restaurant that we had visited many times since. It was now a sentimental place and I would see Dane every time I walked past it. I thought back to the first time we were like this. How he made me feel so much love that I felt no pain. I wished he could do that now. I wished he could wash all my pain away this time.

My mind was in such a state of overdrive that I couldn't find my release. I was too far inside my own head to let myself be in the moment. Dane found his too soon; it could have lasted for hours and it would have been too soon for me. I wrapped my arms around him and held him as tight as I could while our bodies were still joined. Our chests were touching and his heartbeat mirrored mine. After a few minutes, he rolled over on his back and cradled me into his chest. "I love you, Baby," he said, kissing the top of my head. I loved the husky sound of his voice after sex. Everything about him was sexy.

"I love you, too. Don't ever forget it." I lifted my head to kiss his chin. He began to rub circles on my back again until he fell asleep, his body wrapped around mine. I laid there and listened to him breath for a while before freeing my body from his. It physically hurt to be separated from him. He shifted to his side, causing me to freeze in place for a minute until I knew he was still sound asleep. I threw his t-shirt back on and put on the pair of jeans I'd worn into the apartment earlier. I grabbed my purse and disappeared into the bathroom to write him a final goodbye, tears rolling down my face, hands shaking.

Dane,

I am not sure I can ever put into words how much you mean to me. I love you more than anything in this world. I hope you can forgive me some day.

You and I were not meant to be. I can't see you anymore. Do not make this harder than it already is. I wish you the best and hope you know that I will always love you.

Alex

I laid the note on the table by his bed, taking one final glance at the beautiful man lying naked on the bed. I couldn't even begin to put into words how much it broke my heart to know this was the last time I would see him like that. I felt sick to my stomach as I slipped on my shoes and quietly exited the apartment with my things. It took everything I had not to fall to my knees and cry in the three blocks from his apartment to my dorm. My heart felt like it had been ripped out of my chest and thrown in the garbage disposal.

I was grateful Jade wasn't in our room when I opened the door. I wondered when she would be back. She would tell me I was a fool and it would be true. I was a cowardly fool who would continue with her Pre-Med degree to make Mommy and Daddy happy. Jade was going to be upset with me; that was a guarantee. I wondered if she would understand if she had been with me this morning in the study.

I wondered if anyone would understand. The time alone was what I needed to sort through everything.

I left Dane's t-shirt on and pulled on a pair of cotton shorts. Slowly sliding under the covers, I finally let go. I cried because my heart was lying back in his apartment in a million pieces. I cried because I realized that I would never love like this again. Dane had my heart and I would never get it back. I cried because I had happiness in my hand and threw it away. I cried until there were no more tears left to fall down my cheek and slipped back into the numbness that engulfed me before I gave my heart to Dane.

After hours of crying, I must have fallen asleep because I was jolted awake by pounding at the door. I didn't have to look to see who it was. Instead I pulled the covers tightly over my head, willing the sound to go away. "Alex, open this goddamn door! Right. Now." I knew he would be upset, but I hadn't prepared myself for what I would do when he came to my door. He wasn't going to leave here without an explanation and I owed him one. I owed him everything, but I wasn't strong enough to give it to him.

"Alex, Baby, please just tell me what I did." His voice was so pained. My poor, sweet Dane. I didn't want him to think he did anything wrong, but I couldn't will any words out of my mouth. Every minute I looked at his sad expression and heard the pain in his voice felt like another nail to my already fragile heart.

"Alex, I'm not leaving until you talk to me," he said, his voice a little lower. It was quiet for a while before I heard him yell "Fuck!" and what sounded like a fist making contact with the wall outside my door. I winced. I desperately wanted to go out there and tell him everything would be okay, but I

238

knew it wouldn't. My life was stuck in a compressor and I had nowhere to go. I felt so hopeless: I knew exactly what I wanted, but I couldn't have it.

It had been quiet for along time when I heard Jade's voice outside the door. "What are you doing down there?" I hadn't planned on Jade coming home. I scolded myself for not texting her, but now it was too late. I heard Dane's voice, but couldn't make out his words as Jade turned her key in the lock.

Jade walked in as Dane practically shoved her out of the way, making his way to my side of the room in a few short steps and pulling the covers from my face. His eyes were puffy and bloodshot. I closed my eyes, trying to combat my growing guilt. "Why wouldn't you answer the door? Why did you shut me out? What did I do?" He kneeled beside the bed and cupped my cheeks in his hands. "Alex, talk to me. You can't just leave me a fucking note and expect me stay away." I opened my eyes to meet his. They are full of so much pain. "Say something, please."

"Dane, you need to go." My voice was shaky as tears rolled down my cheeks once again.

"I'm not going anywhere until you talk to me," he snapped. The hurt and anger I heard in his voice broke me. For as long as I lived, I would see that pained expression every time I closed my eyes. How could I hurt the man that I loved? Was I really any better than them? Then I remember my plastic heart, the gift from my upbringing. If my family members could do this, so could I. It was time to step back from my heart and detach myself completely. My whole body trembled at the realization, but it was the only way this was going to work.

I would never know where what came out of my mouth next came from. I took a deep breath and squared my shoulders. "I can't be with you, Dane. I can't love you the way you need to be loved; I thought I could but I can't," I said. Each word made my heart bleed a little more. This was draining everything out of me.

His brows pulled together as his forehead wrinkled. "What? I don't believe one fucking word you're saying to me right now." I finally met his eyes again. Had he been crying? "What the fuck is going on, Alex? Talk to me."

"Dane, you need to go!" There wasn't much more I could take before I would completely cave to those glassy green eyes. I was breaking him and I knew it.

"Is there someone else?" Holy hell, where had this all gone so wrong? How could he even think there would be someone else while I was in love with him?

What I did next was wrong. It was so very wrong but Dane had given me an easy way out. "Yes," I whispered, not meeting his eyes. My throat tightened when I spoke and I instantly felt sick. He let go of my face and the anger in his eyes quickly multiplied. I was silently begging him to believe me and leave. This was the hardest thing I had ever done in my life. I had to close my eyes to keep my composure.

"Who? Tell. Me." I didn't answer him. There wasn't an answer to give. He stood there for a second, just staring down at me. "I can't believe you're fucking doing this to me, Alex," he said running his hands over his face before turning around, opening the door and slamming it so hard that one of Jade's pin boards fell from the wall.

"I'm sorry," I whispered, before I started weeping uncontrollably again.

"What the HELL was THAT?" Jade asked. Her voice was controlled, but laced with anger. I knew she would be angry. I deserved whatever she had to say. I was ashamed of what I'd become. "What the hell was that?"

"I can't do it anymore. I can't be with Dane and be what my parents want me to be. They are two different worlds that don't go together; I realized that this weekend. This hurts so freaking bad, but I don't see any other way. I love him, but he deserves better," I replied as tears rolled down my cheeks. It was hard to get the words to pass through my throat. I could barely breath through the pain and tears. I closed my eyes and all I could see was his face before he slammed my door.

I don't know if the look in her eyes was pity or confusion or maybe a mixture of both. She sat down on the end of my bed and examined my face for several seconds before talking. "Why did you tell him there's someone else? You and I both know that there is no one else and you just threw the gasoline on the fire with that one."

"I know. I knew if I said yes, he would get angry and leave. I couldn't just sit here and see him hurting because of me. I made my decision and I have to live with it, but it's going to be hard to do that if he doesn't let it go." More tears rolled down my face. I wondered if Dane was crying right now. What have I done to him? What did I do to us? I was no better than my parents.

"Oh, honey, when are you going to start listening to your heart and quit letting your parents run the course of your life? You know they aren't happy, right?"

"What are you talking about?" I asked, wiping my eyes with my sleeves.

"Just listen for a second. Your parents are miserable. They may have the material things in life, and have everyone convinced that their life together is perfect, but is that truly what you want for yourself? If you can honestly tell me that is what you want, you aren't the Alex I know. The Alex I know wants to be in love." Jade was the second person today to look at me with anger in her eyes. Jade was rubbing salt into the wound, but I deserved it.

"Of course I don't want a relationship like my parents. I need them to accept me. I don't know why, but it's important to me." I sat there chipping the pink polish that remained from my sister's wedding off my nails. I couldn't tell Jade about their ultimatums. She was my best friend and I knew if I told her the real reason I was doing this, she would jump in her car and head straight to Greenwich. If she did that, they would most certainly ruin Dane's life. He didn't deserve that.

"Dammit, Alex, you don't even want to be a doctor! Have you ever heard of student loans? College isn't just for rich kids you know!" Oh, I knew that. I looked it up online one day, but she didn't mention how much I would be disappointing my parents by not becoming a doctor, by staying with Dane and becoming an artist. I didn't need the being-an-artist-is-not-a-real-job talk again.

"I don't want to talk about this anymore. Just leave it alone. I barely got any sleep last night and I have a test tomorrow. Please!" I rolled onto my side, shutting her out completely.

"Fine, but we're not done with this conversation. I can't believe you did that to Dane. Seriously, Alex." And she was gone, off my bed and into the bathroom. I let the tears fall again. I replayed the last few months in my mind, trying to figure out where it all went wrong. I made a choice one-day to give Dane a chance and it changed my life. I now knew what it was like to be in love. I didn't regret it; I could never regret the best months of my life. I only regretted today and everything that had happened that landed me in my bed alone with my tear soaked pillow. This day had been the most draining of all my years and I just wanted it to be over with.

Chapter Twenty-Two

I stayed in bed all day Monday and Tuesday, only getting up to use the bathroom and to grab a drink of water. No part of me wanted to shower, eat, or have any type of human interaction. I even emailed my professor and made up an excuse with hopes of rescheduling my test. I didn't care if he accepted it or not. I could care less about class; I couldn't concentrate so there was no point in going. My phone beeped a couple of times with texts and I had three missed calls, but none were from Dane. I didn't expect him to call after what I had done to him. I just missed him; missed the sound of his voice, the feel of his lips, his hands and his eyes. As long as I lived, I would miss everything about him.

I cried a little less each day, but there was a growing hole where my heart once was. I guess it was hard to cry when your heart was evaporating in your chest. I had lost so much in the last few days and my life was forever changed. I was back to being the old Alexandra, but with less hope and half the heart.

I called my parents on Tuesday night. I needed them to know I made my choice before they had a chance to hurt Dane and cause more issues for him. My mom answered right away, just like clockwork. "Good evening, Riley residence."

"It's me," I replied. My voice was little more than a whisper as the pain of what I'd done yesterday lay fresh on my mind. I didn't want to have anything to do with them, but my hands were tied.

"You sound tired, have you been staying out late?"

"No, it's just been a long couple of days," I said, trying to hold in all emotion.

"Alexandra, have you thought about what we discussed Sunday?" she asked. Her voice was cold, yet amused.

I took a deep breath as I tried to hold myself together, "I did it. Dane and I are no longer together." A chill ran through my body when the words came out of my mouth.

"Good girl. Are you coming home for spring break? Your father and I are heading to Vail one more time before the season is over." I flinched. My heart was broken. I wished just this once she would comfort me or ask how I was doing. My parents had made me choose and had caused this mess. Couldn't she help me just this once? When I left Greenwich to come to NYU, I thought I would have a new beginning. I was naïve to think my parents would loosen their reigns simply because I was no longer under their roof. Since my sister was now married, I was the last one left to control.

"I don't think so. Look, I have to study; I'll talk to you later." I didn't wait for her reply as I set my phone down. I did what she wanted, but she didn't care about my feelings. I didn't know why I expected a different outcome. There was never one. I was starving for their attention right now. I certainly got it when I was doing something they didn't like. But, now that I did what they wanted, life would go back to normal. I would be invisible until they needed me or I did something else wrong through their eyes. I hated that they did this to me. I hated that they did this to Dane.

Wednesday hit me hard. I had to rejoin society at some point, but it felt too soon. I was long overdue for a shower so I conquered that first. I threw on a pair of black yoga pants, a long-sleeve grey t-shirt and my black flats before putting my hair into a loose knot at the top of my head.

My stomach felt hollow so I headed to the campus coffee shop to grab a blueberry bagel and a large latte. I picked a chair by the window and tore off small pieces of bagel as I watched groups of students walk by. Life continued around me while I felt frozen in place. I had everything I wanted one minute and the next it was all ripped away. It was unfair. Do you ever look at people's faces when they walk by and wonder what they're thinking? I watched as one girl walked by, talking on her cell phone. It didn't take much to realize that the person on the other end made her happy because her eyes sparkled as the corners of her mouth turned up. She didn't look like she had a care in the world. I wanted to be like her and go about my life without having to worry about anyone's desires but my own. That wasn't my reality though.

I pulled out my Anatomy book, taking my attention away from the window, and began to study. I had a few minutes before I needed to head to class and the last thing I wanted or needed to do was to think about all the things that couldn't be. I had cried so many tears and ran through so many different ways to make things better, but all I was left with was overwhelming exhaustion.

I was packing up my things when my phone beeped. I looked down to see a message from Jade:

Jade: U OK?

Alex: Y, off to class.

Jade: U going to class???

Alex: Y, test

Jade: Good girl! TTYL

Alex: K

As much as Jade got on my nerves, she was a great friend and I was lucky to have her as my roommate. She brought a pizza home last night and made me eat; I had barely touched food all week. She didn't bring up Dane again and I was thankful for that. Therapists tell you to talk through your issues, but I couldn't; the mention of his name made my stomach clench and made pain shoot through me. I missed him so much that I not only emotionally felt pain, but physically too. It was almost unbearable.

During my walk across campus, I realized I needed to talk to Mr. Thomas and see if I could move to one of the empty seats that were vacated by students who dropped the class. There was no way I could talk to Dane or be that close to him without touching him. If I had to sit next to him for the rest of the semester, it would be a reminder of everything I left behind.

Mr. Thomas was at the front of the room writing today's assignment on the board when I entered the classroom. I cleared my throat to get his attention. "Mr. Thomas, can I talk to you for a minute?"

"Sure, Alex, what can I do for you?" He kept writing while I decided how to say what I needed to say. My mind wasn't as sharp as usual and everything seemed more complicated these days.

"I need to switch seats," I finally whispered.

He quit writing and turned toward me. "Why? Is everything alright?"

"Yes. I mean, it is, but I need to sit somewhere else for the rest of the semester. Mr. Wright and I aren't exactly getting along right now and I need to focus on this class when I'm here." I was nervous that he wouldn't let me move as I started rubbing my hands together.

"I thought you guys were friends." I knew our relationship was pretty obvious, but I didn't think we were that obvious. Not that it mattered now.

"Please, Mr. Thomas," I said, pleading with my eyes. It never worked on my parents, but maybe it would work on him. He seemed like a rational man.

"Okay, go sit next to Brent in row two and Miss Riley, I hope you know what you're doing," he said, turning back toward the board. He was probably one of those hopeless romantics who thought I was being all sorts of stupid right now; I was, but I didn't need him to look at me like that.

Brent didn't talk while we worked on our latest projects, which was fine with me, but I also noticed that Dane didn't show up for class. He never missed this class. A little pang of guilt shot through me as I wondered what he was doing right now. For a second I considered texting him to ask if he was all right, but then I realized that it was not my place to ask that anymore. The thought of anyone else touching or comforting him was like a dagger to my already bleeding heart.

I considered skipping Anatomy, but that would just give me more time to think and, if Sunday was an example of anything, it was an example of what happened when I spent a bit too much time thinking.

Jade wasn't in our room when I returned so I decided to get caught up on some reading. I had read only one page of my Anatomy text before my thoughts started shifting to Dane again. I could see the sincerity and honesty in his smile, smell his clean, but woodsy scent and feel his calloused, yet gentle fingers on my body. For the last few months, I could call, text or see him whenever I wanted. But now that privilege was not mine anymore and a part of me selfishly hoped it would never be anyone else's.

My cell phone rang, making my heart rate speed up. It slowed dramatically when I noticed the caller was my mother. I considered letting it go to voicemail, but she would just keep calling until I talked to her.

"Hello," I said hesitantly.

"Alexandra, what are you doing tomorrow? I was thinking about coming into the city to do some shopping."

"I don't feel like shopping. Maybe some other time." I didn't like to shop half as much as my mother on a normal day and right now it was the last thing I wanted to do. I didn't care what I looked like so why would I want nice things?

"Alexandra, I'm worried about you and the destructive path you've mapped out for yourself." She let out an exasperated sigh. All I had said was that I didn't want to go shopping and all of a sudden I was prone to make bad choices. I just wanted to go outside and scream until I didn't have a voice anymore. My mother was so frustrating.

"Mom, I'm not going down the wrong path. I think the only bad decision I've made lately was dumping Dane." I was seething mad. Why did she have to keep bringing this up?

"Well, it's for the best; you'll see that someday. You need a man with a future ahead of him and quite frankly, that boy wasn't going anywhere." Her words made me even angrier. Dane was going somewhere. He may not be heading to Medical or Law School, but he was talented at what he did and I knew some day he would have a very successful career. Success didn't mean he'd be rich or famous; it meant contentment and respect.

I remained quiet as she continued. "Did you meet Trevor Williams on Friday night at rehearsal? You know, Dr. Williams' son? He's a senior at the University of Massachusetts and has been accepted into Harvard Medical School in the fall. He's single and such a handsome young man." I knew exactly whom she was talking about and handsome would be the worst word to describe him. He was tall, but incredibly skinny and his hairline has already begun to recede at the age of twenty-two. Why did she feel the need to play matchmaker? She didn't care if I was okay. It was more important that I kept up appearances. I was growing more and more angry because I did this to please her. All I wanted was for her to support me emotionally and she was unable to do that, yet again. Really, I would not make them happy until I had been married off to my fake husband who would have my fake love. Just once I wanted someone to care about what I wanted; I realized I'd had that someone and I'd lost him.

"Mom, I have to go. I'm late for study group." I hung up the phone without waiting for her goodbye and hurled my Anatomy textbook across the room, knocking over the lamp by my bed as the weight of what I had done engulfed me. I flinched as the lamp shattered, but didn't move to clean it up. I stared down at all the little pieces on the floor and imagined that they were a part of me. My heart was essentially lying on the floor.

I pulled on a pair of yoga pants and fleece before lacing up my tennis shoes and grabbing my iPod. I used to run all the time in high school as a way to escape my house when my parents became unbearable. College may have put some geographical space between us, but their voices were always in my head ringing over and over like a car alarm. I needed the fresh air and exercise to sort through my thoughts and put some space between my heart and my head.

Every time my feet hit the pavement, I felt a little bit of the tension leave my body. I thought about my childhood and wondered if my parents had ever been proud of me. I thought about my sister and wondered why I couldn't be more like her. Why couldn't I just do what my parents wanted and be happy with it? I thought about Dane and the way he made my heart flutter in a way that I didn't even know was possible. And I thought about my future and what my life was going to be like without him.

My anger began to boil over. I could run for miles and it wouldn't be enough time to get through this mess.

I decided to run back to the dorm and grab my purse. That fake ID was going to help me buy myself a bottle of liquid numbness. It worked before. No one was here to save me. Maybe I was the only one who could save me.

Chapter Twenty-Three

Jade hadn't slept in our room last night or at least I didn't think she had. I started mixing vodka with grapefruit juice after I returned from the store and it didn't take long before I got to the point where I remembered nothing. I was completely and utterly numb. Just like I needed to be. I always wondered how someone could let themselves become an addict and now I understood that some of them might be drowning their issues and pain in the serum of forgetfulness. It worked for a little while anyway.

It was Thursday now. To be more exact, it was Thursday afternoon and I was just getting up; I had skipped so many classes this week, but I didn't care. My head was pounding and my stomach turned as I got out of bed. I felt like a shell of my former self. I felt no happiness or hope like I had a week ago; instead I felt only sadness and loss. No one had died, but it felt like I had. I wished I could be my mother, just for a little while, and feel nothing. How does she do that? Was she ever like me? Had she ever let her heart act as her guide? As much as I tried, I couldn't turn off my feelings anymore. They burned in my chest every minute of the day. I wanted the pain to stop, but I had no idea how to shut it off. It was time for me to at least try to live again, even if it was half the life I had before.

After visiting the restroom, I lied back down under my covers and buried my head under my pillow before I heard my cell phone beep.

Jade: R U OK?

Alex: Just Peachy

Jade: I couldn't wake u up last night and I was worried.

Alex: U were here?

Jade: Y

Alex: Sorry, I guess I drank a little too much.

Jade: Dinner tonight?

Alex: Sure

I couldn't care less if I ate or not, but I didn't want to worry Jade more than I already had. I could see it when she looked at me. Her normally cheerful eyes had been replaced with downcast, sullen eyes. I wondered if she felt my pain or if her expression was meant to mirror mine. She was one of the few people I had ever felt cared for me, honestly cared for me. I made my choice with Dane and I needed to deal with it. Jade might have been the last person I had left in my life who accepted me for me. If I pushed her away, I would have nothing left here.

I showered, brushed my teeth, combed my hair, and put on some decent clothes. I could do this. I could put on my best smile, lift my head up, and have a normal conversation with Jade over dinner. People faked it all the time and if anyone could excel at the art of faking, it was me. It was in my blood.

Jade eyed me up and down when she walked into the room a little while later. A small smile appeared on her face, "You clean up nice." I could tell she was still worried about me. I could see the concern in her eyes.

"Yeah, I thought I could ditch the sweatpants for one night."

"Where do you want to eat? My treat," she said as she applied a fresh layer of lip-gloss. I was up for anything as long as we didn't visit one of the restaurants Dane and I went to on a regular basis; I wasn't ready for that.

"Chinese?"

She eyed me suspiciously. "You never eat Chinese." I didn't. I always complained about the sodium and fat content, but I didn't care about that stuff today.

"Are we going or not?" I replied, placing my hands on my hips.

"Yeah, yeah, yeah. Just let me grab my coat."

The fresh air felt good on my face as we walked to Jade's favorite Chinese restaurant. It was cold, but the wind was nonexistent, making it bearable. The smell of different foods hit my nose as we walked past several restaurants along the way. I heard horns and sirens as people made their way home from work on the busy streets of New York City. It was calming, if even for a minute, to hear something other than Dane's last words in my head. It was nice to have something hit my senses besides the handsome sight of his face and the minty taste of his lips. Maybe getting out more was the key to moving forward.

Jade's phone began to ring right before we reached the restaurant. She motioned for me to give her a minute so I did; I wandered over to a small shop next to the restaurant and peeked through the window. It was a cute little thrift shop with fashionably decorated mannequins. I made a note to come back here sometime to do some shopping. It was not a place I would usually shop, but I needed some change in my life and maybe I would start by dressing the way I wanted instead of the way I was expected to. I heard Jade say goodbye and turned my attention back to her; she looked uneasy. "Who was on the phone?" I asked.

She hesitated for a minute. "Tyler. He wants to join us for dinner. I told him no." She bit her lower lip nervously and looked down at her phone.

"He can join us," I replied. I only said it to be nice; I didn't feel like sitting across from the happy couple all night. Besides, he was Dane's best friend.

"I told him no. I'll see him later. Come on, let's eat." She grabbed my arm and led me inside.

The smell of Chinese greeted me. I usually hated the smell of fried food, but today I welcomed it. Nothing soothed a broken heart like some calories, carbs and alcohol. We sat down and ordered enough to feed a family of five before Jade started her little counseling session. This must be her whole purpose for bringing me here. Well, that and getting me to eat.

She sat back in her chair with her arms crossed over her chest. "Alex, it's time for you to talk. What happened when you went home last weekend? When you left here, you were the happiest I'd ever seen you and then you come back and you're in the worst shape I've ever seen you. Talk now," she said, narrowing her eyes at me. I couldn't lie to her. She knew me too well.

I thought back to the conversation I had with my parents on Sunday morning and the pain and anger surfaced again. I hated that study before, but now I despised it; I would never be able to walk in that room again without a heavy feeling in my chest. And then I thought about his eyes and how they looked the last time I saw them. I would do anything to forget the look in his eyes that morning.

I cleared my throat and told her everything. Her eyes widened as mine closed to keep in the tears that wanted to flow down my cheeks. When I mentioned my mother and her threats, Jade's hands balled into fists on the table. If she'd hated my mother before, she certainly hated her now. I told her about the last night I spent in Dane's room and watched as her eyes filled with tears. Jade was a true friend; someone who felt my pain right along with me.

"Do you want him back?" she asked, sadness wrapped in her voice.

"I can't," I said with a choked voice. "What's done is done and even if I could be with him, I doubt he wants anything to do with me." I used my sleeve to dry my eyes.

We sat in silence, staring at the untouched food on the table. Jade had her hands steepled in front of her mouth, deep in thought. It caught me off guard when Jade suddenly looked up and greeted someone behind me.

"Ladies, care if I join you?" The male voice was familiar. I turned around to see Tyler standing there, sporting a cocky grin.

He took a seat next to Jade, never taking his eyes off me. Jade looked between the two of us, "I thought-"

"I know you said not to come, but I couldn't pass up a chance to talk to two of my favorite ladies. How are you

Alex? Broken anymore hearts lately?" he asked, glaring at me. My stomach dropped. He was here to confront me.

"Tyler, stop!" Jade snapped. I stared behind them in an attempt to concentrate on anything but him.

"You know, you were the only one he let in. He hasn't let anyone get as close as you did. And then you just leave a note and sneak out while he sleeps; you stomped on his trust," Tyler said, his eyes becoming more intense with every word that came out of his mouth. His words cut deep. I shattered someone who was already broken. He continued, leaning forward in his chair so his face was close to mine. "He hasn't eaten, slept or talked to anyone since you left. I hope you accomplished what you set out to accomplish."

"Tyler stop! I mean it," Jade hissed, eyeing him with such contempt. I felt even worse when I realized this was going to cause issues in their relationship.

He continued anyway. "No, she needs to hear what she did to him." He turned his gaze from Jade back to me before continuing. "He loves you and would do anything for you and this is what he gets? You are selfish and disgusting."

His words made me want to crawl into a hole and never come out. I could feel my throat closing up and the overwhelming need to run. "You're right. I'm sorry," I whispered before running out the door.

I could hear Jade yelling my name, but I didn't look back, I just ran. I ran until I was tucked back into our dorm room where I grabbed my bottle of vodka and started to drink. I didn't bother to mix it tonight; I drank straight from the bottle, letting the fluid burn the back of my throat. It didn't take long before my vision was blurred and my mind was numb.

The next day I finally saw Dane for the first time since he came to my dorm room that morning. I was seated in my new desk in Art class when he walked into the classroom. He looked tired and broken. His eyes were completely unfocused and he hadn't shaved in days. My chest hurt just looking at the once happy and confidant Dane, now so forlorn and miserable. I wanted to jump up and hug him, but my feet felt like they were stuck in cement. He wasn't mine to touch and comfort anymore, but God did I want to. Tyler was right; I had completely broken this beautiful man. I tried to meet his eyes, but he wouldn't look at me. He didn't owe me anything, but I needed to know he didn't hate me. A chill ran through my body when I thought back to what he had told me on the way to my sister's wedding. What if he had relapsed because of me and what I did? I couldn't live with myself if that happened. I needed to try to talk to him after class.

Mr. Thomas started class, bringing my attention back to the front of the room. "Today is a discussion day. I would like to talk about inspiration. Artists are often inspired by people, thoughts, history and life events. Think for a moment about what inspires you and let's discuss." My art was inspired by people in my life who caused me pain. No one cared what I had to say as a child and the canvas always listened to me. I hadn't touched paint all week and I knew why. This was the one time I hurt so much that paint and canvas couldn't make it all go away.

I stared at Dane's back, willing him to look at me, but he kept his eyes fixed on the front of the room. "Okay, class, let's go around the room and talk about what inspires us. Starting with you, Sara."

I tuned out all discussion until it was Dane's turn. He cleared his throat as he began to speak, "Life inspires me. Life is unfair, unkind and unforeseeable. It knocks you down when you least expect it. When I create a sculpture, I can control it. I can create happiness even when I can't feel it. It's a way to create what life isn't giving me." My heart clenched at the sound of his voice. I wondered how many sculptures he has created this week.

I continued to process his words and lack of emotion as my classmates shared their thoughts. When it was my turn, I froze. I knew what inspired me, but I couldn't move the words out without tearing up, not when he was in the room.

Dane finally turned to face me, but his expression didn't change at all. He looked dejected and empty. I wanted to hug him, run my fingers under his dark, sad eyes and kiss away all the pain. I didn't have any right to do that anymore, though. I had given him away like an old sweater. The problem was usually you gave away things you no longer wanted, but I wanted Dane more than anything in my life.

My body started to shake as I looked away from his punishing eyes. I ran out of the room without saying a word. A part of me wanted Dane to run after me, but I didn't deserve that. I wished I could take it all back and have his arms around me once again, but it was never going to happen. I was falling with no one to catch me.

I skipped Anatomy. There was always next week to start attending class again. I wanted to wrap myself in my bed and stay there until Monday morning. I didn't feel like talking to anyone, but I accepted Gwen's call when my phone rang.

I thought about letting it go to voicemail, but I hadn't talked to her all week and I didn't want her to call my mother in a panic. "Hi." I didn't even bother to lift my head from the pillow.

"Alexandra, you haven't called me all week. What's up?" She sounded cheery. If only it were contagious.

"Nothing really," I murmured into my pillow.

"What's wrong? You don't sound good." Perceptive one, wasn't she?

"Dane and I broke up." I heard an audible gasp.

"What? Why? You guys looked so happy last weekend at my wedding." I remembered everything about last weekend; the dancing, the night in my bedroom and the night out in the rain. I had never been happier in my life.

"Mom didn't approve and she kind of gave me an ultimatum. I had to let him go." Bitterness streaked my voice.

"Can I be honest with you?" When I didn't say anything, she continued. "I envied you. When I saw you with Dane that weekend in New York, I wanted what you had. I know Mom probably put so much fear in your head that you can't hear what I'm trying to tell you but Alexandra, you had what everyone wants." I gasped as I tried to catch my breath. I expected her to tell me I made the right decision, but instead she was confirming what my heart was telling me. She was another voice being added to the constant soundtrack that plays in my mind.

"What should I do?" I asked.

"Follow your heart," she whispered, surprising me. My heart was torn between loving Dane and protecting him. I was confused and wished there was a way to see into the future. What would the consequences have been if I stayed with Dane?

"Thanks, Gwen. Look, I have to go. Can we continue this later?" I had some thinking to do and I wanted to do it without anyone in my head.

"I know this is strange coming from me, but I love you and want you to be happy." I liked this new version of Gwen, even if I really didn't want to listen to her logic right now.

"Thank you," I whispered before ending the call.

Had I made the wrong decision? I thought I was protecting him, but maybe I was being selfish. Was I more worried about myself than him? I could live without the money; it never really mattered to me anyway. Could Dane defend himself against my parents? I was beginning to think he could; he wasn't as weak as I was. Maybe I gave up on us too quickly.

I tried to call him, but it immediately went to voicemail. I left at least six messages, but after three hours and no reply, I grabbed my phone again and let my fingers hover over the keys before I finally sent him a text.

Can you meet me somewhere to talk? – A

Still nothing. He didn't want anything to do with me and that hurt more than one hundred nails to my heart. Sometimes second chances didn't exist. I had gone past the point of redemption and forgiveness and ruined my one chance at true love.

CHAPTER TWENTY-FOUR

When Jade asked me to go to Tyler's little get together on Thursday, I told her no. The whole time I'd been with Dane, we had never attended one of Tyler's weekly parties. He said it wasn't his scene and I was confident he wouldn't be there tonight, but truth be told, it wasn't my scene either. Besides, I wasn't ready to go out and be around other people who were a lot happier than I was. Over the past several days, I had accepted Dane was gone and wasn't coming back, but my heart hadn't even begun to heal.

Tyler had sent me an apology text a few days ago. I didn't care for how he approached the situation at the restaurant, but he was protecting his friend and I could see where he was coming from. I would do the same thing if someone did that to Jade.

I was getting ready to have another movie night with a package full of cookies in hand. I have avoided alcohol all together after the night I ran home from the restaurant; I felt like I'd been hit by a truck the remainder of the weekend and decided that sometimes the numbness wasn't worth the after effect. I needed to deal with everything without the alcohol; learning to live with the pain was like trying to learn to walk.

"Alex, you're going with me tonight. I'm not taking no for an answer. You have twenty minutes to get ready," Jade said, hands on her hips.

"I'm not going to a party. I'm just going to stay in and watch movies," I pouted, pulling my hair into a ponytail.

"Alex, I swear to God. If you don't come with me tonight, I'm going to invite everyone to come over here. Do you want a bunch of people in our room?" Why did everyone feel the need to threaten me?

"Really, Jade?"

"I'm serious. You're being ridiculous. Now get up and get moving."

"Fine, Jade, but only for tonight and we're not staying long," I said, through my teeth. I pulled on my black sweater, jeans and black stilettos, letting my hair down. It was a cool spring evening, but I couldn't bring myself to put on the leather jacket that hung on my desk chair. I hadn't worn it since I left him lying in his bed, and everything about it reminded me of him; the feel, the smell, the warmth. I didn't feel like I deserved it anymore.

"Ready?" Jade asked, reining me back in.

"Yep, let's go."

I told myself I would avoid alcohol tonight, but the minute we walked in the door my feelings changed. Tyler's place wasn't huge, but there were probably thirty people jammed into the space drinking, talking, and laughing. For the last couple weeks, laughter had been a loud pounding noise in my head. I hated the sound of it because I couldn't bring myself to do it or fathom that anyone was happy when I was so far from it. I was surrounded by lively, intoxicated people and I immediately missed him. I remembered the last party we attended, laughing as we played cards. The first night we said "I love you". I wanted something to drink and I didn't talk myself out of it this time. I wasn't sure how many shots I had consumed, but it was enough to make the numbness completely wash over me.

Jade didn't leave my side and I caught Tyler looking in our direction several times, winking and smiling. Each time she seemed to move her legs off the couch a little more and I couldn't take the sexual tension any longer. "You can go over there. I'll be fine. "

"Are you sure?" she asked, trying to filter her excitement.

"Yes, go!" I practically pushed her off the couch.

"Okay, let me know when you are ready to leave." She gave my hand a quick squeeze and went to join Tyler. I watched for a second as he put his arm around her and placed a kiss on her cheek. I quickly withdrew my attention from them and focused on the rest of the party.

Do you ever have those moments where you are in a room and you feel like you are on the outside looking in? Like those around you are characters in a sitcom and you are just a member of the live studio audience? That was how I felt in this moment. There were sounds floating all around me as I sat in complete silence taking it all in. I got up and stumbled toward the makeshift bar and drank two more shots. I was going for a third when I was startled by a voice behind me. "Slow down there, sailor."

I turned to see Tyler's roommate, Mason, standing there. I ignored him, turning around to grab my next shot before downing it. "You're Jade's friend. Alex, right?"

"You got it," I said, spinning back around to look at him. I made a mental note not to move so quickly next time as the room began to change directions. Even through my blurry vision, I could see he had a smile that would play in most girls' dreams for years. His jaw was strong, he had great cheekbones and a single dimple on the left side of his face; he was cute in the clean-cut, boy next-door kind of way. Definitely the type of guy I used to date with his slightly too long blond hair and dark brown eyes.

"Are you here with anyone?" he finally asked as his eyes traveled down my body.

"Just Jade," I said, grasping the bar to hold myself up.

His smile grew wide as his eyes met mine again. "You look like you could use some fresh air. Want to step outside with me?"

I looked around and didn't see Jade. The sounds in the room were starting to overwhelm me. Maybe fresh air would help. "Lead the way," I said. He grabbed my hand and led me out to a small balcony. The night air was chilly, but with all the alcohol warming my body I couldn't feel it.

I honestly couldn't tell you what we talked about for most of the time we remained outside. He mentioned he worked at an investment firm, but I didn't catch which one. I wondered if he went into it because he wanted to or someone else wanted him to, but I didn't care enough to ask. He looked like he came from money, but that was presumptuous of me; maybe he genuinely enjoyed it.

"It's nice out here tonight," Mason observed as I nodded in agreement. "You're a Pre-Med major, right?"

"Yep." I considered making an excuse to go inside, but the evening air felt good. I didn't come here to talk, but Mason was easy to talk to.

"What kind of doctor do you want to be?" he asked. I didn't know him well enough to tell him the truth.

"I'm undecided," I answered, moving my eyes to the skyline before returning them to him.

We stood there facing each other, hips resting against the old black railing. I felt better than I had in days thanks to the noise, the alcohol and Mason. He didn't know the pain I was in and the things I had done. He talked to me like there wasn't a care in the world and I felt normal. After several minutes a breeze blew past us sending chills through my body and he began running his hands up and down the lengths of my arms. I inadvertently looked up, right into his eyes and before I knew it his lips were on mine.

I didn't know how to react at first. My body stiffened and my instinct was to push him away, run until I was back in the comforts of my own dorm room, but the alcohol froze me in place. As if he knew what I was thinking, he wrapped his arms around me and deepened the kiss. Something about the way he held and kissed me, relaxed me. He was warm and when I closed my eyes, it was like something I had missed out on for weeks was suddenly there. It was comfort, warmth and want. His hands started to travel up my back, then through my hair before cradling my neck.

After several minutes, he pulled away. "It's getting chilly out here. Do you want to find somewhere warm inside?" I just nodded as he grabbed my hand and lead me back inside. I didn't think much about where we were going. There was warmth in my body that hadn't been there in two weeks and whether it was the alcohol or Mason, I didn't care. I couldn't think straight and I didn't question him when we ended up in his room with the door closed. It was quiet again; the sounds of the city muffled with the sounds of those who were socializing outside his door.

My earlier calm had begun to fade as he walked me back until my legs met his bed. He kissed my lips and before I knew what was happening, I was laying on my back with him on top of me. I started to tell myself that I needed to do this, move on from Dane and all the things I could never have. Dane held my heart; he was my first, my one, my only and I couldn't have him. This was the new Alex and I was going to have to get used to it one way or another. He lifted my sweater above my head and I let him. He placed kisses between my breasts and down my stomach while working at the buttons on my jeans. All I could do was lay there with my eyes shut, willing the pain to go away. Dane didn't do this to me. I did this. I put myself here.

As my jeans made their way down my legs, I felt a tear slide down the side of my face. I was about to give Mason something I had only given to one person. I held onto my ideals on love and sex for a long time and now I had to let it go. The numbness I felt before I opened my heart was back and I planned to use it to get through this. I needed to forget everything and feel nothing. More tears fell as I squeezed my eyes shut, waiting. I didn't move. I just laid there as my underwear was removed and then heard him discarding of his own clothes. He kissed his way back up my body again. I was shaking and if he could feel it, he didn't say anything. His hardness was pressed against my leg, but I felt nothing inside. I just wanted this to be over with, but I couldn't move a muscle. It was like I was frozen in place. I wanted to replace all the aching.

With every kiss, I felt Dane's lips. With every touch, I felt Dane's hands. With every second that went by, I felt I was losing a little more of myself and soon there wouldn't be anything left.

He placed one more kiss on my mouth before whispering, "Beautiful" against my lips and I instantly froze. I couldn't do this, not now, not with him saying that to me. That was Dane's word and suddenly I felt like I was being woken from a dream. "Stop! Please stop! I have to go! I can't breathe."

I didn't open my eyes until I felt his body leave mine and even then it was more out of the necessity to find my clothes and get out of there. He looked mortified, standing by the bed completely naked. Hands wrapped around the back of his neck. "Jesus, what did I do?"

"I'm sorry. I just can't." I was full on crying at this point, trying to get dressed as sobs shook my body. I had been stupid to think I could just give this to someone who didn't have my heart or at least to give it to someone when someone else still had my whole heart.

I whispered sorry to him again as I ran out the door, tears still streaming down my face. I should have stopped to tell Jade that I was leaving but I couldn't. I needed to go. As I rounded the corner to the living area, I saw him. My heart fell out of my chest.

I froze. This was more than I could handle right now. I needed to get out of here and go somewhere to be alone. Just as I started to walk toward the door, his eyes went to my face then shot behind me. I looked back to see Mason standing there, looking completely lost. Before I could think or move, Dane was working his way over to me, his face so angry that I walked backward until I was pressed against the wall. I needed something to hold me up; my knees were weak and I wanted to be anywhere but here.

He stopped right in front of me, his face only inches from mine. I pinched my eyes closed; I couldn't be this close to him. I wanted to kiss him and tell him everything would be fine, but I couldn't do that anymore. He pointed his finger right at me, "It was Mason? You left me for Mason? From the look on your face right now, I would say things aren't going so fucking well." He walked toward Mason, punching the wall along the way. This was not going to be good. What have I done?

"Dane, stop!" I screamed, but it didn't stop him. He didn't even flinch. Dane stepped up to Mason and before Mason even knew what was coming, Dane punched him in the face. He immediately fell to the ground and Dane straddled him, continuing to hit him. I yelled for him to stop, but he didn't. I was relieved when Tyler and another guy came and pulled them apart. I could hear Dane breathing from where I stood and when he looked back over to me, I flinched. This was all because of me; it was because of my actions and my lies.

"Dane, you need to leave. Do you want me to walk you home?" Tyler asked as he slowly loosened his grip on Dane's arm.

"No," Dane yelled at him before starting toward me yet again. He stopped and looked right into my eyes. "I hope he makes you happy." And just like that he was gone, walking toward the door. I didn't want him to think I left him for Mason or that I left him for anyone. This hurt me and I couldn't imagine what it was doing to him.

I pushed my way through the crowd toward Dane. I saw him walk out the door and sped up to get to him before he left the building. He was almost to the end of the hallway. "Dane, stop!" I yelled as loud as I could through my tears. He stopped, but didn't turn around to look at me. I walked closer to him until we were only a few feet apart. "I need to tell you something." My voice and body shook uncontrollably.

He spun around to look at me, staring at me with his dark eyes. "I don't want to hear what you have to say. Do you know what you did to me? You broke me, Alex. This fucking hurts, so fucking bad."

Another tear rolled down my cheek. "I know. I'm so sorry, but I need you to know there is no one else. There was only you and there has only ever been you. I need you to know that."

He let out a cynical laugh. "I just saw you come out of Mason Lander's goddamn bedroom and you want me to believe this shit? You told me there was someone else. You said you didn't love me." His last few words made me flinch.

I couldn't take it anymore. "Damn it, I didn't leave you because I wanted to. I had to Dane. My parents would've ruined us both. I didn't want to do it, believe me, if there was another way." His eyes shifted slightly from anger to confusion. I grabbed the front of his t-shirt in an attempt to pull him closer. "I love you. I need you to know that."

His body was tense, but he didn't push me away. "Really? If you love me, what were you doing with Mason?"

"He was a mistake. A big mistake." I tightened my hands around his shirt to pull him closer. I could feel his heartbeat against my fists.

"Did you..?" He was shaking and I knew what he was asking. That was something I had only given to him and he knew it.

"God, no. You still have me. All of me. I couldn't." He let out a huge breath before wrapping his arms around me.

He rested his forehead on mine, his eyes closed tight. "Come home with me then."

"I can't, Dane. I'm sorry. Some choices aren't mine to be made." As soon as the words left my mouth, his arms left me and he grabbed my wrists to free my hands from his shirt. I looked into his eyes and the pain I saw there was unlike anything I had ever seen or ever wanted to see in the eyes of another person, especially one I loved. I could feel myself melting and knew if I didn't get out from under his hot stare soon, I would give him everything he needed and everything we both wanted. The tears rolled down my face as I whispered one more sorry and stepped forward to get closer to him.

All my plans and intentions ended when he raised a hand to stop me from coming any closer. "Don't. Just go! And Alex, you always have a choice. You just made yours." There are no words for how much I hurt hearing him say this. It was like breaking up for a second time. How did I get to this point? I turned and ran down the hall to the steps, not stopping until I was outside. I needed to get home. I was about to break and I wasn't sure anyone would be able to put me back together. How could I have done this to the both of us...again.

The day I met Dane Wright, I fell hard into a bottomless pit. He was the only one who could help me out but now I was left with nobody to hear me scream.

Chapter Twenty-Five

Two Weeks Later

I've always heard drug addicts need to hit rock bottom before they can get better. What happens to someone who hits rock bottom after breaking up with the love of their life? There was no rehab for a broken heart; it was up to me to make things better. The way I saw it, I had three choices – I could live a lonely life, I could find someone else or I could stop all this nonsense and be with Dane.

I couldn't stomach being with anyone other than Dane. The thought of it made me sick. When I closed my eyes, I always saw Dane. I could still hear him telling me that I always have a choice and the feel of his hands on my body. No one else could make me feel the way he did and if my incident with Mason taught me anything, it was that I wasn't ready. Dane couldn't be replaced when he still owned me.

I lived alone before Dane and since I'd lost him, I'd been more miserable than I ever thought possible. There was a hole in my heart that only he could fill; it would be there forever. I always thought the concept of soul mates was cliché, but I believed it now. If I were to lay it out on paper, we wouldn't seem like the ideal match, but he completed me. I could never regret the time I spent with him. He opened my eyes to so many new experiences. He taught me what love was and how to listen to my heart. I would always look back at the decision I made on the ride home from Greenwich and wish my heart had been louder than my head. Life was a series of lessons that lead you to future decisions. I will never make a decision like that again without listening to my heart. Everything I do affects everything I am; I see that now.

As much as I would like to run back into Dane's arms, I couldn't. I had done too much, caused too much hurt. I would be surprised if he could even look at me anymore. For the past few weeks, I couldn't bare to even look at myself. I was slowly starting to forgive myself, but I was not in the position to ask him to do the same; he would always be the one who got away.

So where did that leave me? It was time to figure out who Alex was when all the noise was stripped away. For the first time in my life, I was going to guide my own life and follow my heart. Dane once told me I have to take all of life's lessons and use them to create my own path; he was right. I didn't realize it before all the air drained from my lungs but now it was time to catch my breath.

I started to attend all my classes again. I spent my afternoons in the Art Room, completing painting after painting until my heart didn't feel so shallow anymore. They started out angry and dark, but had shifted over the past few days to something a little brighter. I was gaining more strength than I ever had in the past; control was a powerful, peaceful thing.

Spring break started yesterday. I hadn't planned on going home, but I was on my way there now. There was something I needed to take care of; something I should have done a long time ago. My parents were leaving for their trip tomorrow and I couldn't let them go without talking to them first. There were so many things I had left unsaid and they couldn't remain that way if I was going to move forward. I finally knew what I needed to do.

My hands gripped the steering wheel tight as I pulled into the driveway. I knew this could very well be the last time I would ever be able to come here as a welcome guest. There was a time when the thought of not being welcome in my own house would have punched me in the stomach, but I knew now it wouldn't be the worst pain I ever felt. Nothing could compare to the pain of losing Dane. Nothing.

I parked my car and stared at the front door for a few minutes. I stayed up half the night thinking of all the things I wanted to say. Nineteen years of memories lived in that house and most weren't worth holding onto. I wanted the remaining moments of my life to be mine. I had too much life in front of me to shy away from change. It was time to lay it out there and move on.

I stepped out of the car and let my wobbly knees carry me forward. I heard Jade's words from this morning in my head, "When you let your heart carry you through life, you're never alone", and it propelled me forward.

As soon as I closed the front door, I heard her heels on the marble. I took a deep cleansing breath and closed my eyes as I listened. Click. Click. Click. I used to tremble every time I heard that noise, but I wouldn't allow that sound to affect me anymore. I wouldn't let her dictate my life or my feelings. My mother has never been a listener. Of course, if I told her I was dating a Kennedy or a dashing young doctor, or that I had been accepted into Harvard medical school, her ears would perk up. If it wasn't something she could repeat at the country club, she didn't want to hear it. Today that was all going to change; she was going to listen to my pain.

Her face showed shock as she came into view.
"Alexandra, what are you doing here? I didn't think you were coming home."

"I just stopped by to talk to you and Dad for a minute. Is he home?" I kept my eyes on her and my voice held steady to my own surprise. My nerves were off the charts, but I wasn't going to let her see that.

She eyed me up and down. I never asked to speak to them. I avoided it. "He's in his study. Follow me," she said in her usual cold, detached voice. I propelled myself forward, taking many deep breaths as we walked down the hall. Click. Click. Click.

I replayed everything in my mind one more time so I wouldn't lose my nerve to continue. The study was a reminder of why I was here. It angered me to be in here as everything from the last time played in my mind again. It gave me the push I needed.

I didn't waste any time. "I came here to tell you I'm changing my major to Art after this semester. I don't want to be a doctor and I'm done pretending." I looked over at my mother whose mouth hung wide open. She quickly composed herself and looked at my father who had actually looked up from the paper. His eyes seared into me, but I didn't look away. I wasn't backing down this time.

My mother spoke first. "You will not do such a thing. We will not pay for you to take a bunch of art classes for the next three years. You're better than that. You're a Riley." By the look on her face, she thought she'd won. I wasn't going to let her win this one.

"I don't care if you pay for it or not. I already applied for student loans," I said, raising my voice higher than I had ever allowed myself in front of my parents. There was an audible gasp from where my mother sat. Score one for Alex. "I'm a Riley by blood, but I will never be like you. I'm better than that."

The room was silent for a few minutes. I considered leaving but I had a few more things to say. "And from now on, I will love who I want to love. Dane was the best thing that ever happened to me. He was more than a name. He was my everything." My voice was angry as I leaned forward in my chair. They were going to listen to me.

My father removed his glasses and threw them on his desk. "Alexandra, we're your parents and we have every right to guide you. Where is this coming from? Did that boy put you up to this?" he said, his voice shaking with anger. I smiled; he was still looking at me. This was the longest he had looked at me for years.

"You're not guiding me. You never did. You had a plan for me and I was expected to follow it, whether I wanted to or not. That's not guiding. I didn't know what I was missing until I met Dane and I can't go back to life before him. I may have ruined any chance with him when I let your voices get into my head, but the lessons he taught me will always be with me."

"You're not the daughter who left here seven months ago," my mother began before I cut her off.

"I am the daughter who left here seven months ago. I was just buried inside myself, but not anymore. I won't let you bring me down anymore." The shock on her face made me smile inside. I already wasted so much time on them and their ideals. I was in the midst of the best years of my life and there was no time like the present to take the reins back.

"If you're going to defy us, you can hand over your credit cards and leave your car here. I will not continue to fund this nonsense," my father said, standing from his chair with his palms resting on the desk. His shoulders were tense and I could see the veins in his neck. For the first time since I entered this room, the consequences of my actions were said aloud. My parents didn't want the real me, they never had. It took me a minute to recover from the realness of the situation before my strength propelled me.

I pulled the keys out of my pocket and put them on his desk before taking the credit cards out of my purse, throwing them in his direction. "Happiness is more important than money. Maybe someday you guys will realize that." My mother sat there speechless, her mouth hanging open. I wanted her to say something. A part of me wanted to hear distress in her voice because I know she had heard it in mine many times before. She wasn't about to give me that satisfaction.

"Here's twenty dollars for a cab back into the city. I suggest you find somewhere else to stay over the summer because you're not welcome here," my father said, reaching into his wallet and throwing cash on his desk. I panicked briefly; I had nowhere to stay over the summer.

I composed myself and stood up, leaving his cash on the desk. I took one more look at my mother who was in stunned silence for the first time ever and then to my father who was a deep shade of red and walked toward the door. "I don't need your money. Have a nice trip," I said as I turned the knob and left the study, walked down the hall and out the front door for the last time. I was on my own now. For the first time I stood up to my parents and didn't back down.

There was a bounce in my step as I walked down the drive. I felt freer than I had in years, like a weight had been lifted off my chest and I could breathe again. Fear had dictated what I'd done for so long, but I wouldn't welcome it any longer. There was confidence in faith that can override fear and trepidation. The key was finding that faith and holding on to it when doubt tried to work its way in. I needed to tell myself that every day.

I took one last look around the neighborhood I had grown up in. Each house took up the equivalent of two city blocks, each with a gate and a long, distinguished driveway. The lawns were well manicured and the landscaping was beautifully maintained. I hated everything this neighborhood reminded me of and the memories it held. I didn't care to ever come back.

I sat on the curb and searched for a number to call a cab. I still had my phone, but it would only be a matter of time before they wanted that back to. I made a mental note to purchase my own and mail this one back before they had the opportunity to ask.

"Hey, what are you doing sitting out here?" I turned around to see Ryan standing behind me. He had his hands on his hips as he stood there wearing grey sweatpants and a Stanford sweatshirt, drenched in sweat. His usually perfect hair was going in all directions and sweat ran down his forehead.

"Long story. What are you doing here?" I asked. I was genuinely surprised to see him. I hadn't expected him to come home for spring break.

"It's spring break. I just got back from a run." he replied, smirking down at me. "So, what's the long story? I have time."

I eyed him for a minute, trying to decide how much I should tell him. He was once one of my best friends and I wanted to be close to him again. "My parents kicked me out. I told them I was changing from Pre-Med to Art and they cut me off." Saying those words would have once made me panic, but they didn't now. I'd never had a job or a bill to pay in my life and that was all about to change. I was finally ready to grow up.

He didn't say anything for a minute. "I always thought art suited you more than medicine," he whispered, surprising me.

"What?" I asked, scrunching my eyebrows together and looking to the side.

"Art suits you. You're not like them, you know." Why was he telling me this now? I'd known him for years and thought no one had seen me. But he had. He had seen me the whole time.

"Why didn't you tell me?"

He shrugged. "I guess we were both going along with the act. I've had a lot of time to think since January and I guess I understand you better now."

"I wish we had this conversation a long time ago. It's been a rough month."

"Yeah?"

"Yeah, I left Dane because my parents wanted me to. I let them get into my head and I'm going to pay for it for the rest of my life," I said, holding my head in my hands. It was amazing how much one decision could affect the rest of your life.

"Why does it have to be the rest of your life? I know you have some fight in you." I pondered his response. Could I fight for Dane? Did I even have a chance?

"I did some really terrible things. I don't think he can ever forgive me," I said, feeling the thickness in my throat.

"Do you realize how special you are? I know it's not something you're used to hearing. But Alex, you're worth it. I wish I had fought harder for you, but I realize now that you weren't mine to fight for." He sat down next to me and ran his hands through his wet hair.

For the first time in a long time, I felt hope. If Ryan thought I had a chance, maybe I did. But if Dane rejected me, I didn't know if I could take any more pain after what had transpired the last few months. A part of me didn't think I deserved him.

"That means a lot to me, Ryan." I wrapped my arms around him. "I hope you find someone who appreciates how great you are."

He let out a short laugh. "Me too. You want a ride back to school? I have nothing better to do." He said with a wink.

"Are you sure?" I asked, eyebrows raised.

"Yeah, my mom will put me to work if I go back into that house." Ryan's mom was notorious for putting him to work in the yard.

"Okay."

We hopped into Ryan's Jeep and started into the city. It was like old times, before we had started dating. He was really enjoying Stanford and there was a change in him. He seemed freer and more at peace. In many ways, I think the fact that we were so much alike that meant that we would never work together. We both had some issues brought on by our parents and equally draining self-imposed ones. Staying together would have been a constant struggle; this was much better.

I hugged him one more time before climbing out of the Jeep. This day had turned into a whirlwind of emotions. First, I had all but severed ties with my parents. It was a relationship I didn't think could ever be mended. Things that were never together weren't meant to be fixed. But now I had one of my best friends back in my life. It was strange how life seemed to work itself out.

CHAPTER TWENTY-SIX

Once I'd left my plastic life behind, I spent the next two week thinking and planning. I'd completed thirty-seven paintings over the last several months. If I placed them in order of when I painted them, they showed my rise, fall and eventual rebirth. I rarely showcased my art, but that was about the change today. There was an outdoor art show this afternoon at Brooklyn Bridge Park and I was going to share my art with the world. It was a big step for me.

Jade helped me dress in what she called artsy-chic, whatever that was. She picked out skinny jeans, with a red camisole, black blazer and matching flats. She fought me when I put my black beanie on, but I eventually won out. It was my day after all.

Gwen came for the weekend; it was nice to have her support in my new endeavor. She was there for me when I wasn't myself and now that I was who I wanted to be, she was still there. I realized that I was worth something and that propelled me forward every day.

"Ready to go ladies? Show starts in 30 minutes!" I yelled impatiently from the doorway. I was the first one ready for my own show.

"Coming!" they yelled in unison. I never thought I would see the day the two of them would get along so well. Gwen had relaxed and Jade had accepted her. I think they had done it for my benefit.

We took a cab to the park. Butterflies were working overtime in my stomach as we got closer. This was going to be a big day for me.

After we paid the cab driver, I led them over to where I had set up my paintings earlier in the morning. It was the first time I was sharing my art with either of them. I was surprised to see they both had tears in their eyes after looking at the whole display. I felt accomplished and justified; the people that mattered most were here supporting me.

For the next hour, I played the art guru, explaining my work to the many people who walked through the park. My mind was there, but I felt uneasy. So much was riding on today. I took a short break to grab a drink of water and collect my thoughts.

When I turned around to greet a couple that was looking at one of my paintings, I saw him. My hand flew to my mouth as I held back tears that threatened to fall from my eyes. I begged Tyler to bring him, but I didn't want to get my hopes up. He looked impressive in light colored blue jeans and a fitted long sleeve grey t-shirt. How did that man make cotton look so good? I wanted to run and jump into his arms, but my legs felt like they were rooted in cement. I watched him as he looked over some of my paintings, pointing and talking to Tyler from time to time. He looked better than he had the last time I saw him, but still not back to normal.

I suddenly remembered where I was and excused myself from the couple. I turned to Jade who was chatting with Gwen. "Jade, can you handle this for a few minutes?" My hands were shaking as I glanced back over to where Dane was standing with Tyler. He still hadn't looked my way.

Jade followed my gaze. "Go, we got it."

I still couldn't move. I watched as he looked at the first painting I had done after our breakup when I was finally able to pick up a paintbrush again. It was a rendition of the sculpture he did for our first art project, but the heart was broken and dripping red down the bottom of the canvas. My heart felt like it was being ripped from my chest as I watched his face fall. He scanned the crowd around him looking for me, I presumed, but he didn't see me. I felt a small hand on my back and turned around to see Gwen. "You can do it," she whispered. My attention went back to Dane before I felt her hand give me a gentle push.

I moved slowly, my heart beating faster with every step, until I was less than ten feet away. This was when he saw me for the first time. I could see his jaw working back and forth as I closed the rest of the distance between us. It was hard not to reach up and touch his beautiful face. It looked like he hadn't shaved in a few days, but it looked good on him. Neither one of us spoke as I watched my reflection in his stunning green eyes. I couldn't hold back any longer as a single tear rolled down my cheek. I never thought I would see myself in his eyes again and I never wanted anyone else to see themselves within them. It was my turn to fight for him.

"I'm glad you came," I said quietly, still unbelieving.

He looked to his right then to his left; he was avoiding my eyes. My heart dropped. "Dane, look, I'm so sorry. I'm sorry I wasn't honest with you. The past several weeks have been some of the worst in my life, but the weeks I spent with you were some of my best." I stopped, taking a deep breath and wiping away the tears. My stomach felt sick; he still wasn't looking at me. "I love you. I love you more than life.

Do you know how I know that? I would rather die than live a life without you. You are everything that I'm not and I need you. Please."

He stood there in silence, looking at the ground and working his bottom lip between his teeth. I needed him to say something. "Alex, I can't. What we had, it's over. Once something is this broken," he hesitated, "I'm sorry, Alex. You were very special to me, but I can't. I can't go through that again." He glanced at me for a second, but I couldn't read him through the tears.

"Please," I begged in an effort to change his mind. I needed him more than I'd ever needed anyone.

I watched him swallow before he grabbed my face in both hands and pressed his forehead to mine. "I love you, but I can't. You have to let me go," he said, his voice strained. The emotion in his voice told me he was struggling with this just as much as I was. He let go of me suddenly and I fell to my knees. I didn't care that I was in a crowded park in the middle of an art show. Nothing mattered anymore. The man I loved was standing right in front of me and there was nothing I could do to keep him here. I'd lost him forever.

He started to walk away from me and the dam broke. He was gone. I watched my whole world walk away. I should run after him, but it was useless. My legs were weak and my heart was even weaker. Why didn't I fight harder for him when I'd had him? That question would ring in my head over and over for days as I tried to heal my somber heart.

Sometimes things don't work out the way we want them to. Life was full of truths that don't play out in romance novels. Sometimes we don't get our happily ever after.

❤ ❤ ❤

It had been eighteen day, sixteen hours and twenty-seven minutes since I last saw Dane. He either quit attending or dropped our Art class right after our encounter in the park. The first day I thought he just needed some space, but after that I realized he was never coming back. There wasn't one hour since the day I met Dane Wright that I didn't think about him. He taught me so much in the little time I had known him and even if I couldn't have him, his lessons would always be with me. I was learning to let go and breathe again, but there would always be a big piece of me missing.

"Alex, you ready to go?" Jade stood behind me with the last box from our dorm room. Her parents offered to let me stay at their place during the summer since they would be in Europe. I didn't want to take a handout, but they convinced me Jade would be better off with me than without me.

I walked to the door and took one more glance at my first dorm room. There were so many memories in this room: some good and some bad. I would never forget my first year of college. There was the bed Dane sat on every morning when he brought me coffee and the large mirror behind the door I always caught him looking at me in. Those memories would be with me forever.

I wiped a single tear from my eye when I saw it peeking out from under the bed. When we were in Greenwich, we took the only picture I would ever have of the two of us. I had it printed before I went to confront my parents as a reminder of why I couldn't take in their poison anymore. Dane was one memory that would never fade out, whether I had a picture or not. I grabbed it, rubbing my finger over his beautiful face and tucked it into my bag.

Rain was falling in sheets as we stepped outside. I made no effort to cover myself as we made our way to the car. Her small SUV was packed with boxes as we pulled out of our parking space. My mind focused on the picture as I pressed my forehead against the window. The memory left me crushed, yet again. I'd never been a fighter and I wondered if I gave our relationship my best effort. Why did my first fight have to be the biggest fight of my life?

Something in me snapped. "Stop," I said, clapping my hands together.

"What? Why?" Jade asked, lines forming between her eyebrows. She pulled close to the curb.

I looked at her and understanding passed between us. "I'll be right back," I said.

She nodded as I ran out the door and through six lanes of traffic to get to the other side of the street. I was being irrational, but for the first time in my life I didn't have a plan. It was exhilarating. I didn't bother buzzing his apartment; I knew he wouldn't answer. So I waited for a few minutes before an older gentleman buzzed himself in with a bag of groceries in hand. I held the door open and followed him inside. Running up the stairs I should have been nervous, but all I felt was excitement. I practically bounced down the hall until I reached his door.

My heart sunk when I knocked and there was no answer. I had a quick flash of every possible scenario while I waited to get into the building, but I hadn't imagined the one where he wasn't home. It was now or never for me. I knocked again only to be met with more silence. I was dejected and sick. It was really over. I changed my life and fought for him, but it wasn't enough.

I put my back to the wall and slid to the floor, wrapping my arms around my folded knees. I was so lost in my tears that I didn't hear the door open behind me. "What are you doing here?" a familiar voice asked. I whipped my head around to see Dane standing there in nothing but black sweatpants. His hair had grown longer since I last saw him and he had days of stubble. He looked as dejected as I felt.

"You didn't answer," I whispered as I stood up to face him.

"I worked late last night. What are you doing here?" He rested his arm on the top of the doorframe, never removing his eyes from mine. The contact gave me hope as I pulled the picture out of my purse. "Do you remember when we took this?"

He took the photo, staring at if for a second before looking back into my eyes. "Yeah, it was the weekend you left me."

I winced. I guess I deserved that. "That day I put all my old photos in a box. Do you remember that?" He nodded, drawing his mouth in a straight line. "Dane, I'm not ready to put you in a box. I don't want you to be a memory. I want you to be my reality. What can I do to prove to you I'm all in this time?"

He closed his eyes and took a deep breath. "You hurt me. You hurt me twice, Alex, and I can't go through that again. What happens the next time you get scared?" He didn't have to tell me. I could see it in his eyes; he doubted me. I would have to work really hard to regain his trust.

"I won't. The only thing that scares me now is losing you." I put my hand on his chest; I could feel his heart beating against my palm. "I won't hurt you again."

"What about your parents, Alex?" he asked, running his hands through his hair.

"I don't talk to them anymore. I'm switching my major to Art and they cut me off completely. I did it because of you. That day in the park, I was there displaying my own work. You made me a better person." I cradled his cheeks in my hands, rubbing my thumbs over his cheekbones. He didn't pull back so I leaned forward and kissed his lips lightly. "Please."

He lost all resolve with my last word and wrapped his arms around me so tightly I couldn't breathe. I was back in his arms and I wasn't ever going to let him go again. He pulled back just enough to kiss my lips. That was all the confirmation I needed. All my hopes, desires and expectations were met and I did it by just being me. I didn't have to pretend anymore.

"Do you want to come in?" he asked against my lips, a smile starting to play on his lips. He was so freaking beautiful.

My timing sucked. "Jade is waiting for me downstairs. We're heading to her parents place in The Hamptons for the summer."

He kissed me again. This time it wasn't short and sweet. It was full of hunger and need. He worked his way along my jaw then nibbled on my earlobe before pulling back. "Bring the boxes up here," he groaned.

I pulled back so I could look into his eyes, feeling a warm tingle run through my body. "What did you say?" I whispered.

"Bring your boxes up here. Stay with me." Ten minutes ago I thought I would never see Dane again, and now he was asking me to move in with him. The world works in the strangest ways. I guess there was something to be said about spontaneity. I loved the man standing before me more than anything and I was going to try my hardest to never come between us again.

I thought about Jade sitting outside. What was she going to say when I told her I was moving in with Dane? Then it hit me. I had vowed that if I ever got Dane back in my arms, I wouldn't let anyone get in our way. If Dane was as important as I knew he was, I couldn't let anyone get in our way. "Okay," I finally whispered.

He swung me in a circle, causing a laugh to escape my body for the first time in over a month. "You don't know how happy I am to hear that. It might take you all summer to make up the last couple months. I love you," he said, placing me back on my feet. My heart fluttered as I heard the honesty behind his words.

"I love you, too."

I learned something today. Redemption isn't something that comes fast and easy. You have to put all your effort and heart into it to make it work. It can't be forced or bought; it simply had to be earned. It requires honesty, commitment and trust. Dane and I have some things to work on, but as long as there is effort, there is hope.

Little girls dream about growing up and living in a big house with a gorgeous husband and a pink plastic convertible. It's not until much later in life that you realize what really matters. Love isn't about what you have or who you know. It's about how you earn what you have and how you treat those you love. The material things don't matter when your heart is full of joy and contentment.

My plastic heart became glass the day I met Dane Wright.

THE END

Dane and Alex's story continues in

Glass Hearts

COMING SUMMER 2013

ACKNOWLEDGMENTS

First, and foremost, I have to thank my husband and kids who put up with my lack of cooking and cleaning over the last few months. My characters can make me crazy but they were the constant in my daily life.

I have to give my husband Michael an extra special thank you because he is my rock, my support and the person who makes this all possible. I can't thank you enough for everything you do for me.

I also want to thank my friends and family who supported me through this journey. It's the people we know and meet who shape us so I like to think you all had a little part in this.

To my critique partner Mireya, I am so happy I met you last year. You are not only someone who cheers me on but you are now one of my best friends. I couldn't have finished this without you. You are the crazy to my crazy.

To Angie and Jessica, I don't know if I should thank you or apologize because you were my very first readers of my very "rough" draft. I can never thank you enough for all your help and encouragement.

To Amy, Jennifer, Alexis, Stephanie, Lori, Deanna, Mint and Natasha, thank you for beta reading Plastic Hearts and helping me make it better. You're help was invaluable.

I also want to give a special thank you to my editor Jennifer Roberts-Hall, my cover designer, Michelle Preast and formatter, JT Formatting. You ladies made the process of publishing my first book so much easier than I even anticipated.

To all the bloggers and reviewers who helped me spread the word about Plastic Hearts, thank you so much! I know the pay sucks but what you can do for authors is AMAZING!

I know I am probably forgetting someone so just in case...Thank you to everyone who helped me in this process.

ABOUT THE AUTHOR

Lisa De Jong is a wife, mother and full-time number cruncher who lives in the Midwest. Her writing journey involved insane amounts of coffee and many nights of very little sleep but she wouldn't change a thing. She also enjoys reading, football and music.

For more information about Lisa and her books follow her at:

Twitter: @LisaDeJongBooks
Blog: www.lisadejongbooks.blogspot.com.
Email: lisadejongwrites@gmail.com

2385263R00164

Made in the USA
San Bernardino, CA
14 April 2013